Praise for Bran Hambric: The Farfield Curse

"*The Farfield Curse* brims with mystery, magic, and fun. Kaleb Nation's wry sense of humor kept me smiling, even while the mystical sparks flew. Get ready for lots of surprises and watch out for gnomes!"

—D. J. MacHale, author of the Pendragon Series

"Whimsy, magic, and suspense collide in this breathtaking tale. *The Farfield Curse* is a story you'll want to pick up, but not put down!"

—Kaza Kingsley, author of the bestselling Erec Rex series

"With characters both silly and serious, Kaleb Nation has crafted a world vastly different from our own, where magic sits next to cell phones and gnomes really do travel. *Bran Hambric: The Farfield Curse* is everything a young adult read should be."

—Kim Harrison, author of Once Dead, Twice Shy

"The author tucks in promisingly clever touches (magical power is measured in 'witts,' and weak mages are dubbed 'dimwitts') and has a knack for crafting violent, quickly paced chases and fights."

—Kirkus

BRAN HAMBRIC

THE SPECTER KEY

KALEB NATION

Series design by The Book Designers

Published by Sourcebooks Jabberwocky, an imprint of Sourcebooks, Inc.
P.O. Box 4410, Naperville, Illinois 60567-4410
(630) 961-3900
Fax: (630) 961-2168
www.jabberwockykids.com

Library of Congress Cataloging-in-Publication data is on file with the publisher.

Source of Production: Versa Press, East Peoria, Illinois, USA
Date of Production: August 2010
Run Number: 13362

Printed and bound in the United States of America.
VP 10 9 8 7 6 5 4 3 2 1

To my Dad,
from whom I stole all my best jokes.

Contents

PART I

PART II

PART III

Part I

Chapter 1

The Woman and the Briefcase

Elspeth waited for him at the gas station.

A single row of tall pumps sat in front of the building like rust-colored phantoms staring out into the night. Stalks of wispy grass cut through cracks in the parking lot gravel and waved in the breeze, the windows of the store broken and the car wash devoid of life. No cars passed on that road—no one took that old route through the dark, sandy hills anymore. But it was where Elspeth waited, and it was where she knew he would arrive.

If anyone had passed on the deserted road, no one would have seen her in the darkness. She stood alone, her black hair blowing behind her, a streak of white dashed through it, arms crossed over the black wand hidden inside her long coat. The skies were clear, but the moon hardly shone on her face, waiting and emotionless.

An old gray van pulled off the road, one of the windows taped over with a ripped trash bag that flapped intermittently. The van jerked to a halt in the middle of the lot, and the door snapped open, creaking as a man slid out. He was short and overweight with a greasy face, hair graying and eyes bloodshot from long hours in front of a computer screen. He jumped when Elspeth stepped out, but when he recognized her, he pulled a briefcase from the van. His gaze darted around, wary, as he had every right to be. She was wanted by every Magic Investigational Police officer in the world—but she had offered him a reward he could not refuse.

"Cold night, eh?" he said as he came forward, licking his lips with anticipation, wrapping his torn coat closely to his body. His gaze searched the hills around them.

"I presume you got it," Elspeth said. She glanced at the briefcase, and even that small movement made him shuffle back a step.

"Money first," he demanded. "Like you promised. Had to knife through m'best mate to get these, so I'm not leaving without the money."

"Very well," Elspeth said, drawing a leather bag from its resting place against the worn bricks. She passed it to him, and he took it with shaking hands.

"Count it," she said. "Hopefully it's enough to pay for your friend's casket."

He dug through the bag. It nearly slid from his fat, sweaty hands, but when he looked up, his eyes were bright.

"A casket of pure gold," he said with a harsh laugh. "Combination is 1-1-9 on the right, 1-9-5 on the left." He shoved the briefcase into her hand. She spun the dials and glanced at the contents within. "It's all there," he said to her. "The tapes, the papers, all of it. I broke the passwords to the third level administration of the Mages Council database, but that's as far as I got. If there's anything deeper, no one's going to get it besides the Primirus or the Archmages."

"Everything I need is here," she confirmed after a few moments.

The man nodded his head in farewell, but froze mid-bow, his

gaze trained over Elspeth's shoulder. A pair of searing blue eyes moved in the grass behind her. Elspeth stepped to the side.

"I'm finished with him," she said, and something leapt from the darkness with a shriek that echoed against the hills. The man dropped the money and screamed horribly, falling back to the pavement, cursing and struggling, but the creature caught him by his leg, snarling in his face. The man gave one final gurgling, screamed curse before his voice was abruptly cut short by a crack and a tear. But Elspeth was already reading the papers and paid him no attention.

"Let it feed, Joris," she said as another man appeared out of the shadows of the station. "After it's done, drag what's left to his van and burn it. Let that be his casket."

Joris kept his eyes from the gruner as it fed, a shock of blond hair going to his shoulders and his strong gaze hardly wavering, even as the horrible sounds echoed in the emptiness. Elspeth stepped around the building and held the papers up so she could see the words in the faint moonlight.

Presently, the gruner loped to her side, brushing against her leg, its body like a giant dog standing on its back paws, crouched low, black with sharp bristling fur that flexed across its muscular back and head. Two blade-like tusks protruded from its lips, bearing dirty bits of the man's jacket. Its cobalt eyes were no longer hungry.

"I've covered the van with gasoline," Joris said when he returned. "We should be moving before I set it off."

"Very well," she said. She clicked the briefcase's lid shut. "I have found the answers we seek."

"They have the Key?" Joris asked.

She gave a small, dark smile. "No, they do not." Elspeth's voice carried a hint of resignation. "Which means Emry passed it on to someone before she left—either physically or by desire. I do not know."

A harsh ringing sound near Joris pierced the quiet. Shoving his hand into his pocket, he drew out a silver cell phone. The front was lit with the caller ID, and Joris blinked when he saw it: the single letter T.

"It's him," Joris breathed.

"Answer it," she said. He hesitated but finally flipped it open.

"Hello, Joris, chilly night isn't it?" came the voice of a man on the other end, almost before Joris had a chance to turn on the speakerphone.

"Haven't heard from you in a few months," Joris said flatly. "Trouble with the police?"

The man on the other end chuckled. "I think after nearly a decade they'd have given up on us. Tell me…did my directions lead you to Bran?"

Joris stiffened. "They were correct."

"But he proved to be as difficult as I said, did he not?" the man's voice went on. "I thought you might be able to handle it, but I guess not."

"And how would you know that?" Joris hissed. "You wouldn't be living if you came within a hundred feet of me."

The man on the phone gave another laugh. "Wouldn't I?" he said. "What about sending Shambles alone, twice? You, seeing Bran at the tavern?"

Joris's eyes narrowed, and he looked to Elspeth, who forced him to be quiet.

"Sounds like you blundered it plenty," the man reproved. "I thought I had him sitting on a plate for you. I can forgive others, but when you lost him at the garage—?"

"That's enough!" Joris couldn't contain his rage any longer. "What do you want, before I go back to that house and murder the boy right now?"

"You wouldn't dare try that," the man said slyly. "You know the boy's powers. You can't risk being caught—not with what you have at stake now that Baslyn is gone."

Joris clenched his teeth, and the man spoke again. "Elspeth, I see you're there as well."

She stood up straighter, glancing over her shoulder in a jerk she could not hide. A flower on the edge of the concrete wavered in the wind. Her gaze swept from it to the grass. Nothing.

"I have a proposal for you," he said, his voice soft. "A deal that could get you the Specter Key and Bran at the same time."

Elspeth lifted her chin slightly.

"I see on your face you would enjoy Bran out of the way," the man went on, and Elspeth's eyes darted around, still perceiving no one.

"But you want the Key more," the man finished. "And I know how to get it."

"Oh rot!" Sewey shouted, hitting his head on the bottom of a shelf in the bank vault for the hundredth time that evening.

Bran looked up from his pad of paper just in time to see a money bag come flopping down from the shelf. It burst open, spilling sawdust all over the floor. "There goes another one," he said, tallying it on the pad. "That makes one hundred and four of sawdust and..." He counted his marks. "...only three bags of money."

"Blasted shelf!" Sewey roared, rubbing the top of his head. He kicked the wall with fury. "Bran, I told you not to tally the bags of sawdust! Do you want every bank examiner in Dunce upon us?"

Bran stole another glance at the gray walls lined with shelves stretching high up to the ceiling, filled with bags of what were supposed to look like bank funds, most of which were obviously not. Sawdust had spilled in heaps across the red-carpeted floor along with the random coin or withered sib note. Even seasoned spelunkers might have easily gotten lost if they ventured toward the back, which was filled with precarious towers of cash boxes, some dating back decades.

"You're lucky the examiners don't dare step inside," Bran mused. "We might have a third bankruptcy and the Fourth Bank of Dunce on our hands."

"Rubbish!" Sewey dismissed, sweeping his black moustache free of sawdust specks. "One of my first classes in banker school was Covert Defense of Bank Examiners to the Avoidance of Audits."

Bran knew it was best to keep his mouth shut. He started to scoop the sawdust back into the bag. It felt odd and almost

Chapter 2

The Box in the Bank Vault

The city of Dunce sat directly east of the wild and forbidden West Wood and was generally avoided just as much. Even without terrible beasts and horrifying legends, Dunce was notorious as the only city in the world that outlawed gnomes and magic. Anyone even suspected of being magical was as good as jail-bound, and gnomes might as well have worn big red targets on their backs just for stepping a foot past the sign outside the gates, which proudly declared:

no gnomes
no mages
etcetera

Sewey Wilomas was manager at the Third Bank of Dunce, which was where he happened to be as the sun set on a late Wednesday evening on the fifteenth day of August. All the other employees had quickly left early when Sewey decided to stay late, and anyone on Third Street who happened to be passing by the bank hurried away like scared rabbits. He was in a bad mood, as usual—and since no one else was around to help clean out the vault, fifteen-year-old Bran Hambric was left to take on Sewey by himself.

creepy to be here in the vault, the same place where he had been found nine years ago at the age of six. His very first memory was of Sewey opening the vault door and seeing him there. From then on, the Wilomases were stuck with him, and vice versa. He didn't know what they might do if they found out that his mother, Emry Hambric, had been a magic criminal, killed as she hid Bran in the bank—or what they might do if they found out he was a mage as well.

His secret was safe, though. He had his mother's brown eyes to remind him he was her son and her necklace under his shirt to remind him that she had changed before she died. He reached up and touched the small charm—silver and shaped like a crescent moon. It felt warm today, and it seemed to warm him inside as well.

"Blast it all, I'm through," Sewey grumbled, flinging yet another bag of sawdust aside. He jumped up and, again, his skull was greeted with the bottom of a shelf.

"Great rot!"

The shelf jumped but didn't give in, and he tripped forward, tumbling to the floor and colliding with a mound of sawdust. Bran had to stifle a laugh.

"Stupid shelf." Sewey coughed and sneezed in the cloud of dust. "Must have been put in by—cough!—filthy gnomes."

Bran shook his hair free of dust, starting another storm. His usually brown hair was getting sawdustier by the minute. Sewey kicked some bags out of his way as he steadied himself, then stumbled over to Bran's tally pad, wiping his brow furiously. They were miserable figures.

"This is preposterous," he said. "How do we ever stay in

business?" His eyes narrowed. "And Bran, what the rot did you put down here at the bottom?"

Bran had distracted himself by penciling a sketch of Sewey hitting his head on the shelf, on which was sitting a very grim, dwarfish bank examiner who didn't look at all happy to have Sewey bumping his seat.

"That's you," Bran said. "I got bored."

"Bah!" Sewey snatched the pad and threw it aside. "Enough bags for one evening. We're getting busy with those safe deposit boxes and the crates, before I single-headedly break every shelf in the Third Bank of Dunce!"

Bran shuddered. He was not looking forward to that job. Some of the safe deposit boxes were ancient. Many dated back to the First and Second Banks of Dunce, and since Sewey had never taken the time to clean the vault out before, the new boxes simply appeared in front of the old ones like fresh mold.

"I say we start in the back, get rid of the older stuff," Bran said, following Sewey deeper into the vault. The back room was lit by long, dim lights in the ceiling, but Bran still had to watch his step for the occasional crate, sack, or filing cabinet someone had dumped and forgotten. The air grew darker and mustier the farther they went.

"Blasted piles of junk," Sewey mumbled. "All of it's rot, just rot, and now I've got to be the one who's told to clean it out before Fridd's Day comes along."

Fridd's Day was yet another celebration that—like Twoo's Day and Wendy's Day—was renowned as an event that everyone had to observe or else be talked about behind their backs by all their neighbors. Unlike Twoo's Day, which was celebrated in the park, or Wendy's Day, which was celebrated in a hot-air balloon, Fridd's Day was traditionally celebrated at formal in-home parties, beginning the night before—Fridd's Day Eve—and running late into the next morning. The Wilomases were to host the Third Bank of Dunce's company party at their house that year. The bank had a tradition of inviting all the board members and the fifteen richest investors. Sewey anticipated it with both excitement and dread.

Finally they reached the back of the vault. Some of the stacks of deposit boxes had fallen to the floor and were lying in piles, with no way of telling what they were except for thin tabs stuck on the front, labeled with the name of the owner, the date... or simply a big *X*. The *X* could have meant anything from "This one's expired," to "This one's owner is dead," to "This one's owner is soon-to-be-dead."

"We'll start back here and work toward the fresh air," Sewey said, sniffing. "Anything expired is going up for auction next week, and I don't care whose ghost comes for it afterward. And since old Jim Primbletons ate the pages of our key ledger when we fired him last year, looks like we'll be needing these."

He held up a pair of screwdrivers.

"Time to put on our burglar hats," Bran said with a grin, and Sewey gave him a salute. Bran started for a pile of large crates to the right, but Sewey caught him by the arm.

"No sir, I get the crates," Sewey ordered. "If there's any treasure to be found it's me who's going to find it."

Sewey waved at the pile of cash boxes. "That's where you'll be working, since there probably won't be anything worthwhile in them for you to bungle with. I'll handle the big, adult stuff."

He pointed to a cash box on a shelf in the far corner. "But don't touch that one."

Bran peered closer at the label, on which was written: Sewey Wilomas, Inheritance.

"So you did decide to save it," Bran said, turning to Sewey proudly.

"Of course not!" Sewey said, dashing Bran's hopes. "But since one needs a permit to own or operate an elephant in Dunce, my purchasing plans have been postponed."

Bran sighed and grabbed the box on top, reading the tab.

"Mortimer Snakebob." He didn't recognize the name, so he jammed the tiny end of the screwdriver between the lock and lid. It only took a few twists to get it open, revealing a handful of colorful feathers and some dirty old coins.

"A pirate?" Bran wondered aloud with a smile. He dumped the gold coins into a pile beside him and tossed the box into the back, reaching for the next one.

"Pamela Perkins," he said. Again, he had the lock popped in a minute, discovering that Pamela collected antique western karaoke records and red cowboy boots.

"Throw all that junk away," Sewey commanded.

Bran dumped them out, and at the bottom of the box, he found something else: a handful of glittery gold bracelets and earrings.

Sewey leaned out from the crates. "Great Moby..." he said as Bran added the valuables to the pile. Sewey attacked his first crate and, with much heaving and hacking, finally split it open. It was stuffed with a worthless collection of balloons and streamers. They were so old that the air itself made them crumble to dust. He threw it aside in disgust.

"No jewels here…" he muttered, jealously eyeing Bran's pile. He started on the next crate with vengeance, breaking the lid only to find the box filled with one-eyed rocking horse heads.

"Double rot!" he cried, flinging it away.

Eventually he meandered his way over to Bran's stack of cash boxes and sat on the floor across from him. Piles of things grew around them, and the heap of empty boxes multiplied in the dim light. Sewey reached to the top of the pile, sliding off a box. He peered at the tab and then squinted.

"Hmmm," he said.

"Come on, we're supposed to be doing these quick so we can leave soon," Bran said.

Sewey went on blinking at the box. "What a curious oddity." He looked up at Bran. "Have you been poking about in the vault lately?"

"Not until this evening," Bran said, rattling the lock. "At least, not since…you know…the Accident."

"Well, that's strange," Sewey muttered, "because this one's got your name on it."

"My name?" He was curious, though Sewey was probably just pulling a prank.

"Well, your last name, at least," Sewey said, still perplexed. "It's a different first name."

Bran sat up straight. "What, who is it?"

Sewey squinted at the tag. "Well, it's hard to read, it's so small. But I think it says…Emry Hambric." Bran froze.

It's my mother's.

Chapter 3

Cash Boxes and Gnome Traps

Bran dropped his screwdriver and yanked the box from Sewey's hands.

"Calm yourself!" Sewey spluttered. "What's the matter with you?"

But Bran wasn't listening. He turned the nondescript gray metal box over in his clammy hands. Its contents rattled. Yet it also felt as if there was something large inside that was packed tight so it didn't shift much. His heart was pounding.

Sewey scratched his head. "I thought we searched this town high and low for anyone with the name Hambric years ago, and we didn't find a single one..."

Bran just blinked at it. *Why would anyone leave a box here in her name? Did she leave it there herself, maybe for me to find?* He was anxious to break the lock when he realized that Sewey was right there, staring at him. He caught himself and turned the box over one last time, holding it close.

"It's...probably nothing," Bran said, trying to act natural. "Sawdust, like you said. I'll just open it when I get home."

Sewey peered at him curiously, though he finally relented, shaking his head. "Oh well, I'm exhausted anyway, and famished as well. Leave this, and we'll finish up some other day."

Bran started out of the vault, clinging to the box so tightly that his knuckles whitened. How many years had it sat there waiting for him? Had his mother hidden it there when she had put him into the vault?

Sewey sealed the vault door, and they made their way through the deserted bank, everything neat and in order in the main room for business the next day. The place smelled of the artificial flower scents Trolan, the janitor, had sprayed before leaving. Bran's shoes echoed against the hard floor. In the lobby, he passed by the desk of Adi Copplestone, Sewey's secretary. When Bran's eyes fell on her brass nameplate he knew exactly where he had to go to open the box: the only really safe place in the city.

Adi's house.

She was someone he could trust, a secret mage, just like him. He followed Sewey out into the warm golden rays of the setting sun that fell across Third Street, illuminating the sleepy shops and a lone car parked in the tow away zone. The sunlight made the car look even worse, revealing all the dents and worn paint.

"I just remembered," Bran said as Sewey locked the door of the bank. "I…got my bike all muddy cutting through the park on the way here. I can't put it in the Schweezer like that."

"You bloody won't," Sewey snorted. He reached to his wrist, on which hung a thick shoestring that held his car keys, so he wouldn't misplace them.

"And there's no use dirtying the trunk either," Bran went on. He drummed his fingers on the box as he clutched it. "So I guess I'm stuck with biking all the way home."

"Too bad." Sewey sniffed unsympathetically. "Next time

you'll remember to keep your mode of transportation in tip-top condition." He climbed into the Schweezer and turned the ignition; the car let out an enormous, street-shaking rumble, coughing fire from the exhaust before wheezing to life. Then he switched gears and pulled out, rocketing down the street in a cloud of smoke.

The moment he was out of view, Bran spun on his heels.

"All right, you got the box to me," he muttered under his breath. "I don't know why you did it, but I'm going to find out..."

He started for the alley next to the bank, glancing furtively up and down the street. Before, many months ago, he might have let something like this pass, but now he knew enough to be wary. When strange things started to happen, there was usually trouble lurking around the corner. He ran to his bicycle and carefully placed the box in the basket. Then he hopped on and took off down the street, the pedals wobbling and his heart pounding. He passed the highway and started down a maze of streets that took him into a quiet neighborhood: houses warmly lit, set on grassy lawns.

A short while later, he pulled into Hadnet Lane and parked his bike in front of a two-story, white stone house in the middle of the block. He gently took the box and started to the front door, continuing to survey his surroundings as he knocked. Everything beyond it was quiet until he heard the lock slide. The door opened, revealing a girl his age with brown and blond hair, greenish blue eyes, and a black band around her right wrist: his friend Astara.

"Oh, hello," she said.

Bran was still a little surprised to see her living at Adi's house, a place very different from where he had first met her at Highland's Books. The repairs from the fire were nearly complete, but until they were finished, Adi was letting Astara stay with her.

"I, um..." Bran finally stammered. "I need to talk to Adi. Look at this."

He held the box up so Astara could see the name on the label.

"Sewey found it in the back of the vault," Bran said hurriedly. "I've never seen it before."

Astara read the name. Her eyes widened.

"You're right," she said quickly. She locked the door behind him.

The inside of Adi's house looked like any other regular suburban Dunce home: decorated to the hilt for Fridd's Day—yellow streamers hanging from the ceiling, yellow balloons arranged on the edges of furniture, even yellow flowers in shiny, gold vases on the tables. The chairs were covered with yellow blankets and yellow pillows, and on the walls, yellow flags bearing the inscription "Jolly Fridd's Day!" in big, bold letters.

"Getting ready for Fridd's Day?" Bran half-joked as Astara led him up the stairs.

"Well, it is this Friday," she replied. "I just got home from the bookstore—we were decorating there too. He's hoping to use it as a grand reopening."

"I just got out of the bank," Bran mumbled. "But we weren't decorating, that's for—"

An awful bang from upstairs, partially muffled through the floor, cut him off in mid-sentence.

"What was that?" he gasped.

Astara smiled wryly and pointed up the stairs.

"That would be Polland," she said. "He's working on disarming a gnome trap."

"By shooting at it?" Bran asked.

"No, just disarming it." Astara shrugged and pushed open the door, revealing a room with floor-to-ceiling bookshelves. There was a large fireplace at the far end; chairs and a sofa were neatly arranged in front of it. The fire was out, though sitting in the middle of the floor was something new: a row of bright orange traffic cones. They stood in a long line, ten of them, though three were in a very odd state. They looked as if they had gotten themselves turned inside out. A stench of gunpowder clung to the room, and a gentle cloud wafted in the air. As it rose to the ceiling, Bran spotted Polland lying in a heap in the corner. Adi was helping him to his feet as he spluttered curses under his breath.

"Blasted bramble of gnome traps!" Polland spat, holding his tall red cap on his head with one hand. He wore a green shirt underneath a pair of dirty, brown overalls with black buttons, and a pair of thick goggles over his eyes; the lenses were coated by a dusty film. Polland was the size of a seven-year-old child, at most, but his thick beard and ruddy cheeks proved that he was one of the very things Dunce stood against: a gnome hiding within its own walls.

"You got two yesterday without any trouble," Adi consoled him. She looked up at Bran.

"Hello, what a surprise," she said.

Polland pushed her hand off and dusted his clothes.

"Gnome traps...disguised as traffic cones?" Bran questioned.

"Another ghastly invention by the Decensitists, no less," Polland grumbled. "You can't even tell which are traffic cones and which are gnome traps."

"The Decensitists think that gnomes are so stupid," Adi explained, "that the moment they see something reddish and cone shaped, they'll immediately run forward and give it a hug."

"And then..." Polland grabbed a book off the shelf, aimed carefully, and threw it at the gnome trap. It hit against the side of the one closest to them, but instead of knocking it over, there was a pop like a pistol shot and blast of smoke. The gnome trap sprang up, inverting itself and swallowing the book in midair. Bran jumped.

"What a poor fellow who should happen to fall into its clutches!" Polland said, lifting his goggles to reveal a patch of clean skin underneath. "Might very well pin his arms so he can't escape even if he turns to stone!" He drew himself up proudly. "I've been practicing tactics of disarmament."

He reached down to the floor for a long stick that looked like a pool cue, held it out at arm's length, biting his tongue as he did, and gave the top of the next cone a sharp thwack! The instant he cracked down the gnome trap gave a wobbly little jump but didn't close and fell back to the ground like a limp rag doll.

Polland rushed forward and seized it immediately. "Disarmed!" he announced. "Just whack the top, and it turns it off. Trick is to not hit the sides by accident...as I learned the hard way."

Bran laughed, imagining Polland flying across the living room, arms flailing. Adi noticed the box in his hands. "And what's that you've got there?" she asked, stepping closer.

"Read the name," he said. He held up the box so Polland could read it as well. A dark mood fell over the entire room.

"Where in the world did you find this, Bran?" Adi whispered.

He told her about the vault and how he had come to her house to be safe before opening it.

"Smart thing to do," she muttered. "We'll take it up to my office. Do you have a key for the box?"

"I think a screwdriver will work fine," Bran said with a hint of dryness. He followed Adi into a messy office, papers strewn about and the window uncovered, the last bits of sunlight poking through. This room, too, was littered with books, and also held a large cage on one wall that housed Adi's crow, Ginolde. The crow was still, though Bran knew she was alert, her golden beak darkening in the setting sun.

Adi grabbed a hidden handle in the bookshelf, pulling the door open to reveal a long set of stairs. Everyone followed her up to the attic and her secret office.

The air was rather comfortable, though tinged with the scent of wood. The television was muted; on-screen a reporter from the Mages Entertainment Channel 0 jabbered silently. To the left of Adi's desk was a birdcage-shaped object covered with a blanket and to the right were boxes of tightly packed books on magic—all kept secret from the City of Dunce.

Bran set the cash box on her desk, and they gathered around it. Polland produced a screwdriver, and Bran pushed it into the lock, expecting to break it open as quickly as the others in the vault, but this one wasn't as simple.

"A regular picklock, aren't you, Bran?" Astara said, trying to lighten the room. He dug the screwdriver farther, giving the lock a sharp wrench. All eyes were on him, the air filled with anticipation.

What if it's nothing? he thought, but then the latch popped.

"There," he said, setting the screwdriver aside. He flipped the lid open and drew back so everyone could see.

It was another box, made of thick brown wood, the dark grains of it stained and smoothed to a perfect shine. As Bran lifted it, he could feel there was something inside, sliding about. He turned it and saw that at every corner there was a brass fixture, and around the rim that joined the lid to the base, another length of flat brass, dull and etched with designs. Opposite the hinges was a thick clasp with a keyhole. Whatever this box was, it was ancient and captivating.

Taped to the top was something very out of place—a folded scrap of paper, which Bran couldn't help but peel off. When he did, the burned shape of a crescent moon, carved into the box's surface, was revealed. It was the same shape as his mother's necklace.

"Odd..." he said, studying the mark and brushing his finger across it. It was very plain, but the black burn of the shape was so perfect, even to the points, as if seared by a master artist.

"That is odd," Adi agreed, her eyes filled with alarm. She knew the dark past behind Bran's necklace. His fingers ran over where the lid was clasped. There was no key to be found.

"I guess I'll have to break this open, too," Bran said, but Adi seized his hand.

"Wait, Bran—this box is probably very old," she said. "It might be better to leave it up to a professional lock picker."

Bran nodded slowly in agreement.

"I'm on the job," Polland said. He took Bran's screwdriver

and slid his cleaned goggles back on, which magnified his eyeballs like fish eyes. Then he set the box on his lap and inspected the lock closely in the light.

"Look, Bran, there's something written on that paper," Astara said. In his haste, he hadn't even taken the time to look at the sheet. She moved beside him as he carefully peeled it apart, revealing two words in smooth, crisp black handwriting.

"Nigel Ten," Bran read aloud, and he looked up. "Who is that, Adi?"

She furrowed her brow. "I haven't heard of any Tens living around here."

"Me neither," Astara said, looking at the page curiously. Bran glanced at Polland, who was struggling with the lock. He had the screwdriver jammed into the latch and was gently trying to pry the lid apart. It didn't budge, and all of a sudden an invisible force seemed to spit the screwdriver back at Polland, knocking him against the chair.

"Bother! Stuck tight, that's for sure," Polland growled. "I've used every trick I know, too."

"What if I try magic?" Astara asked, and Polland perked up.

"Wonderful idea," he said. "I'm sure there's a Netora magic to open the lock."

He slid out of the chair, sucking his sore thumb, then retrieved a thick book off the shelf behind Adi's desk and paged through it rapidly until he found what he was looking for.

"We don't keep Netora books around here," he murmured. "But this one is a compilation, and almost every book has an unlock spell. If we're lucky there should be one here..."

He went to the index, using his goggles like reading glasses, and finally found what he was looking for, spreading the book on the desk. There were two columns of words on each page; most of the type was small and hard to read. The pages were very thin, and the text was muddied, but Bran could still read the title that Polland laid his finger on.

[158-N] Norton's Netora Unlock—Norton

Very useful and simple spell to open the locks of doors and otherwise

Hand Out: *Lock coming undone*

Onpe likoca

"Easy enough," Astara said, stepping forward.

Bran repeated the words in his head, knowing that they might be very useful at some time or another, as Astara carefully placed three of her fingers on the surface of the lock. She paused for a moment and took a deep breath to gather up her magic.

"*Onpe likoca*," she commanded.

There was a great flash of green light, like a blast from a strobe tower, and arcing out of the box, through Astara's fingers, came an enormous, crackling flare of energy. A sharp breaking sound like thunder exploded through in the room, hitting the ceiling. It broke plaster and sent it raining down in dust, and then suddenly, another thick arm of the green energy burst out and seized hold of Astara, throwing her backward across the room.

Chapter 4

The Unbroken Lock

A scream escaped Astara's lips as everyone fell, a tremor knocking their feet from under them as the ceiling plaster fell on their faces. When Astara hit the wall, she knocked over a stack of books that came tumbling to the floor, and in the same split second, the green energy vanished back into the box, leaving Bran, Adi, and Polland coughing on the floor.

"Astara!" Bran shouted, crawling toward her. She rolled over, spilling more things as she did. Bran got to her side and tried to help her up from the floor as she struggled to steady herself.

"What happened?" she asked aloud, still trying to catch her breath. She pressed her hands against the floor, the crackling magic gone, though she still looked to be in the last fading edges of pain.

"Are you all right?" Adi burst, rushing forward. Astara pushed Adi's hands away and brought herself back up, Bran next to her in case she fell again. For a moment she was unsteady and had to catch herself against the wall.

"Did I say it wrong?" she asked, blinking.

"Forget that," Bran said. "Are you all right?"

"I'm all right!" she said, pushing away. "What happened?"

"That box nearly killed you, that's what!" Polland exploded, and all eyes turned from Astara, back to the desk. The box was still there, all the way across the room, like it hadn't done anything at all. The clasp was still locked tight.

"I said it wrong, that's what happened," Astara said.

"No, you didn't," Polland replied, his voice lowering. "In fact, you said it perfectly..."

Polland glanced around to Adi, hesitating with his words. "I think that lock is enchanted."

Bran stared at the box from across the room, none of them daring to get closer to it. The box was silent, though Bran felt as if it had eyes, watching them, ready to strike again.

"Then how are we supposed to open it?" Bran asked. Adi gave a frustrated shrug.

"Not much we can do about that," she said. "Without the key, that lock can't be opened, and it's made to withstand anything, even magic, from attempting to break it."

Bran hesitated. "What do you suppose she's put in there?"

Adi tried to speak, but she couldn't seem to make any words come out. Bran looked from one to the other, but neither Adi nor Polland had an answer for him.

"So we might never get that box open?" Astara said grimly, voicing the thoughts that were running through all their minds. Adi slowly shook her head.

"Maybe your mother didn't mean for you to open it after all," she said.

If my mother didn't mean it for me, Bran thought, *then why put it in the vault?* He slowly drew himself toward the desk, gently touching the box. When nothing happened, he lifted it, turning it over, but there were no other markings. The others came around him, and though there was deep disappointment within Bran, there was more of a drive to find the key to the box, wherever it was. At that moment, it seemed absolutely hopeless, because he didn't have a single idea of where to look.

"Well, either way," Adi finally said, "it is getting late, and the others might…you know."

"Right," Bran nodded, and Adi started for the door as he bid Polland and Astara good-bye. Astara was hesitant to let him go, glancing at the box.

"I'd keep away from that," she whispered to him. "It's probably going to cause trouble."

"You, afraid of trouble?" Bran whispered back with a slight grin.

"No, I'm serious Bran," she said, looking at him intently. "Do you really want to know what's inside that box, if she's made such an effort to keep it locked?"

Astara's words were ominous, and they instantly made Bran's expression turn grim. He didn't reply but followed Adi through the house and outside, where the entire city of Dunce had now entered the darkened hours of the early night. The wind had gotten a little chilly as Adi unlocked her trunk for Bran to put his bike in, the back tire hanging out.

"Don't put the box in there," Adi said. He kept it in his hands as she started the car, and they drove off, her headlights illuminating the dim streets. The drive was very quiet for most of the way until Adi spoke up again.

"Now you know I probably shouldn't let you keep that box," she said bluntly.

"Do you think I'm going to just let it go because it isn't safe?" Bran said. "It's from my mother—probably one of the few things she left behind. I have to keep it, even if I can't get the thing open."

Adi still looked uneasy but relented.

"All right," she said. "Only because it's from your mother. But whatever you do—"

She glanced from the road to him "—don't try to open it."

Bran nodded at her reassuringly. But as he held the box in his arms, he was thinking otherwise.

Adi dropped Bran off at the corner of Bolton Road so the Wilomases wouldn't suspect anything. By that time, the whole street was dark save for the streetlamps and the lights from the homes, but he knew the place well. Parked far down the road, in front of the thirteenth house on the end of the right side, was the Schweezer, resembling a miniature metal elephant in the dark. The neighbors on the left side had recently moved out, and there was a big FOR RENT sign in the front yard. Bran wondered what poor souls might end up there and be forced to deal with all the noise next door, or if they were prepared for the car chases, burglars, gunfire, and spontaneous explosions that seemed to follow the Wilomases everywhere.

The lights from inside his house were bright on his face as he came up the walk, and his eye caught something that had been stuck on the glass next to the front door. It was a set of stickers pasted down toward the bottom, the first of a tall, red triangle with a circle and a line over it, and next to that, another of a long, slender rectangle with stars floating out the end, again with a circle and a line over it. The first meant "no gnomes," and the second meant "no mages," and to complete the collection, there was one final rectangular sticker below these, the words ABSOLUTELY NO SOLICITORS printed in bold lettering. The Wilomas family didn't beat around the bush when it came to gnomes and mages and especially solicitors, a term which had commonly come to refer to anyone who supported either of the first two.

He stepped inside, and a huge racket was coming from the kitchen.

"Help, help!" Mabel was screaming. Bran spun just in time to see a blast of black smoke explode through the kitchen door like a grenade going off.

"Oh no, she's tried cooking again," he said. With Rosie gone, the Wilomases had been forced to cook for themselves. Everyone had quickly become accustomed to bread bricks or delivery food.

"Mabel, if I've told you once, I've told you a thousand times!" Bran heard Sewey bellowing and coughing from inside the kitchen. "You've got to keep that far away from any source of flame! Now look at this awful mess!"

The whole house was filled with a clamor from the ruckus the two of them were making. Mabel began screaming and coughing.

"Oh! Oh! It's sending me into a Hotron fit!" she shouted, knocking things off the counter. She went on shouting, and Bran turned and saw that someone else was in the room with him: little three-year-old Baldretta Wilomas, sitting at the bottom of the stairs, already in her pajamas with a pink Mandrita-Wingans

Bondersnitch rabbit doll in her arms and some candy being chewed between her teeth. She was looking at him glumly.

"Been like this all evening?" Bran said.

"Blawthi," she said, nodding dismally, her brown hair tied with a loose red bow. The noise from the kitchen just went on and on, like the clamor of an iron pot-sorting warehouse.

"Don't worry," he said. "Rosie will be back sometime, and then we can start eating food again."

Baldretta shrugged. She looked quite content with the candy and might have been able to survive on just that if they had left her to it.

There was a table next to the front door that Bran had been ordered to put out earlier in the week, the only preparation the Wilomases had done for the impending Fridd's Day party. Since the party guest book wasn't there yet, Sewey had taken it upon himself to dump the postcards from Rosie and Bartley all over it, so he wouldn't have to look at them every time they sat down for dinner. The top of the table was covered with them, splashes of colors and stamps from all over the world with photographs of Rosie and Bartley: one of them in ski gear in front of the mountains, another of them in scuba gear far underwater, another of them in lava gear deep in a volcano, and piles and piles more. Bartley, always the festive one, wanted to make it the biggest honeymoon ever, and possibly the longest one, as it had been many a month and they still hadn't returned.

Bran shifted them around, but there wasn't anything new, so he started up the stairs past Baldretta, hearing the television, in front of which he presumed Balder could be found. He thought it was probably best to hide the box in his room before Sewey or Mabel appeared, so once he reached the top he started across the hall to his ladder that went to the attic. It was quite a complicated matter going up with the box in his arms, but he made it with some difficulty, and when he poked his head through it was pitch black. He had to feel his way to his desk, running his fingers along it until he found the switch to the lamp. When he turned it on, his room was immediately bathed in light, casting shadows across his pencil sketches pinned to the board on the wall.

He sat on his bed, underneath a bright painting that hung over the bed frame: it was his Friendship Gift from Polland, a picture of the first time he had visited Adi's house and found out the truth about his past. Bran turned the box over, hearing the contents rattle about, and he studied it from all angles. It was clean on all sides except for the moon on the top. He ran his fingers cautiously along the edge where the lid met the base.

"Now how am I supposed to get this open?" he asked himself. There was no answer, not even in the deepest parts of his mind. His senses in recent weeks had become honed so that he could feel parts of magic within him that he had not yet harnessed—though even these seemed to be blocked by the box so that he could not penetrate it.

He knew it would do him no good just to sit there staring at it and quietly set it on his desk. As an afterthought, he turned the box over so that the moon shape was underneath.

No point letting anyone see that if they happen to come up here, he thought, though it was highly unlikely anyone would venture into his room.

He was just placing his foot on the first step of the ladder when suddenly—CRASH! There came an abrupt noise behind him that broke the stillness of the room and sent him spinning around.

"Who's there?" he demanded. There was no one. His eyes searched the room, darting from one thing to the next, until he noticed something out of place: the box had fallen off his desk.

He thought for sure he hadn't put it close enough to the edge to fall. He lifted it from the floor and situated it closer to the middle, turning it over again so that the emblem was hidden.

"Stay there," he commanded, feeling a little silly after he did. He started to turn but then stopped, looking back. The box was still there. Shaking his head, he moved for the ladder again.

Strange happenings on Bolton Road again, he thought wryly, starting down the ladder.

CRASH!

Bran froze in his tracks, halfway to the bottom. He spun, his eyes now level with the floor of his room. And there, across the wood, was the box.

He had put it in the middle of the desk that time, he knew for sure. Nothing short of a miniature earthquake could have made it fall off. Yet there it was, sitting on the floor—the emblem facing up again.

He felt a strange sense of deep foreboding urging him to run from that box as fast as he could. But at the same time it seemed as if the box was alive and calmly studying him and his actions. Bran couldn't move for a minute, and when he did, he jumped up the ladder again and stood across the room. The box didn't do anything, even as Bran cautiously drew nearer.

"Now what's going on...?" he asked softly. The room replied

with nothing, empty stillness like a buffer around him. Slowly, carefully, Bran picked up the box again, and this time, he set it on the desk, the marking facing up where he could see it.

He slowly drew away from it, never letting his gaze fall. When he got to the ladder, Bran started to turn, placing his foot on the ladder, and still it did not move.

"This isn't right..." he said quickly under his breath, pushing from the ladder and walking over to his bed. Grabbing a thin blanket, he tossed it over the box, covering it and the marking altogether. He hurried to the ladder, rushing down, and even as he got to the bottom and started down the stairs, there wasn't a sound from his room or the box again.

Chapter 5

The Sound in Rosie's Room

Bran hurried to the kitchen and nearly collided with Sewey coming through the door.

"Watch out!" Sewey bellowed, balancing a steaming silver tray in his hands and swinging it over Bran's head so it wouldn't spill. Bran dodged out of the way as Sewey tripped through the door, his face darkened with ash and his hair wild.

"What an absolute latecomer you've become today," Sewey scolded, twisting around and looking like some space monster from the volcano universe. "Go stir the potatoes. Mabel is on that blasted apparatus again."

Bran pushed through the kitchen door without replying and heard the whizzes and whirrs of the latest of Mabel's health crazes. She had recently invested in a device advertised in *Fitness Witness* magazine called a tarbofluximator. The ad promised to rid anyone's body of crinkets and snivs, touted as the secret cause of all the world's problems. Sewey, who had been forced to put all twelve thousand parts of the hideous device together in the middle of the kitchen, had first mistaken the instruction manual as a conspiracy novel, though Mabel would hear no objections.

Obviously, the tizzy she had flown into over cooking dinner had immediately warranted some much-needed detoxing, and so she was hooked up to the new machine when Bran entered, a wired headband strapped around her scalp and bunching up her red and black hair. The device was composed of four miniature cranes with magnets dangling down from wires. So far, the only real effect it had had was on the Wilomases' bank account.

"Don't look in my direction!" Mabel hissed the moment Bran stepped through, and he quickly averted his gaze.

"Stop thinking about it!" she shrieked. "You're ruining the tarbofluximation!"

"It's hard not to with all the noise it's making," Bran protested, trying to be heard above the huffing and puffing and beeping.

"Stop thinking!" Mabel screeched. "Stop thinking this instant!"

That would be so much easier if I were a Wilomas, Bran thought, but he drained the potatoes and tried to ignore her. He dumped the food into a glass dish and covered it with aluminum foil. He started to wash his hands.

It was in the midst of this, however, that above his head the lights in the kitchen started to flicker. He stopped and looked up at them quickly, fearing a dying bulb that he would have to change out.

"Bran, stop fooling about with the light switch," Mabel demanded, opening one eye.

"I'm not even near the switch," Bran said.

"Change the bulb then," Mabel snorted. The flickering stopped for a second and then started again, fading out and then back.

"It's not the bulb," Bran said, shaking water off his hands and then looking up at the ceiling. "Look, there, it's fading out in both lights."

"Well, I don't care what it is," Mabel snapped. "It's ruining my tarbo—"

It was then that Sewey came back through the kitchen door, visibly befuddled.

"What's all this?" he said, and Bran could see through the open door that the lights in the downstairs living room were also fading and flickering in the same time as those in the kitchen. It was as if the power in the entire house had begun to fluctuate madly. He could hear Balder going into hysterics upstairs as the reception on the television kept going in and out, and Baldretta stumbled in and clung to Sewey's leg, visibly frightened.

Bran, who had never seen something like this before, immediately tried everything he could to get it to stop. He turned off the running water in the sink, and though the lights stopped flickering for a moment, they were half dimmed and then immediately went to full brightness and then out again. It seemed to follow no pattern.

Mabel's machine had begun to make garbled noises as a result, so she started to slap its computer box to get it to stop, and it died. Immediately the room was abandoned to silence, which only made the flickering lights more eerie as they all stared up with nothing to say.

Suddenly, just as quickly as it had begun, the lights gave one final, dim hiss and then sprang back to their full brightness, causing the whole family to blink. Bran hadn't realized how tense they had all gone until he tore his gaze from the ceiling.

"Well, I..." Sewey stammered. He blinked a few times, and then his face soured.

"Power fluctuations," he said, dismissing it with a wave of his hand. "Probably a nearby thunderstorm."

"Or it's that ridiculous device," Bran said, waving his hand at Mabel's contraption, which had whirred back to life.

"My tarbofluximator does nothing of the sort!" she roared, turning up the dial and covering her ears with the attached headphones to block him out. Bran grabbed the steaming dish of potatoes and carried it upstairs, worried the power might go out again. They had flashlights and lanterns, but he was irritated that a little power failure had scared him. Ever since he had touched the box, his nerves had been on edge. Everyone soon went up to dinner, and nobody talked about the electricity troubles. For a while, they just sat there. It had been a long time since Rosie had left, but still no one had gotten used to getting their own plates. Nothing felt the same without her.

The feeling of emptiness could have quite possibly been shared by all save for one in the room. Balder Wilomas—chubby, eight years old, and with a head of dark brown hair—had entrenched himself with a battery-powered black-and-white television safe from power troubles; the antenna extended many feet into the air and had a ball of aluminum foil on the end for better reception.

Sewey finally coughed and started to reach for the tray of roast beef.

"Might as well get started, shall we now?" he said, trying to break the silence, though it didn't do much good. He stretched in his chair for the tray but couldn't reach far enough. It sat directly in front of Balder, but he was too engrossed to even dream of helping.

"Balder," Sewey finally burst. "Come on, pass the beef before I pull a muscle."

Balder looked up, bending out a headphone. "What?"

"The beef." Sewey gestured. "Hand it over."

"But I'm busy watching the portable," Balder whined, swinging the antenna. Baldretta ducked just in time.

"Hand me the food right now!" Sewey demanded, and Balder banged on the table.

"Wait till the commercial!" he shouted. Bran let out a loud breath and shoved the tray toward Sewey.

"There," he said. "Let's all try to eat in peace for once."

"Daw, grumbles," Sewey growled incoherently, spearing some roast onto his plate. Mabel took it afterward, sprinkling a bag of herbal tea over hers, and Bran helped fill Baldretta's plate and cut her meat. Any other time, juicy roast beef, buttery corn, and sweet carrots would have been wonderful—except today there were none of those. The beef looked more like jerky, the corn like tiny black marbles, and the carrots were covered in piles of oatmeal flakes Mabel had mistaken for sugar. The only thing that had turned out right was the potatoes.

Balder, who could not survive on much less than a prince's ransom of food, eventually got to work eating, headphones still plugging his ears and the screen propped up against his glass. Mabel rattled a bottle of food enzymes about halfway through the meal, but it wasn't until Sewey was almost finished that anyone spoke.

"Fridd's Day is impending," he alerted them. "Balder, do you know what impending means?"

Balder couldn't hear him. He was still watching the television. Sewey scowled.

"It means that something that could be quite terrible is rapidly approaching," he went on. "Think of a big train coming around a bend while your car is between the crossing guards."

Baldretta giggled. They'd experienced that before. Sewey coughed.

"And since this party is impending upon us this Friday," he went on, "it would be best if we make a few plans for it before it impends itself upon us too harshly."

Sewey reached to his left, where his day book sat. It was actually not on the table but resting on top of a miniature mountain of envelopes that was so tall it had built itself up as an additional wing of the table. If someone had let out a great sneeze he could have possibly blown a snowstorm of bills throughout Dunce. The advantage of having such a large pile of bills next to one's table was that it could be easily exploited by Sewey, who had decided to make it useful and placed a salt shaker, a lamp, and a few extra napkins on top so they were close at hand. He also had his glasses there, and he swooped them up and placed them over his eyes as he paged through his day book.

"As planned," Sewey said, "we will have caramel popcorn and yellow streamers and balloons decorating the house. There will be a dance to the Fridd's Day Song and maybe even the Saltine or a waltz. And you, Bran, will dance with Madame Mobicci."

"But I don't know how to dance," Bran protested.

"Well, you had better learn," Sewey retorted. "This is Fridd's Day, and we jolly well will look good to these rich people or else!"

Bran knew better than to argue any further. When they had finished eating, he picked up the dishes and started for the kitchen. It was already late, and there were piles of things to be washed. None of the Wilomases lent a pinky to help—except Baldretta, who helped carry silverware down the stairs.

It took over an hour for Bran to get all the mess cleaned up from Mabel's cooking fiasco, and by the time he was finished, the rest of the house had gone quiet, the Wilomases having gone to bed for the night. Sewey, taking an unannounced interest in conservation after the lighting incident, had turned off every bulb in the house for fear the world was running out of power. When Bran finally left the kitchen, he had to feel his way up the stairs.

He slid his hand across the wooden railing of the balcony as he headed for his ladder. The carpet upstairs was soft under his toes, and the house was very still. When he came to the ladder he started to pull himself up, yawning.

Just as his foot hit the second step, there came a low but sharp sound from down the hall. It immediately made him stop and stare into the darkness. No one was there, not even Pansy the cat—but there was one door at the end of the hall. It was the door that had once led to Rosie's room.

The door was closed, as it had been since she had left. No one wanted to think of using the room for anything else—it just didn't feel right. But as Bran stood there, frozen against the ladder in the darkness, he heard the sound again: a sharp tap.

"Balder?" Bran whispered. No one replied. He stepped down to the floor, pressing himself against the side of the wall, fearful and curious at the same time. The tapping had ceased. But then he heard it once more, sharply. Someone was in Rosie's room.

He tightened his fingers into fists, and the instant he did, he felt the powers within him slide into his grasp. They came more easily now, like drawing out a sword the moment his mind triggered that he might need them. He knew he couldn't let himself do magic, at least not if he could be seen, but it was ready nevertheless.

He started toward Rosie's room, hesitant with each step he took. Everything had gone silent again, so he almost turned back, but he reached the door and stood very still, listening. Nothing. But he knew he had heard something. He touched the door handle. It was cold, and he gripped it tightly, listening for anything that might tell him if he was walking into a trap.

Very slowly, he turned the handle, and it twisted silently. Cautiously, he pushed on the door, swinging it inward on the hinges, and the moment he did, there was a sudden flurry of clicks in the room beyond.

He's seen me, Bran thought. He didn't want to give a second for the intruder to regroup his senses and, with a quick push, shoved the door open all the way. He jumped through, ready for anything.

His eyes swept the room. It was tranquil and clean, the furniture still where Rosie had left it. Empty. Not a thing out of place. He turned quickly, alert for any movement. A single, plain picture of a flower was on the wall next to the closet, the doors of which were closed. There were two windows, one directly behind Rosie's old bed and another on the far wall, curtains drawn over the glass.

He thought if it was a burglar, he would have gone out through the window, and so Bran quickly moved for it, pulling the curtains aside. They swept apart, light from the moon pouring in over his face, but the window was closed and locked. All the houses down Bolton Road were dark and still, not a single movement outside to tell him if someone had escaped. *What made that noise?* Bran thought with alarm, turning to look at Rosie's bed, then to the dresser, hoping to see something that might have caused it. *Maybe I imagined it,* he thought. It made him feel a bit ridiculous.

Suddenly, there was another loud tap, only inches behind him. It made every muscle in Bran's body tighten and freeze at once, every inch of his skin feeling as if it had been pricked by an icy needle. He spun to see who was there.

Still, as before, he was alone in the room. His gaze jerked along everything he could see, to the closet, to the door, to the dresser, down to the desk across the room. His eyes caught on something sitting on Rosie's desk.

It was her typewriter, old and rusted, the blue paint peeling and the round keys without labels—the old one she kept mostly for sentiment's sake. There was a single piece of paper in it, situated about halfway down the page. Bran couldn't imagine why it would have made a sound. He peered closer, the moonlight illuminating the page, and it was then that he noticed a long row of *X*s printed on the previous line.

"Strange..." he said. He hadn't noticed it before, but then again, he hadn't been in there for a while. What puzzled him the most was how the typewriter had made a sound. It wasn't like the fancy electric ones, or else he would have blamed it on the strange power surges earlier. The only way a key could have moved was if someone had pressed it.

Then, right in the middle of Bran's thoughts, there came a sudden flash of movement from the typewriter that made him jerk back. One of the keys had been punched, as if someone had struck it, sending one of the metal arms up onto the page, printing a letter. Bran gasped with shock, and then there came another tap, and another, all on their own.

It tapped twice more and then stopped, the keys moving right before his eyes with no one pressing them. He didn't know what to do, and when the movement ceased, he was still frozen in place, feeling the back of his throat go dry and his palms begin to sweat.

Very slowly he stepped forward until he could see the paper clearly in the light of the moon.

And printed on the page were two words:

Hello Bran.

Chapter 6

The Typewritten Message

Seeing the words on the page sent a shiver across Bran's skin.

"What's going on...?" he whispered, reading them and not entirely believing what he had seen. Bran was very alert now, sleep forgotten.

The keys had been typing *X*s before he had come in the room; it had known he was there and had drawn him in. Fearful, he took another step closer, reading the page again and looking around the room. Was it a ghost? Something trying to communicate with him? Bran moved until he was standing right in front of the desk, looking down at the words.

Suddenly, as if to prove to him it wasn't imaginary, the carriage gave a jump, sliding across the page to a fresh line. The keys started to press down by themselves again, the little metal arms striking against the page with rapid speed. The keys were pressed so quickly it was like a motor, the carriage jerking back into position in less than a second.

There isn't much time.

Bran swallowed hard, staring at the freshly inked words. It knew his name, which was enough to send terror through his skin.

"W-what's going on?" he asked aloud, unsure if it could hear him. There was a second of a pause, and then the keys flew to the page once more.

Help us.

The carriage leapt back across to a new line. He took a glance around the room. He was alone. He didn't waste another second, pulling the chair out and sitting in front of the typewriter.

"What's happening to you?" he whispered frantically, talking to the typewriter as if somehow they could hear him through it. The letters clicked across the page in a fury.

We cannot escape.

It went to a new line. Bran read the words, every nerve on edge. He couldn't think of what to say next. But he didn't want to let them go, whoever it was on the other end, so he stammered for something.

"Where are you?" he asked, keeping his voice low. The keys moved again.

Trapped.

It leapt to a new line.

She has enslaved us.

It crossed again.

Help us.

And then, in a furious scramble of keys:

There isn't much time.

New line. He felt the intensity of the room begin to grow. The page was almost to the end, and he didn't know how much longer whatever magic was at work would stay active.

"Who put you there?" Bran asked. Then the keys moved again, typing only four letters:

Emry

He blinked at the page, unable to do anything but read the name, twice, a third time, not believing what was there. His heart was racing, his hands shaking.

What can they mean by that? he thought with alarm. He saw that the typewriter had moved to a new line. They were almost to the bottom.

"Who are you?" he asked aloud. There was hardly room for one last line on the page. Sweat was gathering on his forehead. He gripped the sides of the chair in anticipation, hoping that it wasn't too late, staring at the last words on the page. Had the spirits left already?

But the keys snapped twelve more times. Before Bran could read it, there was one final push given to the page, and the paper went out the top and started to slide behind the typewriter. Bran caught it, bringing it up into the moonlight, so that he could see the final words written there.

The Specters

And that was all. The typewriter was out of paper.

Bran stared at it in his hands, almost as if it wasn't real, but it was there, as much as he didn't want to believe it.

"The Specters..." he said. An abrupt rushing sound filled the room, like a gust of wind, and a great, bright green glow erupted from the paper between Bran's fingers. It burned to the touch, and Bran reflexively threw it onto the desk. In a second he saw that it had ignited with green fire, eating the page as if a torch had been held to its center.

The glow blasted onto Bran's face, and he leapt back, searching for something to throw on it. But in a second he was already too late, and the glow ceased just as quickly as it had started, engulfing the room in darkness once more. All that was left of the page and the words written on it was a crumpled, ruined piece of paper. Bran seized it, but the paper was so brittle it tore into pieces, still hot enough to make him drop it to the desk again.

He quickly looked to the typewriter, but it was only metal and ink once more; whatever had possessed it had lost its strength and departed.

Bran could find no use for the shreds of paper, but he kept

them anyway, the darkened edges leaving black markings on his palms. He was bitter that his only clue had just burned itself up. He knew there was magic at work, strong magic, and someone who needed his help.

He went up to bed, but he certainly couldn't sleep, so he thought he'd do as usual and sit at his desk for a while until he was over it. However, when he got to his desk, he saw his blanket.

The box, he thought immediately, sweeping the blanket off. It was still there, the shape of the moon facing up. It felt almost as if Bran had uncovered the face of a corpse instead of a box. He had just brought it home and already strange things were happening—strange magic seemed to surround it, as if something within was trying to break free.

The Specters. Bran turned it over in his head. There was no disregarding what he had seen. He didn't exactly know how to react to what had happened. The box could be haunted for all he knew. Perhaps something inside of it was listening to his thoughts at that very instant, waiting to be broken free. The label said Emry Hambric, after all. In one startling thought, Bran wondered if it hadn't been left for him but contained something cursed from his mother's criminal past. Perhaps the Specters were actually spirits trying to twist his mind into breaking them free.

It scared Bran how little he knew. The desperation in the words on the typewriter played on his sympathies, despite the warnings in his head. He repeated what he remembered from them: "She has enslaved us." If it was someone, or something, that his mother had cursed before her death, could they be reaching out to him as a last resort?

The confusion nearly made him wish he had left the box with

Adi. He ran his fingers along its intricate metal ornaments at the corners. He was at a loss for what to do next, so he finally set it back and just stared at it for a long while, presently pulling out the piece of note paper that had been taped to the top.

The words Nigel Ten stared back at him: this mystery man that nobody had heard of. Perhaps he had the key—or at least knew about the box? But how to find him, Bran did not know.

The next morning he decided to go to Highland's Books, where he knew Astara would be helping Mr. Cringan get ready for Fridd's Day. Luckily, Mabel needed a new quart of echinacea, and the nearest herb shop was on that side of town, so he was easily able to use that as his excuse. It was a sunny day that smelled of freshly cut grass, since everyone was eagerly getting their houses ready for Fridd's Day parties.

There was a small group of people around the bookstore making up what remained of the repair crew. The outside had been completely rebuilt, with rows of shiny new windows on the front and red bricks all around. Already there were displays in the windows, waiting for the store to open, and some of the repair crew were doing bits of cleanup work outside. Over the door was a brand new sign with a banner pasted in front.

HIGHLAND'S BOOKS
GRAND REOPENING – FRIDD'S DAY EVE

Bran smiled when he saw it, for he knew that once the store

was open, the last bit of remaining damage from what had happened to him months before would be gone. He parked his bike in the front and went inside.

"Hello, Astara, anyone home?" he called. The workers inside ignored him as they went about, finishing up the hardwood flooring in a corner. Everything was brand-new, with rows of books already on some shelves.

"Over here, in the back." Bran heard Astara, and he started down the steps toward the door marked Employees Only—not that it had stopped him before. The back was more like a warehouse with towers made up of boxes of books, as well as files of public records which Cringan kept stored in the back. It was much emptier than it had been, mostly because it was where the fire had started and done the most damage.

"I'm over here," Astara said, and Bran spotted her at a long table with boxes of books surrounding her. There was music playing from a radio on the desk beside her, and as he made his way over, she lifted another box and ripped it open.

"Cleaning out?" Bran asked, sliding to the other side.

"Sorting it, mostly," she replied, looking at a book and then tossing it into a large pile on the floor. "Most of these have been here for ages and won't get sold. We're getting rid of what we can and putting out the rest for sale."

"You sure you'll be ready to open up by Fridd's Day Eve?" Bran said.

"Of course." She nodded. "There's not much left. We've already got most of it out. We're just waiting on the flooring to finish up. And I have to watch the—"

She jerked her head toward the wall nearby, behind which

Bran knew was a hidden room containing illegal books on magic. Astara nodded at him gravely: she was there to make sure none of the workers accidentally stumbled upon it, as Bran himself had done before.

"Are you going to move back in to live here, then?" Bran asked.

"Not sure yet," Astara said. "Most of my things are all right. Just a corner got burned, but half of it is ruined from the fire department. It's going to take some cleanup, and Adi said I could stay at her house if I wanted."

"Do that then," Bran said.

"It'll be really different," she said, twisting her face. "I liked it here. I won't get to hear cars rumbling by all day."

"Your commute to work will certainly get longer," Bran said, grinning, and she pushed the box at him but smiled anyway.

"What are you doing here?" she asked. "How'd you escape?"

"Mabel wanted some more medicine," Bran said. "Who better to send than me? But I really came here because I wanted to show you this."

He reached into his pocket and drew out the tattered pieces of the burned paper. He had carefully folded what was left so that it didn't break anymore, but it was still brittle, and he held it out so Astara could look.

"See any writing or words on those?" Bran asked her. She looked closer, taking the pieces and laying them on the table.

"Been playing with matches?" she asked, turning them over. Bran shook his head.

"No, this paper was all in one piece last night," he said. "It burned up all by itself."

He told her what had happened the previous night.

Unfortunately he couldn't remember all the words that had been typed, except for his mother's name and what they had called themselves: the Specters.

"What do you think it means?" Astara asked, looking closer.

"Either I'm losing my mind," Bran said, "or there's something in that box that's trying to talk to me."

"And we already tried getting it open," Astara said. She stared at him, both of them thinking hard.

"You didn't tell Adi, did you?" Astara asked. Bran shook his head.

"No, she'd take it away for sure," he said. "She didn't even want me keeping it. But there's no way I'm letting this out of my sight. Not now."

He let a deep breath out. "There's just something not right about all this."

"What's not right, now?" a voice broke in, and Bran spun. Astara swept her hand across the table and hid the pieces of paper in her hand just as Mr. Cringan stepped up to them.

"Can't be anything wrong with this week, can there now?" Mr. Cringan said, a smile across his face. "Fridd's Day's coming up, and it'll be the best one ever!"

Mr. Cringan had yellow hair on his head and through his cleanly cut beard, and white teeth shone when he grinned at them. He held two big boxes of books in his muscular, tanned arms. Bran jumped forward to grab the one off the top and set it on the desk.

"There we are now," Mr. Cringan said. "Nothing better than the smell of all these pages. And seeing an extra helping hand!"

Mr. Cringan chuckled merrily. He was much happier these days it seemed, and Bran knew it was because his bookstore was finally about to open again. Fortunately, Mr. Cringan had gotten a generous insurance policy, or else he might not be so jolly.

"We've got everything planned to perfection," Mr. Cringan boasted. "Hardly a detail left out. Yellow streamers and balloons and five yellow cakes, all laid out on a yellow table with corn tortilla chips and cheese sauce. Gigantic bowls of cheddar popcorn and caramels, and everyone dressed up in yellow like no one's seen!"

"Sounds like a real party," Bran said, and Mr. Cringan looked up.

"Well, you are coming, aren't you?" he asked with a smile. "You've got to come."

"You have to," Astara insisted. "We're going to have the biggest party in town. And you know how hard it is to get Duncelanders near any place with books."

"I wish I could," Bran said. "But Sewey has already drafted me into dancing with Madame Mobicci at their company party. I'm pretty much stuck."

"Oh well," Mr. Cringan said. He was clearly disappointed, though he tried to cover it up as best he could with a laugh. He started to walk away, stepping behind some crates. The moment he was out of view Bran spun back to Astara.

"That was close," he breathed, and she quickly slid the burnt scraps back to him.

"We've got to figure this out," she whispered. "There's something big going on. Last time this happened, this store burned down."

"That's not going to happen again," Bran vowed, shoving the pieces down in his pocket. There was something else in there, and he was reminded of the other paper. He brought it out for Astara to see.

"That's our clue," Astara said, looking at it. "It's the only real thing we've got."

"Right," Bran said, taking a deep breath. "If only we knew who Nigel Ten was."

"Well, Nigel Ten's not a person," Bran heard Mr. Cringan chuckle behind him.

Bran stiffened and turned, not having realized that he could still hear them.

"It's not?"

"Of course not," Mr. Cringan said, slapping some books onto a crate. "Where'd you get an idea like that?"

Bran blinked at him, and then he glanced at the note paper. "I just...found it."

"No, no," Mr. Cringan said, coming forward and wiping his hands. "The Nigels are a set of apartments that were owned by millionaire Nigel Stoffolis over by the docks. They were converted out of a mansion, and the rooms are rented out by the year to sailors and travelers and whatnot. There's about sixty rooms I'm guessing, all in the manor."

"So Nigel Ten isn't a person at all," Bran stammered.

"No," Mr. Cringan spread his hands apart. "Nigel Ten is a room."

Chapter 7

Finding Nigel Ten

The idea had never once occurred to Bran, and now he felt as if he was hotly onto something. Mr. Cringan saw that it was important and turned to the wall, where a calendar and a big, tattered map were pasted.

"Look, it's over this way, not too far," he said. "Don't see why you're interested in going to the Nigels, though."

"It's not really that important, I guess," Bran said, though he knew his face told the opposite because Mr. Cringan lifted his eyebrows. There was no fooling him. But he was the type of person who wouldn't meddle into anybody's business unless they asked for it, and so he finally relented and traced his finger along the road.

"But if it ever does in the future become of any importance," he said pointedly, "the best route is to follow along this way here, by the marina."

"Good thinking," Bran said. He knew he was already caught, even as Mr. Cringan turned again and walked off. Bran looked at Astara. Neither of them spoke.

"I'm going there," Bran finally said.

"I'm coming," Astara added, not leaving any room for him to refuse. It was close enough to lunch that she had an excuse to leave for a while, even though Bran could see that Mr. Cringan had his suspicions. Astara had a bike that was just about as cheap as Bran's own, black with parts of the paint worn off, but he was so used to cheap things he didn't really notice. It was a warm trip that was mostly flat ground and easy riding, until it got to a few more hills as they got closer to the docks.

Bran had gotten down this way before but usually only came to this side of town when he had to get something special for Mabel at Larak's Bakery. There were tall hills around with mansions dug into the sides, overlooking the river like bird nests. He knew the streets well and found the one Mr. Cringan had pointed out, biking down halfway and then skidding to a stop.

"Here we are," Bran said, catching his breath. Both of them paused on their bikes for a moment. Off to their right and ahead a way, the road had a sharp drop-off. A steep hill bordered the harbor, with boats parked in docks and people all about. That was Lake Norton, which flowed downstream until it reached the ocean many miles away. There was a muddy beach somewhere down there, though it wasn't close enough to see.

Off to their left, however, between a bunch of fancy seafood restaurants and buildings lining the busy street, stood a large, white mansion with tall columns in the front. It was significantly worn and old, parts of the roof sagged, and bits of the steps were broken in places. It looked as if at one time it had been something breathtaking but had aged in recent years. There was a wide wooden sign sticking out of the ground in front that read simply: The Nigels.

"There it is," Bran said.

"It's an ugly old thing," Astara noted.

"But why this place?" Bran asked aloud. She shrugged.

"No one would suspect anything strange here, I guess," she offered. It was the perfect place to hide something.

They crossed the street and leaned their bikes against the side of the building. The steps creaked as they went up, and Bran pulled the door open. A chilly artificial air blew out, wafting with the sounds of an old record playing inside.

"Close it, please," an old man's tired voice commanded. He was sitting at a desk to the left and didn't look up from his crossword puzzles. Bells around the handle jangled about as the door closed, mixing with the sounds of oldies music from the phonograph on the desk. Bran rubbed his arms in the cold.

"Good morning, sir," Bran said, looking about. The inside was all wood of an old design, with intricate carvings on the ceiling and cluttered with antique furniture. Hallways branched out in all directions, and stairs on either side of the room led to more. The creaking floorboards made the room echo as Bran turned slowly, taking it all in. A large stained-glass window on the front wall threw colors across the room.

"Morning," the old man replied, still not looking up. He found a word and penciled it in.

"How's business today?" Bran asked, searching for anything to say.

"Usual," the man said.

"Should be more travelers with weather like this," Bran mused.

"Perhaps." He erased a word and replaced it with another. Bran took a glance around the corner and saw that there were rows of doors on each side with numbers on the front.

"We're looking for a room here," Bran said.

"I've got plenty of 'em," the old man replied.

"Which ones are open?" Astara tried. The man looked up. His face was pale and bony with bits of gray hair poking out on his dirty chin. He was mostly bald, and his eyes narrowed as he looked them over for the first time.

"Aye," he said. "You want a room? We only sell rooms to folks old enough to have driver's licenses. Go get your parents."

"Oh, this," Bran stammered, "is my...sister. We're...apartment hunting, for our parents."

The man blinked and didn't look as if he was entirely convinced. Bran grinned stupidly, hoping he looked brother-like, and finally the man relented and started to look for his ledger book. He coughed roughly.

"Twenty-three's popular," the man said. "But it's filled. Forty-five's filled too."

"What about ten?" Bran asked. The man flipped through the book.

"Taken," he said. Bran's shoulders fell a bit. Taken? He hadn't been prepared for that.

"Who's got it?" Astara spoke up.

"Can't say that." The man shook his head.

"Come on," Bran said. "It's just a name."

"No, honestly, I can't," he said, squinting at the paper. "This bloody ledger's all smudged out for some reason. It's been there a long while, too, that's why. Whoever-it-is paid in advance."

"When will they be leaving?" Bran tried.

"Hmmm," the man looked in the book. "Oh, they've got that one booked for the next two years, it looks."

"Two years!" Bran gasped.

"On for longer than that, too," the man went on. "Ten's been taken for the past nine years at least. Probably some sailor who thought it'd be his home."

"Do you ever see anybody going in there?" Astara pressed.

He shrugged. "Never look," he said. "There's so many rooms I can't keep up with them. If they pay, they stay; it's been paid, so I don't care if they live there or not."

"You don't check on the tenants?" Astara asked.

The man furrowed his brow. "What they keep in their room's their business," the man declared. "There's rooms in this place I haven't been in since I started working here nineteen years past."

He nodded strongly. "But eleven's open, if it's any recourse."

"Great," Bran said. "Let's have a look at it."

He thought instantly that if they could get into eleven they'd at least be closer to the room than they were now. If anything, they could find a way to glance inside. The old man dug about for a key in one of the drawers, pulling out an intricate one with a metal number 11 welded into the handle.

"Second floor, right this way," the man said. He started to stand up but began to cough again and had to sit back down, raising a handkerchief to his face. Astara suddenly slid closer to Bran, dropping her voice to a strong whisper in his ear.

"He can't come," she hissed. "He'll take us there, and we'll never get to ten."

"What do you want me to do?" Bran whispered, as the man hacked into the handkerchief.

"Make him stay here," she said. Bran instantly knew what she meant by her tone: she wanted him to use magic on the man and convince him to stay behind. The man stopped coughing and shook his head, blinking to clear it from his sinuses. Bran was still hesitant, though, and Astara let out a breath and turned.

"How about you stay back here?" she suggested. "We can show ourselves up."

"No, no need," the man said, trying to stand. "I'll go up there and open it for ye."

"No, I insist," Astara said. "We can show ourselves up just fine."

"No, I'm all right," he said adamantly. Astara was getting nowhere, and Bran knew she was right. If the man went with them, their chances of getting to Ten were slim.

"Come on, just sit down," Astara insisted. "It'll be much easier, and you can rest."

"Thank you but no," the man said. "I'm not too old to walk up a—"

"Maybe you should listen to her," Bran broke in, and he slid command into his voice: it was something he had not done before with magic, but he knew that in his powers he also held the mental abilities of the Comsar: to communicate, to read minds, and perhaps to alter thoughts. The crossword puzzles in the *Daily Duncelander* obviously didn't do the man's mind much good because it took hardly any effort, and his eyes went blank.

"On second thought," the man lifted a finger, "perhaps she is right."

The man slid down back into his chair, his face confused. Bran pushed harder on the magic with his mind, feeling as if he connected with the man's thoughts, suggesting for him to stay behind, until he had fought down the man's mental barriers.

"We'll be back soon," Bran said, starting to pull Astara

toward the stairs. "Why don't you have some fun with more crossword puzzles?"

"Yes, yes," the man nodded, taking his newspaper up again and looking at it. Bran and Astara hurried up, the steps creaking under their feet. Bran felt it was a wonder the balcony even held up, and the whole place seemed like it could fall apart at any moment.

The hall was lit by a window at the end and some old light bulbs, so it wasn't particularly creepy or dark. The floor was covered with a thin red carpet, and there were doors on each side with numbers, none of them Ten. At the end, it went in both directions, almost like a miniature maze.

"Your sister?" Astara finally said. "Couldn't have come up with anything better?"

"It's the first thing that came to mind," Bran defended, though he saw she was actually trying to hide a smile while they searched. They turned the corner at the end, staying close together, although no one seemed to be up there who might notice. The halls were very wide and quiet except for their shoes against the wood, and the hallway at the end was lined with windows that showed the marina and the lake quite fabulously. They had to turn again, going down another passage until they finally found it.

"Ten, right here," Bran said. The door was closed. For a moment Bran looked at it, up and down, and listened for anyone beyond it. When he heard nothing, he pressed his ear against the door.

"Hear anything?" Astara whispered.

He shook his head and glanced both ways. "Let's go in."

"Let me get the lock," Astara insisted. "It'll make me feel better after not getting that stupid box to open."

Bran obliged, and she stepped to the door, placing her fingers around the lock, as if to feel its inner workings. Bran listened closely for anyone who might be coming.

"*Onpe likoca*," Astara whispered. She obviously had the spell down, because the lock clicked on command.

"See, you can do it," Bran said encouragingly. "As long as the lock is old and feeble and easy, of course."

"Don't even start," Astara hissed at him, and she took the handle and pushed the door open.

The room was dark save for the long lines of sunlight poking through broken slats in the wooden blinds. There was furniture all about, couches and chairs and tables, all made of wood and expensive upholstery, the seats of many covered with dirty white sheets. Littered across the floor were various scraps and notes, and, stepping inside, Bran's foot brushed against a piece of paper, the sound of which made them both jump.

"Sorry," he said in a whisper. The floor was dusty, the walls decorated with drab paintings that seemed like the artificial pieces of art found in dentist offices—and banks. On some of the tables sat sad looking vases, each holding a single, nearly dead flower drooping over the side. If the room had been a person, it was now a corpse.

"What is this place?" Astara whispered, her eyes sweeping the mess. Bran slowly pushed the door closed behind them, so that only a crack was left for them to hear if anyone was coming. He surveyed it all.

"I have absolutely no clue," he finally said. "It's all strange. More like a storage room than an apartment."

"Maybe your mother left something here, years ago?" Astara said. Bran wasn't sure. He still hadn't seen any evidence that anyone might be living there, so he started to step farther from the door. He came to one of the couches that didn't have a sheet over it, and he saw that there was something sitting on the cushion. It was a copy of the *Daily Duncelander*, opened to a certain page. "Astara," Bran said lowly. "Come look at this."

He gently picked the newspaper up so she could see.

"A newspaper?" she said.

"Look at the date."

"This week," she whispered. "Someone has been here recently."

Bran nodded, letting his eyes dart around the room, into the corners he had not checked before. He noticed something then: a long table on which were scattered papers and pens and discs. There was a television screen as well, next to a bed with tattered sheets, but Bran's attention had been caught by something else—

He dropped the newspaper into Astara's hands and started to it.

"There's no way..." Bran said in a low voice, hardly believing it.

The pile of papers was a mixture of colors and shapes, some torn and others bound by staples. There were charts and maps, ink markings and notes spread across them all, pressed down in places by strange mechanical devices and tiny surveillance camera lenses used as paperweights. There were many photographs in the pile as well, but the one that caught Bran's attention was sitting on the top.

The face in the picture was his own.

Chapter 8

The Music Box

In the photograph, Bran could have been no older than thirteen. He was outside their house on Bolton Road, holding a trash bag tightly in one hand and obviously in the process of taking out the garbage. He was in motion, but the photographer had captured his face with extreme clarity, even in the dim evening light. Bran felt like he had looked out a window and seen himself staring back.

"Astara, look at this," Bran hissed, waving her over. As he felt his hands begin to shake slightly, he knew that he was onto something much larger than he had thought.

"What is it?" she asked but then needed no answer. She looked from it to him.

"That's me for sure," he said, meeting her eyes. She looked as frightened as he was.

"Someone's been watching you," she said. She looked down at the pile of papers and slid them around, uncovering more documents. Her fingers stopped on a large, folded map, and she pulled it to the top. Bolton Road was circled.

"Whoever-it-is knows where I live," Bran said.

They leaned over it. There was a thin ink marking that started at Bolton Road, pulling from it onto the main street. The line went on down the street, and Astara quickly turned the map, unfolding and laying it out on the table.

"Look, it starts there," she said, and both of them pressed their fingers on it, sliding across, trying to see the faint line in the dimness of the room. Bran's heart pounded furiously, following the line, moving down the table to the end until they had to unfold the map more. The line led straight into a side of Dunce Bran had been to before; seeing it again stirred a memory he didn't wish to recall.

"The warehouse," he hissed, stopping his finger.

Astara looked at him quickly.

"See, that's where it's leading," Bran said. "The warehouse where Joris and his men took you."

"You think it's related?" Astara asked. Bran was about to speak, but the line didn't stop there. It started up again, making a corner and weaving down the streets. He followed it down until it came to another familiar location: Third Street. It circled an address.

"He's got the bank, too," Bran said. The line made a cut across the street, through the buildings, and onto the next street over.

"The alley," Astara observed, following the line as it came out the other side. The map didn't have the alleys marked so the line seemed to cut through the street itself and then make a quick turn on the next road, heading off in the opposite direction.

"Over here, it's going through the city," Bran said, moving to the other side of Astara and anxiously following the line. It took a sharp turn and then another, getting onto the highway and off again, then making a sudden turn and reaching the edge of the map. It stopped there, where another address was circled: Border Gates of Dunce.

"That's it!" Bran said, snapping his fingers. "I can't believe I didn't see it."

He tapped the final marking. "Look, it goes straight from my house, to the warehouse, then to the bank, and out of the city. Just like what happened months ago, when they kidnapped you and took us to Farfield!"

"Do you think it's them?" Astara asked.

Bran quickly shook his head. "They had us both here." He pointed to the bank. "They wouldn't have gone on tracking me."

"Someone else?" Astara said.

The thought sent a chill down Bran's back. It was very strange, but at that moment he recalled something from a conversation he had tried hard to let go—one he had with Baslyn, the man behind the Farfield Curse. Though the man was dead, Baslyn's words seemed to resound in Bran's head, words he could never forgot, and he remembered something Baslyn had told him the night he had died, about Shambles, who had tried to kidnap Bran: "He wasn't the only one who knew where you were, either. Someone else did, and he knew the house."

Is this that person? Bran wondered, throwing the idea about in his mind and trying to find an answer. It had to be. But who was it?

He found that in his concentration, his blank stare had come to rest on something sitting on the edge of the bed, mostly out of view because of the table. It was a wooden box, and it caught his attention immediately because it had metal all along the edges, just like the box he had found in the bank vault.

He slid toward it, and Astara didn't notice because she was

digging through the stack of documents. Gently picking it up, he saw to his disappointment that there was no marking of a moon at the top and no keyhole on the front. The design was similar, though, despite the fact that this one was more of a boxy cube, and as he turned to look for the lock he noticed a little metal arm sticking out of the side.

A music box, he realized.

He looked up, hesitant for the sound it would make, but at that moment he almost didn't care if someone did come—perhaps it would reveal who had been following him. So he gently took the handle and started to turn it.

The sound that came forth was sweet and like no other he had heard before, mellow and soothing. It brought Astara's head up sharply, but she said nothing as he went on turning it. He had started off fast, hoping to get the box open as quickly as he could, but the song was slow, and his motions slowed to match. Each chime of the instrument seemed tiny but perfect, muffled inside the box. Bran felt disappointed when it came to the end, though the click of the lock jarred his senses back to reality. He gripped the lid and opened it.

The inside was hollow, the instrument lifting up with the lid and the handle. He could see where it connected to the locking mechanism, the wood thick and strong even on the inside. There was nothing inside save for one object: a small, withered flower with yellow petals, sitting at the bottom.

"Anything in there?" Astara asked. He shook his head sadly.

"Just a flower," he said, about to close the box.

Suddenly, the flower gave a jerk. He looked back down into the box quickly, the motion catching his eye. It had gone still.

He reached to close the lid again, watching the flower. Again, it gave another jerk and flipped over.

He opened his mouth but couldn't speak. The flower leapt a third time, and part of it burst out like new stems, the leaves folding backward and the flower petal folding inward. The sides contorted into legs and the stems into arms, the flower blossom into a head, until in less than a second, it was no longer a flower but a tiny figure of a person.

The leaves had folded behind her back into tiny wings, though they were green and dull like the leaves they had been before. She was mossy almost, no more than three inches tall, colored in dry, leafy hues, like a living plant more than a living creature. Bran's eyes were held captive by the transformation so much that even when she shook her pale head and blinked her eyes, he almost could not make himself speak.

"H-hello there," Bran finally stammered. The creature's eyes shifted up and met with his. She blinked, her eyes tiny and bright, crystalline green. Her wings were so thin they were slightly translucent at the edges, and they twitched as she took a startled step backward upon seeing his face.

Astara hurried over and looked down into the box. The creature looked from one face to the other, fear in her eyes as she fell against the wall of the box.

"A fairy?" Astara whispered.

"I think she's scared of us," Bran said, gently setting the box down on the table. He stared at her for a moment.

"Maybe she's hurt?" Astara said.

Bran gently poked his finger into the box, trying to see if he could lift her out. In a flash of motion, the creature leapt forward, striking his finger with her teeth. It stung like a needle stab, and Bran jerked his hand back out.

"Obviously not hurt too badly," Bran said, scowl. The fairy's teeth had drawn a tiny droplet of blood so he held his finger in his fist. The fairy backed farther into the corner of the box, breathing hard with fear. She wiped the edges of her lips with her tiny hands, licking the bits of Bran's blood that had stained her teeth.

"Look, we don't want to hurt you," Bran said. "I'm trying to get you out of the box. Can't you see that?"

He gave the music box one half-turn, the first few notes of the song playing again. The fairy searched with her eyes for the noise.

"See?" Bran said. "I opened it. You can come out if you want or just stay in there."

But his words were not needed. Before he even finished speaking the fairy leapt out of the box, darting through the air and over Bran's shoulder. He spun around as she dashed across the room, like a very large fly. She knocked some papers off the table and jarred the hanging pulls of the lamps as she circled. Bran almost couldn't keep his eyes on her.

"What's she doing?" Astara said, fearful of the noise. At that moment, the fairy dashed straight at Bran's head. He didn't have a second to move clear, but he felt her run into his face, grabbing hold of his nose: the impact was hardly stronger than a falling leaf.

He blinked. Her face was so small that when she came close, he could see it clearly. She tilted her head, looking into his other eye. Bran was very still, unsure of what to do.

"Hello again," he said. "Who put you in that box?"

She blinked at him, as if she couldn't understand. There was a clicking noise that came as she folded her wings behind her back, almost like a cricket.

"You can't talk?" Astara said in a low voice, coming up beside Bran. The fairy shook her head somewhat remorsefully, putting one hand on her throat.

"But you can understand us?" Bran tried.

She nodded quickly.

"That's good," he said, glancing at Astara. The fairy crawled a bit down his nose, getting a better look at his face.

"You think she knows anything about who's in this room?" Bran said in a whisper to Astara as the fairy studied his face.

"She's got to," Astara said back. "He's probably put her in there until he gets back. But I don't understand why she—"

Astara stopped because the fairy had started to crawl across Bran's shirt, down to his hand, where she had bitten him. Bran stiffened as her feet and hands clattered across him, unsure of what to do, until she came to the wound. She circled the spot with the dried blood and then suddenly bit again.

"Hey!" Bran hissed, knocking the fairy away.

She leapt into the air, hissing at him through her teeth, leaping back at his hand and diving at the tiny droplet of blood. He swatted her away again.

"What in the world are you doing?" Bran said, his finger stinging again. "That hurts!" he hissed angrily, but the fairy was furiously wiping her lips, licking up every bit of his blood she could get.

"She's hungry," Astara realized. "She needs blood."

"But does it have to be mine?" Bran protested. The fairy darted around, shaking her head, and finally landing on his face again. He was about to hit her in case she was going for his nose this time, but she simply crawled up his cheek. She looked into his eyes again, as if they were mirrors. Bran was very tense, but he couldn't bring himself to brush her off.

"Don't bite me again. Understand?" Bran said, lifting his finger. The bleeding had stopped, but it still throbbed slightly.

"That hurts me," he said. It felt pointless trying to communicate with the creature, but he thought he saw her face change to remorse.

"You don't have to worry now," Astara said, looking closer. "A couple drops of blood could sustain her all week. Bloodfairies usually get it from animals, so she must be starving. I can't believe there's a fairy here, given how rare they are outside the woods."

"If she could talk, maybe she could tell us who's been snapping the photos," Bran pointed out.

"Perhaps if she could write it—" Astara began, but then the fairy opened her tiny mouth.

"Nim," the fairy said suddenly, and it made Bran jump. It was such a tiny voice: soft as a whisper, but perfectly clear.

"Nim?" Bran repeated.

She nodded, scampering onto his nose again.

"You can talk," Bran said quickly. "C-can you say anything else?"

"Nim," she said again.

"Is that who put you in the box?" Astara asked. The fairy shook her head.

"Nim," she insisted, looking at Bran and insisting with her eyes. Bran knew it then.

"Is that your name: Nim?" he tried, and at that she nodded

again quickly, leaping away from his nose and hovering an inch from his face. Her features were green and blue in places, a mottled color against the paleness of her skin. She didn't have to flap her wings more then once every few seconds, as if her body was lighter than air. Neither Bran nor Astara really knew what to say. Nim wasn't something they had expected to find at all in ten.

Bran heard a scrape from down the hall.

"He's coming!" Astara hissed, and both of them dove to the floor, jumping behind one of the couches. Nim moved as well, and as Bran fell she flew up next to him, clinging to the back of the upholstery. All three were very still. Bran held his breath as the door pushed open slightly, the soft creak like a scream. Bran could hear Nim's breathing. He held his hand up quickly, and she closed her mouth, biting her lip as she did. The door creaked open another inch.

"Ten, hm," a voice said. Bran recognized it: the old man at the counter. He closed his eyes and let his breath out softly.

"What a mess they've made of the place," the old man said grumpily, and Bran heard the key rattling. "Hucksters. Hucksters, the lot of them..." He went on cursing as he struggled with the lock, then he slammed the door closed behind him. Bran let his head fall against the back of the couch when they were alone again, and they heard the man continue down the hall.

"That was close," Astara said.

Nim began to breathe quickly. Bran got to his feet.

"He probably came to and went looking for the key to eleven," he said. "We've got to get out of here before he comes back."

"But we haven't even come close to finding out who lives

here," Astara said. "You saw it: he's been following you for months, maybe more."

"I know," Bran said. "But if we're caught in here it's over. I've seen enough."

Nim slid up around the back of him and stepped on his shoulder. He stopped.

"But we can't leave her here," Astara said strongly.

"He'll notice she's gone," Bran replied, looking at Nim up and down and thinking hard.

"She was trapped in a box," Astara pointed out. "He couldn't have cared much."

Bran took a deep breath. He knew Astara was right. Nim looked back at him imploringly.

"Nim?" she said softly.

Bran nodded. "We've got to hurry, and you've got to stay out of sight."

In that instant, understanding his words, Nim popped her arms to her sides and they seemed to mesh back inward, her head melting back to the blossom it had been in the box. In less than a second she was a withered flower again, and Bran had to bring his hand up to catch her before she fell off his shoulder. He gently put her into his pocket, trying to be as careful as he could.

"Be very still," he whispered. "Remember, you're illegal here."

They hurried to the door. Taking her out of the room might set the person who had been taking photos hot on his trail. But she was so small, so seemingly helpless.

They slipped out into the hall and crept down the stairs. The old man was back in his chair, still at the crossword puzzles with the record playing as if nothing had happened.

"Visit the Nigels sometime again," the old man said as they passed.

Bran nodded back at him as he pushed the door, but just as he was stepping outside, Bran's shoulder collided with another man coming in.

"Oh sorry!" Bran apologized. "I wasn't watching where—"

But the man didn't even turn to look back at him, trudging ahead. It had happened so fast Bran hadn't even seen the man's face, but he caught the back of his head: he had messy, dark hair and a black coat. Bran rubbed his shoulder where they had hit.

"You all right?" Astara asked.

"Yes, I'm fine," he said, stepping outside.

"Anything wrong?" she pressed.

"No, nothing," Bran replied, but something within him kept saying otherwise. He tried to shut it out, but it went on whispering a warning. He dismissed it as his nerves from narrowly escaping the room upstairs. The wind was beginning to get stronger and smelled of the water nearby.

"That man coming in was rude, wasn't he?" Astara said. "Ran right through you."

"Did you see what he looked like?" Bran asked quickly.

Astara blinked at him and then shook her head. "No, I wasn't watching either," she said. "Why?"

Bran shook it off. "No reason."

But inside an indefinable feeling kept pulling at him, and he felt an urge to look at the Nigels one more time. It was as if he could sense someone watching him from the house, though he kept walking briskly to his bike.

Chapter 9

Nim

That night, two thick cotton balls swiped from Mabel's medicine cabinet served perfectly as a bed for Nim. Bran stretched them apart and laid them flat on his windowsill, and she rolled around in the fluff before pressing her face to the window. The glass was almost the size of a cathedral to her. She was curious about everything; she could stare at things for hours.

"Nim," she said again, turning to Bran and pointing out the window. He was sitting on his bed, watching her closely. The light from his lamp reflected his face so he could hardly see anything through the window.

"The house?" he suggested. She shook her head and tapped the glass, insisting he come closer. He did and put his hands up to block out the light in his room. She was pointing down toward the road, where he could see the Schweezer parked askew.

"That's Sewey's car," Bran said. "It's a ferocious thing. Run when you see it coming."

Nim shook her head and went on tapping at the window.

"Garbage cans?" he said. "I see a car, garbage cans, the road, Mrs. Hortibury's garden, and then the next house. That's it."

Nim gave up and fluttered back down to the windowsill.

Bran went on looking outside, but there wasn't anything that he could see. Nim turned her attention to the board of drawings next to his desk, flying up and hovering there for a minute. She gently lifted the edge of one that had been falling so she could see it better and then moved to another, touching the pencil marking and then looking at the gray it put on her hands.

"Those are my drawings," Bran said softly, turning from the window. She wiped her other hand across the pencil shading and got it gray as well, and then she darted over to Bran, holding her hands out with a terrified expression on her face.

"Look, it's just pencil," Bran said. "It doesn't hurt."

She didn't look convinced. Bran gently rubbed her hand between two of his fingers. The gray wiped off instantly.

"It comes right off," he assured her. Bewildered, she looked at her hands. Bran sat down at his desk, ripping some paper off the roll beside it. He waved Nim over, and she stepped onto the paper, looking down as he gently shaded a long streak with a pencil.

"See?" he said, pointing to it. She got down on her knees, looking at the gray closely. Bran wondered how she could have not seen a pencil before. Had she been trapped in that box all her life?

She rubbed her fingers in the gray, but this time she smiled widely when she saw them. She wiped her hands on a clean part of the paper and looked delighted when they left a faint mark.

"Hold on, sit over there," Bran said, unable to keep from smiling. "I'll show you."

She slid back on her knees, watching him very closely. He started to carefully draw the lines, glancing at her every few seconds and seeing that she was held enraptured by his motions. His pencil swept across the paper until very slowly he had formed a likeness of Nim, kneeling down just as she was at that very moment. He shaded her wings in with deep strokes, and then her wide eyes.

"Look at that," he said. "I think it's you."

"Nim," she said excitedly. Bran carefully added the three letters that spelled her name to the bottom of the sketch, and she stood before her likeness, still staring at it.

"Like it?" he asked.

"Nim," she replied. She crawled off, and Bran pulled the drawing up to put on the board, sticking it in the bottom corner so she could see it from the desk.

What am I going to do with her? he wondered. He hadn't wanted to ask the question, but he knew the real danger he had brought to himself. If she was seen he would be off to jail in no time. He heard a sound and glanced at the box and was startled to see Nim peering into the keyhole.

"Wait, no!" he burst, leaping forward and seizing the box from her. His rush of motion caused her to fall over. He dropped the box onto the desk again with alarm.

"Are you all right?" he asked frantically, but she was already getting up. She shook her head, looking to be very dizzy.

"You can't touch this, understand?" Bran said severely, but the harshness in his voice caused him to stop. She blinked up at him, confused, and he bit his lip.

"Listen, this is just very, very dangerous," he tried to explain. "There's something in here, and I don't know what it is. It could hurt you—or me."

She didn't look as if she really understood, but the fear in her eyes told him that she knew from his reaction that it was something important. He covered it with the old blanket again. Nim fluttered up to pull the corner over the other end. When he was finished, he glanced at the clock.

"It's late," he said aloud. "I've got to get to sleep. Since you're staying here you probably should as well."

He reached to the lamp switch and turned it off. Instantly, two circles of blue appeared as a glow in the night, resting on the edges of Nim's wings, almost like eyes. Bran was surprised to see the color. As Nim breathed in, it went green, and when she breathed out, it went to blue again, like a softly pulsating lamp. She had flown to the window and was looking out again.

"What's out there now?" he asked. She shifted her head, crawling up the window and then tapping on the sill. He sighed and went back over.

"Look, there's nothing out there," he said after studying the lawn and road again. "There's not even a squirrel or a cat."

"Nim," she insisted, trying to keep his attention.

"Look, it's really late," Bran said, checking the window one final time. "I need to sleep. Tomorrow we can go out there and look if you want."

Nim sighed and gave up trying. She settled down into her cotton ball bed and folded her wings softly over her like a blanket. The glow of her wings continued, but it was so soft and Bran so tired that as he settled into bed, even it didn't keep him from falling asleep.

Very early the next morning, Bran awoke to a huge racket downstairs. He almost leapt up but felt something on his cheek.

He didn't move, expecting a wasp or a mosquito, but found Nim curled up on his face, sleeping.

"Wake up ye and feel the cheer! Tonight's the feast 'cause Fridd's Day's here!" a chorus of voices roared in song downstairs, banging bells. Bran blinked and shifted his eyes up—not even daylight out.

"Fridd's Day Eve already?" he groaned. The singing voices were far too in tune to be the Wilomases; it was probably Ms. Hattie and Her Roaring Chorus out caroling and paying back the neighbors for never going to her parties. Bran very gently slid Nim onto his pillow, stealing down the ladder. He overheard Sewey give a nervous chuckle by the front door.

"Thank you everyone, thank you and bravo!" Sewey called out, the front porch light illuminating the visitors in the dark. "Wonderful performance. Five stars. Stupendous." He clapped frantically. "I feel practically full of Fridd's Day cheer already and it's not even four o'clock! Not even four o'clock!"

The people laughed and whacked their bells, not catching Sewey's drift. He winced at the clamor and gave another fake laugh. Mabel came out of the bedroom, squinting and wrapping a robe around herself. The neighbors waved. Mabel did not.

"Look, Mabel," Sewey said, turning to her. "These people have come to wish us Fridd's Day cheer. Come: happily sacrifice precious hours of sleep with me."

Mabel furrowed her brow. But the most important thing in the world to the Wilomases was to appear at least as respectable as, if not more than, their neighbors, so she forced a smile. First went up half of her lip, and it fell. She tried a second time. The muscle trembled from lack of use.

"Like you, it is about this time every year," Sewey went on, "I actually feel like climbing out of bed at some unholy hour and waking my neighbors with an accolade of metal instruments! Truly a—"

The lights on the front porch started to flicker, causing Sewey to lose his concentration.

"Ah," Sewey said. "Truly a remarkable—"

It happened again. Not only were the lights on the porch starting to dim, but the lamp Sewey had turned on downstairs faded as well. There was a night light plugged into the wall next to Bran's foot, and even it buzzed in and out.

The neighbors looked at one another awkwardly and then up at the lights. For a moment, the flickering seemed to have stopped.

"Erm," Sewey tried again. "A remarkable feat to—"

But then the lights went out entirely, with a horrible fizzing sound that caused the carolers to jump. It sounded like the hiss of an angry cat. It was followed by a strange rumbling. The noise seemed to be coming from all the walls at once, like a great stone being rolled across concrete, reverberating around them.

The neighbors began to shuffle about nervously, and Bran could not deny the fear that crept up his back. The sound kept growing louder and more horrible, grating at his nerves. Then, suddenly, the lights came back on. Sewey jumped, and the sound was gone again.

The neighbors gave a collective gasp and turned to one another, as if checking to make sure they were all there.

"Totally sorry about that," Sewey stammered. "I, uh, it must be something with the power lines."

The neighbors had begun to whisper, and Bran caught tidbits about "overdue bills" and "Wilomases getting poorer" and "city cutting off their power."

"Oh, nothing of the sort!" Sewey stammered.

The neighbors did not look convinced. The Wilomases appeared to be in an even worse financial state than before. One of the neighbors even came forward with her checkbook, offering a donation. Sewey nearly went into hysterics but finally got them all off his porch and closed the door with the lightest of slams.

"It's mad!" he whined. "What the rot is going on with our lights?!"

Bran, still in shock over the strange sounds, was beginning to be convinced that it had something to do with the box. He tore himself from his thoughts and came down the stairs, hoping to get some cereal. Sewey, however, followed him into the kitchen for coffee—but the moment he stepped through the door, he reared up like a mad goat.

"It's that bloody *machine!*" Sewey roared, jerking his finger toward Mabel's tarbofluximator.

Mabel gave an enormous scream, casting herself in front of it. "*It is not!*" she squealed as loud as she could, causing the cups in the cabinet to rattle.

Sewey leapt toward the machine in a frenzy, as if he might tear it piece by twelve-thousandth piece with his bare hands.

By the time Balder and Baldretta awoke a few hours later, the tarbofluximator had been tossed outside in the backyard rot heap behind Sewey's shed, with its wires hanging down like a sad spider. The separation left Mabel in tatters as well, and she sat by the window that faced the yard, occasionally reaching out toward it.

Sewey was in a far more delightful mood now, and he came back inside with grease and dirt on his hands.

"Good morning children," he said.

"Monster," Mabel hissed at him, going upstairs and slamming the door. Sewey felt no remorse and instead grabbed the newspaper and carried on as if nothing had happened.

Mabel didn't appear for breakfast, so they all had cereal, much to Balder's dismay. To make up for it, he doused his in three heaps of sugar, while Sewey ranted and raved about something in the newspaper.

"We've got that rotten party tonight," Sewey grumbled as he ate. "The whole rotten thing's going to be a mess. All those rich people and their gold buttons and fancy watches."

"You could always rent a fancy suit and watch tonight," Bran suggested.

"It's just all rot," he said. "Decorations and cooking and Friddsbread to get."

"From Larak's?" Bran said, perking up. "I was just down on that side of town—"

Bran caught himself and stopped, but Sewey had already heard it.

"What the bloody rot were you doing down there?" he gasped.

"I was...seeing a friend," Bran said, which was basically true.

"A friend?" Sewey stammered. "What the rot does that word even mean? You could have been out picking up our Friddsbread order from Larak's instead of cavorting with hooligans. Now you've got to bike all the way back there this morning."

Bran didn't feel like protesting. He finished breakfast, cleaned up, and went back up to his room. Nim was waiting for him, and she zipped around his head.

"Shh," Bran said. "I've got to head out somewhere today." He knew he couldn't leave her there alone. "You've got to hide if you want to come along."

She seemed eager to join him, and Bran set off outside. Larak's Bakery was a good way off, very close to the Nigels—so close Bran wanted to kick himself for having to go all the way out there again. It was the rougher side of town, where the roads were bumpier and there were more dogs and fewer businessmen. Bran had to swerve his bike to avoid pockets of dingy men arguing in the streets. When he started to smell something burning he knew he was getting close. He came to a large building with a sign hanging over the street and blowing in the wind, which read:

LARAK'S BAKERY

OVER 95 YEARS OF BREATHTAKING SERVICE

It was, in fact, so breathtaking that people stumbling out of the building seemed to have trouble breathing at all. Smoke poured out of the windows like they were chimneys. Bran coughed as he made his way in and saw three other people already standing inside with drooping faces. The smoke was so thick Bran couldn't see the ceiling. The sound of breaking pots and dishes filled the bakery with an echoing clamor.

"Leave it open!" Larak the baker shouted above the noise, wiping his hands on a cloth. He was short and in his mid-thirties, with a walrus moustache and big ears that stuck out the sides. His clothes were stained from head to toe. Gigantic blimps of smoke were pouring out of the oven behind him, but he wasn't even paying attention; instead, he was furiously scribbling on a yellow notepad.

"How goes the new play?" Bran asked, but Larak only waved his hand to silence him until he had finished what he was writing.

"Well, Bran, very well, thanks," he said. He shoved the pad in his pocket with a dissatisfied huff. "This one's for the big stage, it is. Full house, that's what. I see the reviews. Sizzling. Wonderful. Hottest play of the season."

"There's something else that's a bit hot in here," Bran said, nodding toward the oven.

Larak blinked, and, spinning around, he leapt forward with his oven mitts. Out came a solid black, bricky loaf of bread—amid a stream of curses. "Blasted ovens!" he roared. He tossed the pan onto a cooling rack and fanned the smoke toward the window, coming to the counter. "You're here for the Friddsfeast, I'm sure. Everyone's wanted my Friddsbread."

"Only the best," Bran said.

Larak snorted. Bran covered his mouth and went on breathing in the smoke; his eyes were beginning to sting, and he felt a little dizzy.

Bran felt Nim jerking about in his shirt pocket. He quickly turned to face the wall, fearful that someone might see but instantly disregarding it: the smoke would cover almost anything.

"What's wrong?" he whispered, pulling his pocket open. He couldn't see much in the dark room, but she thrashed about, and he dug his hand in quickly.

"Are you all right?" he said, setting her in the palm of his other hand. She went limp for a second, and for a terrifying moment Bran thought that she had suffocated to death. But then she rolled over, jumping to her feet.

"There, now are you OK?" Bran said urgently, but she didn't look at him. Instead, she shook her head, and Bran noticed that her eyes were glowing.

It wasn't the usual green he had seen before—not the brightness or happiness that had been there. It was something behind her eyes, like a storm that was beneath her pupils, fierce and violent. Seeing this sent fear through him.

"Wait!" Bran hissed as Nim flew straight for the wall. She hit against it a few times like a trapped fly. Bran stumbled forward to catch her, thinking the smoke might have hurt her. But she leapt out of his reach and found the open door, zipping outside.

"Come back!" Bran called, loudly this time because he really didn't care who heard anymore. There was terror in his veins—not for himself if she was seen but because something was so clearly and gravely wrong. As he dashed out of the bakery he caught a glimpse of her rushing ahead of him.

Please, don't get out of sight! he thought. He saw her looking about for a moment, confused and lost, unnoticed by the crowds of people passing on the sidewalks below. It gave Bran just a second to leap onto his bike, hearing Larak calling out after him.

Nim shot off at full speed. Bran pushed on the pedals to follow her.

Chapter 10

Watched

No matter how fast Bran pedaled, Nim flew faster. She went sporadically, dashing from one way to the next, never stopping for breath, the green glow behind her eyes always present. It seemed as if madness had overtaken her.

Bran wasn't really watching where he was going and narrowly missed hitting a few people. He couldn't lose sight of her—not in the city. Even though it was only a few minutes, it felt like hours before Bran saw her make a final turn, and he realized where he was.

"Here again!" he gasped, out of breath but still pedaling. He saw the Nigels just up ahead.

"Wait, Nim, please," he pleaded, but she had gone deaf to his voice. He plowed right through the crowd on the sidewalk, causing people to jump out of the way and shout at him. He dropped his bike in front of the Nigels as Nim struck against the front door. He thought that he finally had her, but she found an opening in the mail slot and popped through it.

Bran darted up to the door and blew through it.

"Come back!" he commanded, but the echo of his voice was like a slap. He was struck to silence by the sheer emptiness of the place. The old man was not at the desk. The record player was still on, though it had gotten stuck and was skipping.

"Hello?" Bran called, stepping forward, barely catching sight of Nim as she flew around the corner at the top of the stairs. He started after her but skidded to a stop.

The old man was there—slumped over the desk, unmoving.

Bran's eyes widened. "H-hello…" he said in a hoarse whisper, terrified at what he was seeing. The record continued, skipping against the man's right hand. Bran grabbed his arm and jarred the record so that it stopped. He began to shake as he pushed the man forward onto the desk again, searching for a telephone to call the police. Out of the silence that had overtaken the room, there came another sound: the soft strains of a music box coming from upstairs, and Bran recognized the melody.

"Nim…" he breathed, rushing for the stairs and up to the hall. He came around the corner, his shoes pounding against the wood. He heard the song come to a sudden halt, which made him run faster. He saw the door to Ten ajar and, without caring what happened, burst through.

"Nim!" Bran hissed. She flew at Bran and began circling his head as she had before. He tried to grab her, but she was too excited, finally stopping in front of him. There was a smile on her face, and the stormy greenness behind her eyes had once again subsided.

"Nim, what's going on?" Bran demanded.

The smile disappeared from her face. She tilted her head as if she didn't understand what he had asked, blinking as if she didn't know where she was at all. The moment her eyes looked at her surroundings, she shot toward him, grabbing onto the shoulder of his shirt in terror.

"Why'd you bring me back here?" Bran asked. He wasn't so much angry as terrified. He wanted to call the police. He felt as if eyes were watching him from every corner and at any moment someone might leap out at him. He let his eyes sweep the room and saw that nothing had changed since yesterday—except for one thing. Across the room, beside the bed, Bran saw the faint glimmer of light: a television.

His eyes had caught a glimpse of the video playing, and the movements were so familiar that he instantly recognized it. He inched toward the screen. The video was filmed from an odd angle, slightly crooked but very clear. Bran could see what was happening.

"Look, we don't want to hurt you," he heard his own voice say in a low volume. It was he and Astara in that same apartment, the window slats casting dim light across their faces. He watched, enraptured by the image; it was as if an invisible camera had followed him in there. The blood in Bran's fingers felt like it was draining away as he watched with wide eyes. He felt violated. Nim had stopped on his shoulder and was watching the screen with him.

"It's got everything..." Bran gasped. He tore his eyes from the screen, scanning the room but too afraid to move. He could see no cameras, though there were plenty of places that one could have been hidden. Just as that thought crossed his mind, there came a bright sound from behind him that caused his eyes to freeze: the music box. Nim leapt into the air and shot behind Bran, but Bran froze in terror. He could feel another presence. Someone had entered the room.

The song played slowly, the sound of the metal wheel turning like the screech of a rusty hinge to Bran's ears. The song reached the end.

Standing there, leaning against the frame of a door to another room, was a man.

His hair was dark and long but turned back off his forehead, making him appear hardly more than thirty, though the small flecks of gray suggested he was perhaps far older. The man's face was a few days unshaven, and his eyes piercing and so dark they almost seemed black. He was tall and hardened like a soldier, though he looked amused. As Bran stared at him he only stared back, the music box held between his hands and Nim clutching onto the man's right shoulder, her eyes a wild, animal green again as she crawled robotically up the man's black coat.

"Look at that," the man said, his voice warm and sardonic at the same time. "Looks like Nim brought the prize in after all."

Nim looked back at Bran over her shoulder, still clinging to the man's coat. There was no recognition in her eyes, and she bared her teeth at him. When she smiled, it was the same smile as the man held: as if Bran had fallen right into their trap.

"Looks like she's just dragged you along with her," the man said. He started in Bran's direction, and Bran tensed up, ready to spring for the door, but the man only passed him to set the music box on one of the side tables. He opened it and turned the wheel, and Nim rushed forward and into the box again, and the man closed it and set the lock.

"Nim here is a troublemaker," the man said. "Not so much unlike yourself, Bran. Perhaps that's why she's gotten attached to you so quickly."

"Who are you?" Bran demanded. There were so many emotions at once: anger for being led into a trap, brokenness for whatever had happened to Nim, fear for what the man was going to do to him. Bran knew well that there were many undesirable characters in the world who wanted him for the powers he had inherited from his mother. The man only looked at him once and then shook his head.

"I don't think you're in a position to ask me questions, Bran."

"I can ask you whatever I want," Bran said, the anger within him winning out over any fear he had. He knew that with magic, he could escape this man, if he was merely a mercenary or someone who had been sent to kidnap him. But if this man was a mage—Bran did not know how to tell either way—then it could become messy.

"Aren't you afraid I'm going to kill you?" the man asked abruptly. It was said in such a blunt manner it felt like the man threatened people every day, as if shooting Bran and hiding the body would be no different than turning off the television.

"I've had close scrapes with death before," Bran said, trying not to let his voice waver.

"Not as close as here with me," the man replied.

"So you are going to kill me?" Bran asked. "Like the man, downstairs. You killed him too?"

The man gave a slight laugh and moved for the other table, on which had been scattered piles of papers the day before but which was now mostly cleared off. There were a few things left, which he gathered and put into a thin, leather bag, next to which was a dark sack that looked to be filled with something thick.

"That man isn't dead," he replied. "He's only unconscious for about ten more minutes. Just enough time for me to leave this place with no money in the cash register."

He shrugged. "Unfortunately, he hit the panic button, and the police will be here in about the same amount of time, if they can draw themselves from lunch long enough."

Bran was appalled at how natural it seemed to this person, talking to Bran as if he had known him for all his life.

"Who are you?" Bran hissed again, his voice demanding an answer. The room went very still at his words, but he did not back down.

The man looked to his bag, drawing from it a single videotape. He approached Bran slowly, and Bran forced himself not to shrink away.

"Take a look at this," the man said, holding the tape out. Bran hesitated, so the man reached past him and punched on the VCR, exchanging the tapes himself. The screen shifted.

"Watch," the man insisted, gesturing to the screen. Bran didn't want to, but he finally turned to look. The video fizzled to life and began to play.

On the screen, Bran saw stacks of boxes and crates, all lined up. The angle was from above, like something perched on the top of a roof support. It took Bran a few seconds before he realized he was looking at the back warehouse of Highland's Books, before the fire.

Bran saw himself on the screen, walking in through the darkness, looking wary. Out of the corner of the screen, there came a hand that grabbed Bran from behind, and in a flash of motion, he had spun about, swinging his hand out and throwing the person into a stack of crates behind him. In a second, he was thrown off his feet as well, and Bran realized what this was.

"You," the man said, "at Highland's Books, meeting the girl named Astara."

He punched a button on the remote control, whizzing backward, and the scene shifted.

"We'll go back more," he said. "Highlights of the day before?"

Now it showed the park, right in the middle of the Duncelander Fair, just as it had been months before. The scene cut to the second when Bran leapt in front of the huge truck coming toward Rosie: his hands came up, and a thin, translucent blue wall appeared. The truck hit against Bran on the screen, nearly throwing him back.

In his shock as he watched, Bran slid down to sit on the edge of the bed.

"Ahead a bit?" the man asked, and he punched the button before the scene finished. It changed to show Bran being led through the side door of Farfield Tower with Joris and the men around him.

"A bit more?" the man asked, skipping to another time. The scene changed angles, watching through the window of an office, at the very second that Baslyn shoved Bran through the glass and into the rain. Seeing it happen all over again sent pain through Bran, as if he was reliving it.

"Want to see more?" the man asked. "How about Shambles closing the door? How about you and Astara running down the stairs? Or do you want to see something different, perhaps Joris and Elspeth at the van, just as the bombs go off? Or maybe you at Adi's house, when—"

"What do you want!" Bran suddenly shouted, jumping from the bed and turning on the man, his hands in fists now, ready to fight. He had seen enough to know this man could be the most dangerous person to him in the world—even if he had no intention of killing him there.

"Are you going to show it all to the police?" Bran said, backing away. "Are you an officer? Have you been watching me all this time?"

The man said nothing. Bran was breathing fast, anger built up inside of him; how stupid he had been letting someone watch him that closely and not once even suspecting it. If one minute of that tape was to ever fall into the hands of a police officer—even someone in the Magic Investigational Police—it would be over for every person he knew.

The man stepped forward, and Bran inched back into the corner.

"No, stay away," Bran hissed. The man narrowed his eyes and then took another step closer. Bran backed away by instinct, but the man only reached for the television and ejected the tape. He slipped it into his bag.

"Never," the man said, "ever, ever, ever think no one is watching."

He turned. "We are always watching."

"I want to know who you are right now," Bran said through clenched teeth, not afraid anymore, because he had had enough of being afraid. He came forward, but the man didn't move, calmly zipping his bag. The man looked up.

"Are you going to Comsar me?" he asked sharply. "Why don't you throw a bit of magic in with your words and try to make me tell you then. Magic seems to have served you and Emry quite well, hasn't it?"

The man's words hit Bran like a train—this stranger even speaking of his mother was an insult.

"Don't you dare talk about my mother," Bran said. The man seemed to shrivel under these words, drawing back slightly.

"Your mother," he spat, and his calm voice became interjected with anger, though he tried to hide it. "Look at where she is now. Dead. Because of magic. You keep up with it and maybe you can follow in her footsteps."

"My mother died trying to save me," Bran said. "You know nothing of her!"

"Your mother died when the magic caught up with her," the man shot back. "It does to all of us mages one day or another. She was just on the wrong side when the killings begin."

He zipped another pocket on the bag. "As for my name, I'm Thomas, though most people just know me as T."

Bran recognized it instantly. He remembered months before, when he had stolen Joris's silver cell phone, that someone by the name of T had called, just before Shambles had first shown up at their house.

"I know what this is now," Bran realized. "You've been following me ever since my mother left, and you told Joris where to go. Didn't you?"

Thomas nodded without remorse.

"Unfortunately, I am that person," he said. "But I'm someone worse than that, Bran. I'm also your father."

Chapter 11

The Man Called T

The word caused Bran to shrink back, as if the man had reached forward and slapped him. But recognition struck him in that same instant. Though their eyes were different colors—Thomas's a slate gray—and there were no deep physical similarities between them, there was something to his voice, something Bran hadn't perceived before but was clear as day to him now. The revelation drew no reaction from Thomas, and though Bran deeply wished to deny it, he knew that the man's words had been the truth.

"M-my father?" Bran stammered.

Thomas didn't nod, didn't even turn to look at him. He just picked up his bag and the sack beside it and the music box and turned to the door.

"Wait!" Bran said. His voice cracked. The man continued out of the apartment, and Bran rushed after him. "If you're my father, why haven't you come? Why did you leave me there and watch me work in that house for years and then tell those men and Shambles where I was?"

Inside, a part of him was weeping, but at the same moment he was angry, knowing that his own father had done this and was now walking away yet again. His mind did not know how to react. He felt he was in a nightmare but couldn't break free.

He had waited all his life to find someone—anyone—who was actually a part of him. But this stranger had called Bran his son just as he might have called him his neighbor or his dog.

"Bran, there are higher things at stake here than you, I'm afraid," Thomas said, not looking at him as he locked the door to Ten. "Much higher things."

"But...you've been here," Bran said, trying to restrain the emotions that were hitting him at once. "I've thought you were dead all this time."

"No, you haven't," Thomas replied, starting down the hall with Bran close behind. "You haven't really thought about me too much, I don't think. You've been far too concerned with Emry."

"I have," Bran countered. "But she left me with a note—and you left me with nothing. Now you come out of nowhere with no answers, and you expect to just disappear again?"

"There are higher things at stake here," the man said again.

"Enough to put my life on the line?" Bran said.

"Possibly," Thomas replied. "And it worked. You drew Joris and Elspeth out of hiding."

"So I was the bait," Bran said sharply. "You set me up because you knew they would come to get me, and then you'd know where they were."

"Precisely," the man said. "But don't worry, they'll be dead soon enough."

"Dead?" Bran demanded, coming around the corner. "Whose side are you on?"

"No one's side but my own," Thomas said, looking straight ahead with a half smile. Bran followed, hearing sirens in the distance. Instead of going for the front, Thomas took a sharp turn toward the back of the building. At the end, Bran saw another door that led outside.

"So you're just going to leave again?" Bran asked as Thomas pushed outside. Everything there was rocky gravel, with an open view of the streets on both sides. Thomas moved for a dark gray car parked near the back entrance.

"Are you?" Bran pressed. "Just leave and take Nim with you?"

"Perhaps," was all his father would say, opening the door and dropping his things in as the police sirens got closer. Thomas turned the sack over and dumped all the money out into the music box, taking no care to avoid smothering Nim. He then dug around and scooped out a handful of the money and stuffed it back into the sack.

"Hold this please," Thomas said calmly, shoving the sack at Bran. He slammed the door and brought the music box to the front with him. "I am leaving this place. And if I was you, I'd leave quickly as well."

He reached for the driver's side door handle.

Bran shook his head. "Then I wish I hadn't even met you. You're a horrible father."

Thomas's hand stopped, the door pulled halfway. Bran could see the reflection of his father's face in the window.

"I was called that once," Thomas finally said. "By your mother."

"And now she's dead," Bran said.

For the slightest of an instant, the hardness behind Thomas's eyes seemed to shift in the reflection, as if his features fell for just a split second, before stiffening once again.

"So she is," he replied. "And soon there will be a few more dead because of it." He yanked on the door handle, his heart a brick wall once more.

The engine roared throughout the lot, and Bran stepped back. Thomas pulled the car out and onto the gravel, the wheels throwing up some of the rocks as he drove away, spraying hot pebbles and a cloud of dust upon his son.

Bran kicked the rocks with anger he couldn't hold in any longer, but a flash and loud noise jarred him. He spun and saw two police cars coming around the other end of the lot, their sirens blaring and their lights spinning. His first reflex was to point the police in the wrong direction so that Thomas could get away. The reaction shocked him, that he would even consider helping this man.

"He went that way!" Bran forced himself to shout, contrary to everything his confusing heart told him but obeying what his mind demanded. He pointed down the road, trying to get them in the right direction. It was at that moment he realized that in his right hand he was clutching a sack of money.

"Oh no…" he said, as he realized what was happening, and looked up and saw that the cars were coming straight for him. A deeply fearful thought came upon him: what if they tested him for magic somehow at the station? They would know he was a mage.

In a flash he spun around, dashing off before they could get a good glimpse of his form, dropping the bag as he did. He heard their engines roar, but he already had a head start, shooting around the corner and down the side street.

The cars weren't far behind, their tires scratching and sliding on the rocks. He felt his heart pounding as he ran, heat rising up and causing him to sweat. He could hear the sirens bearing down, and he leapt through a grove of bushes, falling and rolling into the yard of a small white house.

He hadn't lost them yet. The cars screeched to a halt, and he heard the lumbering officers dash out in pursuit. The bushes provided him with hardly any cover. He ran even faster around the side of the house. *Great, running from the police now,* he thought, panting for breath. *Can things get any lower?*

Just then Bran slammed into a tall wooden fence. It knocked the breath out of him for a second, but there wasn't any time to lose. He grabbed the top, pressing his shoes against the gate's handle and flinging himself over.

"Come back here!" the officers roared, but he was already running again through the yard. There were a swimming pool and a swing set but thankfully no people. The opposite end was gated as well, and Bran pushed through it, dashing out onto the next street. The officers were still shouting, trying to find a way past the fence.

There was a large wooded area just across the next street, and he headed for it, turning back toward the main road before he lost his bearings. He was nearly out of breath, but he managed to get deep enough into the trees and brush that he couldn't be seen from the road. He fell to the ground that was covered in a bed of pine leaves and sticks, and sat there bent over, trying to catch his breath.

Cars rumbled by on the road, and he stayed still even though he was hidden well. It had been such a close call that it was hard to slow his speeding heart. He heard the police sirens getting closer and getting louder. He was very still until he heard them pass, and slowly he was able to calm himself.

He knew he was in one of the parks but not one that had many visitors. He could see the shapes of houses through the trees and across the street, and the roof of the Nigels poking above the gates and rooftops. Already, there were ambulances and fire trucks gathered outside: at least he knew the man at the counter was getting help.

When he finally thought it was safe, he stood up but found that in his frightful run, much of his strength had been spent. He stumbled and had to catch one of the trees for balance, getting golden sap on his palms. He didn't care; somehow, he had escaped.

He made his way through the trees carefully, creeping along the edge of the road until he reached a corner far from the Nigels, and made a quick exit onto the sidewalk. He tried to look casual as he did it, though no one was around to see him anyway. Everyone must have scurried home for the Fridd's Day parties already.

It reminded him of why he had come that far in the first place and only made him feel worse about the condition he was in. He tried to brush the sticks from his clothes but ended up smearing his shirt with tree sap. Still, he felt it was best to get as far away from the Nigels as he could, so he headed for the road and caught the first bus that arrived. Thankfully, he had the money that was meant for the Friddsbread. The driver eyed his clothes but drove on. Bran didn't even know where he was going. He just didn't want to go home and be interrogated by Sewey.

So he sat there, facing out the window on the bus, as its tires squealed at each stop. People filed on and off, carrying groceries or pulling along children. The city became a blur as it passed, and Bran continued to stare out the windows, glimpsing the tiny form of his reflection in the windows of the shops that were closing early for the celebration.

How did I end up here? Bran thought, too bitter inside to offer himself any answers. Anger was mixed in with sadness and fear for what might happen—but mostly betrayal. It was his father's fault Bran was running from the police. His father had planned it all along; he simply didn't care what happened to Bran.

Knowing his father was alive and cared nothing for him hurt worse than thinking he was dead. Part of Bran wished he had never met his father—if Thomas Hambric even deserved to be called that.

The rumble of the engine continued to lull his thoughts until the exhaustion set in and he fell asleep leaning against the side of the bus.

When evening fell on the thirteenth house on the right side of Bolton Road, Sewey was peering out the windows. Bran still hadn't turned up. And this meant there was no Friddsbread.

"His head," Sewey muttered between clenched teeth. "Off with it. Off with it *now!*"

As all the stores in town had closed, Sewey was left with no choice but to accept his fate and hope the guests forgot about the Friddsbread. It was a slim chance, like forgetting candy on Halloween or torches at a book burning.

He was forced to hang up the decorations himself and ended up tying himself in knots of streamers and having to be unwrapped by Baldretta. Mabel threw the food out onto the tables downstairs. The house very quickly became one big, yellow madhouse.

Bran still did not show. The hour grew later, and then the telephone rang.

"Shush, everyone!" Sewey hissed. "It's the rich people calling!"

He went for the telephone in his office. They had recently purchased a new one with a big caller ID display on the front. It was one of those fancy gizmos Sewey had no care for, but the picture on the front of the package showed a banker, and he looked like he had gobs and gobs of money, so Sewey bought it. He hummed to himself, hoping it would make him sound cheerful and obliging, as he slid his glasses on his nose to read the caller ID screen.

Dunce Cops

Sewey gasped.

"What the rot?" he said fearfully. "What have I done now?"

It rang again.

"If I don't answer it, maybe they'll go away," he whimpered.

It rang.

"I'll get it then!" Mabel screamed from upstairs.

Sewey was seized with a terror. "No, Mabel!" he roared, grabbing the phone off the hook and then immediately dropping it again to hang it up. He fell back in the chair, wiping his brow.

"That was close," he said. But then the phone started again.

"Dah!" he shouted, leaping up.

It was the police again.

"Don't answer it!" he boomed, and he pulled the plug on the phone and then dashed to the one in the kitchen, pulling its cord out also. He went all throughout the house, disconnecting every phone there was.

"No police officers are ruining this Fridd's Day party!" Sewey huffed.

When Bran awoke, he didn't know where he was. The bus hit a bump, jolting away the grogginess. He looked around only to discover that the sun had all but set. Everyone else had gotten off the bus except for one other person, who was sitting across from Bran and staring at him in an odd manner. The man's thin figure was like a human pencil broken into a sitting position, and his small head was nearly eclipsed by an enormous puff of sandy hair. It stood out in all directions, as if the bus walls buzzed with static electricity.

Bran blinked, but the man did not. He just went on staring. His face spelled confusion so much it might very well have been written there.

"Hello," Bran said, his voice echoing.

"Aye," the man replied with a quick nod.

"Where are you headed?" Bran asked, digging for anything to say. He felt that if he kept this man talking, he might not think about leaping at him with a hatchet—or whatever else he had planned.

"Out of here," the man said. "Just got released from the Dunce Jails."

"Ah," Bran said, nodding slowly. His gaze darted to the bus driver—a scrawny, college-aged boy who looked as if he could barely lift a pillow, much less fight off an escaped lunatic.

"I was innocent," the man went on. "Got me on indecency. I was masquerading as a man who was masquerading as a man who sold...things."

"Doesn't sound so bad," Bran said. "What'd you sell?"

"Papers," he replied.

Bran lifted his eyebrows incredulously. "Well, then," he said. "I'll remember that next time I scribble on a notepad."

The man shook his head.

"Not just any normal papers, no siree." He looked around, and then put a hand up to the side of his mouth. "Magic papers."

Bran coughed. He'd heard that before.

"The name's Rat," the man went on. "Mr. Rat."

Bran coughed into his hand again at the name, blinking. "Mr. Rat?"

The man nodded slowly.

"The same Mr. Rat," Bran went on, "who tried to sell magic papers on Twoo's Day?"

Mr. Rat blinked. He did it again and about two dozen more times, as if the marching beat in his head had skipped and he now had to get it back on track.

"I can't really remember," he said. "'Tis all muddied up."

"You probably don't want to remember it either," Bran consoled him.

"Yes, yes..." Mr. Rat repeated, as if recalling some wistful memory. His face twisted up. They rode in silence for a bit, and Bran quietly plotted various ways of escape if Mr. Rat jumped at him.

"And it was such a useful invention, too," Mr. Rat lamented after a while.

"Well, you're out and about," Bran said. "So they must not have thought you were much of a threat." *Or they were too afraid to keep you,* he considered silently.

But Mr. Rat shook his head. "Nah," he said. "There's a whole lot more magic in this town than they know of, and I ain't the deepest threat. None too harsh on Mr. Rat. I was let go after some community service, and now I's heading off to Yarrow for a job at the subways."

Bran nodded, unsure of what to say. He felt a bit uncomfortable when Mr. Rat mentioned the magic in the town, but he was certain enough that Mr. Rat was not hinting at anything. The bus came to a stop just in time.

"Fifth and Main Street," the electronic voice said from the ceiling.

Bran looked about—he hadn't realized how close the bus had brought him to home. Two passengers got on at the front of the bus, so he stood and headed out the back door, thinking he could stop by Highland's Books and maybe use the telephone. The streets had already darkened. As he walked back to the corner and the main road, the streetlamps seemed to follow him, flickering on one by one as he went. It was coincidence, but it warmed him inside, as if the lamps were in some way trying to comfort his heavy steps.

The sidewalk was deserted, with most people heading off to parties or to the grand celebration in Givvyng Park, where the mayor would ring the Watling Bell and light off some fireworks. Much more interesting than anything the Wilomases might concoct. And the longer Bran stayed away from the house, the later it would be for him to get into trouble. As he walked, he felt intensely lonely. He'd grown so used to Nim in only a day that not having her with him felt like he was missing a piece of himself. The streets seemed far colder and far emptier than usual, but he trudged on and tried not to think about Nim back in the music box.

Several cars turned at the corner ahead on Fourth Street. Bran realized with a start that Mr. Cringan and Astara were having a Fridd's Day party of their own. He had completely forgotten about it. He started toward the street with renewed vigor, only to glance down and realize that he was not dressed in yellow, but in fact was dirty and covered in tree sap, dust, and bits of sticks. No way could he show up to the party.

Still, he cut in at Third Street and took the alley around the back, hoping he might get to at least pull Astara aside for a minute and say hello, and maybe take a sip of the Friddspunch, since all the running had left him frightfully thirsty. The back door to the bookstore was unlocked, so he just went through.

He could hear the loud sounds of revelry. There was rock music playing from in the main part of the store, and people were laughing and shouting at each other. A pang of wistfulness shot through him; he wished he could be a part of it. There were long tables in the back warehouse of the store on which were ice chests and plates and extra cups.

"Bran?" Astara's voice called. She was already there, holding an empty tray with plastic silverware and plates piled on it, about to put it into a huge garbage can.

"Happy Fridd's Day," Bran said, hastily brushing off as many of the sticks as he could from his clothes. Astara dumped all the trash and rushed over to him.

"So you got away after all!" she said, sounding thrilled, even as he went on brushing the mess onto the floor. She was dressed in light jeans and a clean yellow shirt, and had gotten her hair done in curls. She looked different; Bran had only ever seen her when she was working or on an errand—or when they were running from people who desperately wanted to kill them.

"Yeah, I, um, barely managed to escape," Bran stammered, partly because he didn't know what to tell her anymore and partly because he felt embarrassed about how he looked.

"Well, that's good," she said. "Feel like joining in? Mr. Cringan's about to start some of his horrible karaoke."

"Actually," Bran began. "Well...I don't know."

Astara seemed to have picked up that something was not entirely right, so she set the tray onto the table. "Just want to talk?"

It always struck Bran the way Astara seemed to be able to read his mind, so much that sometimes he doubted she was a Netora at all, but really a Comsar in disguise. Still, he shrugged.

"Not really," he said.

"How about somewhere else?" she suggested.

"No, I don't want you to leave the party." Bran shook his head.

"I told you, Mr. Cringan is about to do karaoke," Astara replied dryly, placing the lid onto the garbage can. "Let's go to Givvyng Park, and we'll see the fireworks before it's too late."

Bran almost smiled. On Bolton Road, he would never have been allowed to simply leave and head off to the park without running errands along the way. But with Astara he felt as if he had some power in the strength of the two of them, and he no longer feared what was going to happen when he got home. So he agreed, and she smiled, and they started out the back door in the direction of Givvyng Park.

Chapter 12

A View from the Water Tower

Astara knew enough about Bran not to talk about what was troubling him. There was a chilly wind, but the park was not far away. There was a large and bustling crowd already, with a stage set up in the middle of the grass and people gathered all around it. Mayor Demark was on the stage, giving a roaring speech about patriotism and Duncelander spirit, and at the end of each sentence the crowd would shout in approval and ring bells and shake yellow maracas.

The crowd was vastly different from the sort Bran was accustomed to with the Wilomases and the wealthy people they tried to impress: there were people with children, some carrying cotton candy and ice cream. It struck Bran how odd it was that a group of Duncelanders could seem so happy and yet innately harbor such a deep loathing toward those outside their walls. Seeing the cheerful and smiling faces almost made Bran feel as if each of them was wearing a mask, covering up some dark secret. These same happy neighbors might turn on him in an instant if they knew who he was.

Every person was wearing something that was yellow: jackets or shirts or shoes, even a few with yellow pants. Bran felt uncomfortable and out of place again. Astara looked about for some place to sit with a good view.

"It doesn't have to be close," Bran said. "We can see the fireworks and miss hearing the mayor's speech at the same time."

"The concert," Astara said. "There's going to be a concert after he speaks, from Hillins Frugal. We came all this way, so we might as well enjoy it."

"Sheesh," Bran said. "So we'll suffer through the speech. But we won't be able to see, look at the size of the crowd."

Astara pointed off to the right. "How about up there?" Her finger was tilted upward at a dangerously high angle.

"Beside the water tower?" Bran asked hopefully.

"No, on top of it, you gat," she said.

He laughed. She did not.

"Wait..." he began, but she had grabbed his arm, pulling him and ignoring his protests.

There was a sea of tall grass surrounding the tower, nearly up to their knees, waving in the wind as they brushed through. The tower was a small one compared to most, no longer in use and its fence long gone—but the city thought it too expensive to take down the rusty metal monstrosity. At one time, it had been a frequent spot for rowdy teenage boys from Droselmeyer High School. They would test out their manliness by climbing to the top and doing various stupid things, like jumping jacks during a tornado or leaping off with a garbage-bag parachute. However, after Bingo Rondle had fallen and broken eighty bones the summer before, kids had pretty much avoided it.

Astara did not seem anxious at all, and Bran wasn't about

to let her go on without him. He wasn't afraid of heights, but as they stood at the bottom of the water tower and when he looked up, he couldn't help but feel dizzy.

"H-how do we even get to the top?" he asked.

"There's a ladder," she said, gesturing to its obvious spot.

"There's not one for the lower part," Bran pointed out. The company who had built the water tower had been smart and chopped the ladder off above where most people's heads would have reached; the local teenagers usually brought their own ladder.

She still looked at him as if he were stupid. "Come on, Bran. It isn't that hard." She turned her back to him, and then leapt into the air—far higher than any normal human.

Bran spun around to make sure no one was watching. "Astara!" he hissed at her, but she didn't seem to care and had already started scrambling up without him. So he took a deep breath and jumped; the powers came naturally to him as if he used them all the time. He shot upward and grabbed hold of the rungs. They rattled with his impact, and when he realized just how high he had jumped he clung to them tightly.

"Come on, Bran," Astara insisted. He huffed and started to clamber up, trying not to look down as he rose higher. The ground slowly got farther away, until he reached the top and swung over the edge. Encircling the perimeter of the tower was a thin walkway with bars—but even with the bars, Bran felt his heart beating faster, and he clung to the railing.

"Over here," Astara called.

The wind was cold on his face. The mesh flooring rattled below him as he made his way around, and he saw that Astara was already sitting with her back against the tower.

"You're late, he's just finishing," she said with a grin.

"Oh no," Bran said with fake regret. "I feel horrible missing it."

She shook her head at him, and he slid down next to her. Their shoes hung out over the edge of the tower, and he heard the crowds below give a rousing cheer as the mayor finished. The mayor traded places with a set of four band members with guitars, all dressed in yellow suits with yellow ties, who started to play a rocked-out version of "Here Comes the Yellow Squid," a traditional Fridd's Day classic.

But even with the loud music far below, all felt silent on the tower. Complete darkness had set in, so that the only lights on their faces came from those of the party below. Even though it was cold, everything was still and serene.

"Nim's not here," Astara said, not looking at him. She had finally noticed—or else she hadn't said anything before on purpose.

"Nim went back to the man who owns her," Bran replied after a while of silence. Astara continued to stare down at the concert as the lights began to flash with the guitar rhythm.

"Why did you let her go?" Astara asked. Bran didn't know how to reply.

"Because," he said, "the man who owns her is my father."

And that was all. That was the only reason he knew. Thomas was his father. And by revealing that, Thomas had disarmed Bran of every weapon and defense he had.

So Bran told Astara how it had happened. She said nothing as he spoke. He almost felt as if his eyes should get teary thinking about it, but the cold wind on his face and the bitterness in his heart left no room for crying.

Bran fell silent. The song changed below and then changed again—and still, Astara didn't speak. It wasn't until the fourth song that she did.

"It will all work out," she said.

Bran didn't feel so sure. "What about the box?" he said. "We still haven't gotten anywhere with it."

"So let's bury it," Astara said, taking Bran by surprise.

"Bury it?" he repeated. She nodded.

"Why do we really need it?" she said, her eyes still staring down at the musicians. "I mean, really. Problems started again the moment you found that in the vault."

Bran took a deep breath. She was right. She finally turned to meet his gaze.

"Do you really want to go on forever trying to win a war that people have fought for thousands of years against this dark magic?" she said. "They'll go on fighting until they get what they want."

Bran was left open-mouthed. He didn't know how to respond.

"So we're fifteen now," Astara said. "Is it really right for us to get into this war—to find out who these Specters are, why they want you? How do we know they're not just tricking you? Do we really want to be involved in the war that ended your mother's life?" She shook her head. "I say we bury it now and try to go on and forget about it. Next time, they might not leave any bookstore left to rebuild."

Bran sat there for a while, letting the emptiness creep over them once more. He was shocked to hear those words come from Astara of all people. It wasn't like her to give up. Bran could hear that she was afraid, perhaps not even for herself, but for what might happen to him.

"I can't give it up," he said. "This might go on forever, but we've still got to fight, because if nobody fights, then we all will lose." He let out a deep breath. "It's because of what happened to my mother I've got to do it. Because I believe what I read on that paper, and I may very well be their only remaining hope. It's my duty to help them—because of my mother."

They were strong words, and held a resounding depth.

Astara seemed to accept this. She leaned back and closed her eyes, letting the sounds below take over again. The band ended their last song, and the announcer said that the fireworks display would begin soon, at the stroke of midnight, after the mayor rang the Watling Bell. A crew began to wheel the ancient bell onto the stage. It was inscribed with many great and epic scenes of the history of Dunce, most of which were concocted tales about grand victories and battles against gnomes and mages.

"I just don't want them to hurt you, Bran." Astara broke the silence.

"Hurt me?" Bran said. "How would they do that?"

"I don't know." Astara shook her head. "They almost had us a few times. Or have you already forgotten all about that trouble you caused?" She punched him on the arm, and he faked being hurt, falling to the side before coming back up again and lightly knocking her back. She laughed quietly.

Bran felt better seeing her smiling again. "Come on, Astara," he said. "You know that, together, we can't be taken down by just a bunch of guys with guns."

"But what if they do get to you again?" Astara asked, unable to hide her fear.

"We made it out all right," Bran said.

"But what about now?" Astara asked. "Your father's suddenly here? This strange box? I just have such a bad feeling inside, like something horrible is going to happen."

"Look," Bran said, "we've saved each other before. We can do it again if things get bad."

Astara let his words sink in, and they seemed to comfort her.

"I just don't want you to think for one second," she said, "that if they get you again that I'm not going after you. Because I will, even if you don't want me to."

Her voice was grave and resolute. Bran wanted to argue with her but found he couldn't bring himself to speak. Behind her eyes, there was not only a fierceness but sadness as well.

"I'm going to be all right," Bran said, trying to smile again. "On the other hand, if you're so concerned about me dying, maybe we shouldn't make climbing water towers a habit?"

She mustered a faint grin at that, and then they heard the mayor on the loudspeakers.

"May I have your attention, please," the mayor bellowed. "Fridd's Day is about to begin. On my ringing of the Watling Bell, the great day will have officially started! Countdown begin...now!"

The crowd started counting down from eleven, as was tradition. When they reached zero, the mayor lifted the gigantic paddle and gave the bell an enormous whack, which sent him spinning and caused the floor of the stage to shake. The bell was so loud it rang high up onto the top of the water tower, and everyone cheered and screamed with joy—and the fireworks exploded, sending up a storm of yellows and golds.

"You know," Astara shouted over the noise, "I might want to have another go at that box."

Bran looked at her with horror. She was grinning though.

"Not with magic," she said. "Maybe if we hang around it we'll figure something out."

"How about tonight?" he shouted.

Astara seemed all right with the idea. She stood up with the fireworks still blazing and, before Bran could stop her, swung herself over the edge of the tower.

Bran gasped and jumped to the edge, his heart nearly stopping. She stumbled a step on the landing but caught her balance.

"I hate how you do that," he hissed, trying to make himself breathe. Astara started to wave her hands, beckoning him down.

"Here goes my death," he said and swung himself over the railing. In a second, his arm was twisted so that he was forced to let go, otherwise he might have just dangled there. He plummeted through the air, the wind beating at him, pushing his hair all around as he flew. He felt weightless, like he was falling from the highest diving board at the city pool. The ground came closer and closer, and just as he neared the grass, magic slowed his movement, bringing air between him and the ground. He landed heavily on both feet, tumbling forward onto his knees.

"Ooh, that hurt," he said.

"You baby." Astara laughed. He grumbled and got to his feet shakily, and she finally offered him a hand. Starting around the tower, Bran instinctively glanced to where he normally parked his bike. It wasn't there.

"My bike..." he said. "I left it in front of the Nigels." The police might track it back to him! But a moment after, his mind was put at ease. "Oh." He remembered with a grin. "It's still got Sewey's name carved on it."

Chapter 13

The Green Light

Back at Bolton Road, things were going magnificently. The guests had arrived in limousines and sedans driven by chauffeurs with white gloves. Even the hubcaps were polished to mirror-like perfection, so that Sewey could see his reflection as he peeked through a slit in the blinds.

The Board of Directors of the Third Bank of Dunce had shown up first: a mess of cranky old men and even crankier old women, the smell of cigar smoke and perfume following them indoors. The men were mostly overgrown sausages, their coats bright yellow and snugly tailored to fit their planetary bodies. Some had military badges and sashes over their coats, and others had ink pens tucked in the edge of their pockets for quick stock exchanges. The women wore high, beehive wigs and had powdered faces, with long curled fingernails and bright yellow dresses that hung loosely about their corpse-like figures.

The Wilomases ushered the guests in, and soon the house was bustling. Sewey scuttled about, making sure the wine glasses were constantly full.

"Enjoying yourself?" he asked a member of the board when she appeared at the food table.

"Hardly the Hotel Lumiere," muttered Madame Manchini,

studying the selection of food on the table. She lifted her nose even higher than usual and sniffed so strongly it pulled Sewey's hair forward like a draft of wind.

"The Lumiere?" Sewey tried to chuckle. "That old place. Probably couldn't throw anywhere near half the party."

Madame Manchini's eyes widened. "I own the Hotel Lumiere," she scoffed. She spun and left. Sewey was left petrified.

I'm finished, he thought.

"Well, fool?" came a familiar voice, and Sewey turned quickly.

"Oh!" he gasped. "Madame Mobicci!"

She tapped her cane on the floor, and it seemed the earth threatened to crumble beneath it. Madame Mobicci wore no beehive wig, no makeup, and no yellow—but instead wore the same black robe she had worn every single day of every single month of every single year for as long as Sewey could remember. Her old skin would be the envy of any prune.

"We telephoned," she said. "Nobody answered."

"Did you?" Sewey said, spluttering. "I didn't hear the telephone ring."

"Sewey disconnected the phones!" Balder bellowed like a trumpet from the stairs. "The police kept calling!"

Sewey narrowed his eyes on Balder but let out a fake chuckle. "All this Fridd's Day jolly has gone to the boy's head," he said. "Silly idea, police calling!"

"Police?" said a voice near Sewey. The man was round as a beach ball and wore a row of metal badges and awards like a shiny billboard. His soldier's name tag, placed precisely where everyone could see, read Colonel Brumtoppa.

"No, no police," Sewey assured him, attempting to smile.

"Yes, yes police," Colonel Brumtoppa said, taking Sewey by surprise.

"No, Colonel," Sewey insisted. "No police."

"*Yes!*" the Colonel nearly roared. "*Police!*"

He jerked his finger toward the window, where suddenly Sewey saw a cacophony of flashing blue and red lights reflecting against the blinds.

There came a loud pounding at the front door. Most of the guests instinctively recoiled, their past business sins returning to haunt each of them.

"Do not worry!" Sewey shouted. "Everything is under control!"

"What is the meaning of this, Wilomas?" Madame Mobicci demanded, catching his arm. "Are you set on ruining the entire Third Bank of Dunce's Fridd's Day party in front of all the richest people in town?"

"Not at all!" Sewey stammered in horror, thinking of how many times his head might roll in punishment. "Probably just a parking ticket for a limousine!"

But the whispers had already grown so loud she could hardly hear him. Sewey tore through the jabbering crowd and finally made it to the door, with Mabel, Balder, and Baldretta stumbling behind him.

"Open up!" an officer demanded. The crowd gave a gasp.

"We could barricade the doors!" Balder suggested.

"Open up or else!" the officer said. Sewey, not wanting to take any chances, brushed his hands down his suit, straightened himself up, and pulled the door open.

"Yes?" he said.

There were at least six police cars and a dozen officers, all spread out and in full gear. The glare of all the lights fell upon the sea of the people behind Sewey.

"Mr. Wilomas?" the chief officer growled. Sewey was relieved to find that it was not Officer McMason, who was probably off for the holiday. But the man at the door was just as intimidating, nearly half a head taller than Sewey, with three times the muscles down his arms.

"Ahd, udh..." Sewey stammered. "Yyeesss...?"

"I'm Officer Rex," he said. "We have reason to believe you were downtown by the marina this evening."

"Sorry, wrong house," Sewey said swiftly, starting to close the door. He was stopped by a well-placed elbow from Officer Rex.

"We also have reason to believe," the officer continued, "that you are a suspect in a robbery that happened just this morning."

This accusation caused the crowd behind Sewey to gasp at once.

"Preposterous!" he bellowed. "My entire household has been here the entire day. No one was anywhere near the marina or any robbers whatsoever!"

"Well, then!" the officer said, becoming annoyed. "How do you explain this?"

At that, one of the deputies behind him wheeled forward a familiar, rusty contraption: two wheels, handlebars, and a few metal shafts and gears. Upon further examination, Sewey realized that the old piece of junk was a bicycle on which was carved the name SEWEY WILOMAS. The officer coughed. Sewey felt the blood draining from his face.

"I'm afraid," the officer said, "that I will be arresting you now, Mr. Wilomas."

Sewey opened his mouth to protest, but the lights in the doorway blinked out for a moment. The officer jumped.

"Erm..." Sewey had lost his concentration. The light flickered again, this time going out and then returning with a half-glow—and inside the house, the lights flickered as well, all of them going out at once, then returning.

"Are you trying something funny?" the officer growled, rattling the handcuffs as he pulled them out. "Now by the order of the Great and Glorious City of Dunce, I hereby arrest you, Mr. Sewey Wilomas, for—"

"What's this?!" Colonel Brumtoppa roared.

Sewey spun, the officers looked up, and everyone else began to stumble backward. Right above the Colonel's head, the ceiling had begun to glow. It seemed to be a trick of the light, but in a second all doubt had been erased, because the glow expanded at a rapid speed, seizing the wall and growing to the floor. It was like a ring of fire that did not burn, and it cast a strange greenness upon their petrified faces.

"Great Moby..." was all Sewey could say.

The glow caught the wallpaper, spreading down the halls, up to the ceiling, growing in brightness, as if everything were catching flame.

The officers, breaking from their fear, suddenly shouted from outside, and Sewey saw that the green had lit up the yard and street. He shouted, and the guests screamed and began to run for the door. Sewey was pushed aside in the frenzy, the green growing brighter and stronger.

A slow, rising, high-pitched sound squealed in Sewey's ears. The bright, fiery glow blinded him. He finally reached the door, surrounded by the piercing green light, the noise, and the screams from the people around him as they dashed out of the house in a mass panic.

When he staggered outside, his strength returned and he found himself running with Mabel beside him. He discovered that in his arms he was carrying Baldretta, though he had no memory of picking her up. They spilled into the street, and Sewey spun, looking back at the house amid the shouting and sirens. He squinted in the light.

The entire house, from the bottom of the open door to the highest point of the roof, was a piercing green. He looked up and saw that there seemed to be a source: a deeper, darker glow, from which the illumination seemed to originate. It was the attic window.

"Great rot..." his voice finally returned, though he couldn't even hear himself over the shouts and screams of those around him.

Bran and Astara arrived back at the bookstore, though Bran stayed in the back room, still feeling out of place. Astara fetched Adi, who was happy to drive them both back to Bolton Road for the remainder of the Wilomases' party.

As they approached Bolton Road, he spotted something strange ahead.

"Look at that," he said, pointing upward. Right above the rooftops of the houses, they could see a strange, green glow on the dark horizon.

"Wow," was all Adi could say. "Are those fireworks?"

"But it's green," Astara pointed out. "All the fireworks for today would be yellow."

Their confusion only grew as the brightness of the glow became more pronounced. Bran spotted blue and red lights ahead.

"Oh no…" he said.

Adi turned onto Bolton Road. And he saw the madness. People were running about screaming in party clothes. There were police with guns shouting into radios, jumping into their cars; guests were falling onto the grass, dashing across the street, doing anything they could to get away from the light.

Adi gasped, spinning into the street and gunning the engine. Bran could only stare at the house. The brakes on Adi's car screeched to a halt, but Bran had his door open a moment before, leaping out and stumbling forward, shielding his eyes as he did.

An enormous, high-pitched tone pulsated from the house, cutting into his ears. Bran fell forward, dodging behind a police car when he could go no farther. His skin was bathed in the light, and his heart pounded harder as the fear rose within him. *The box!* his mind screamed. The noise and the light were so strong that he felt he would be pulverized by it. But then the sound began to take forms in his mind.

It became a mixture of high, garbled screams, like a crowd of people being murdered, screaming in agony at the same time.

"Hammmbriiiic," he caught: a whisper floating among the agony. He heard it again, and a third time. There were so many voices that he could not decipher any other words, just a mass of torture.

There was a great, deafening shatter, as the windows of the

Wilomases' house exploded outward. The people screamed and covered their faces, the yard littered with bits of broken glass that sparkled like gems in the green light.

"Hambricccc!" the voice called again, sick and hurting. It twisted around Bran like a whirlwind.

Out of the corner of Bran's eye, he saw someone move. Astara stumbled to her feet, wavering for a moment.

"Get down!" Bran shouted, but his voice could not be heard above the screams and echoes coming from the house. Astara didn't even notice him, her face stony and pale, as if she was seeing something everyone else could not. Her eyes locked on the open doorway, and Bran shouted for her again, but she stumbled forward a step toward the house.

"What are you doing?" Bran yelled, but Astara pushed forward, the power rushing against her with the strength of a thousand winds, blowing her hair and shoving her back—but her gaze remained focused ahead, as she took another heavy step closer. Bran pulled himself up; she was nearly to the door, the lights from inside the house silhouetting her in their glare.

"Stop, Bran!" Adi tried to grab his arm, but he pushed her away, fighting his way toward Astara, covering his face with his arm.

Astara didn't notice him. Her clothes were being buffeted by the powers that fought against her steps. Bran tried casting magic outward, anything to pull her back, but the magic did not come. She stopped at the door, the green glow now so bright that Bran couldn't see anything but the black outline of her form.

"Astara!" he yelled, one final time.

But before her name had left his lips, Astara stepped across the threshold.

In an instant, she was enveloped by the green, like a wave of water crashing over her. She was lifted from her feet a few inches, her body bending as if a cord had wrapped around her waist and pulled. Bran continued to fight, but the power from the house leapt forth even more fiercely than before, throwing him off his feet. The scream of the crowd became intermingled with the screams of the voices, the scream of Adi, the scream of Bran…as Astara was consumed by the light.

The moment Astara disappeared, a glow burst from the house like a bomb. The roof right above Bran's bedroom exploded outward, and everyone leapt for cover as bits and pieces of shrapnel rained down. Bran had no cover and threw his arms over his head, trying to shield himself. From the hole erupted a deep beam of green light, piercing the sky. Black clouds swirled around the light in a fiery storm.

The beam crackled and fought like a beast waging war in the sky. There came one final, great blast of light and a roar—and then it was gone. The noise shriveled up. The voices ceased. The glow shrank back through the hole in the roof, like the fading of hot embers in a fire, and the streetlamps, which had been blown out, flickered back to life until the road was once again filled with their friendly yellow glow.

And there, lying still on the doorstep, was Astara: her face solid white, her lungs drawing no breath, and a blank, glassy stare.

Chapter 14

Her Death

Every muscle within Bran cried out as he pushed himself to his feet, screaming Astara's name. He rushed for the house, but Adi caught him. He fought, but she held him back, so he struggled against her with magic, caring nothing for anyone who saw them. Before he knew what he was doing, his powers shoved Adi through the air, where she hit the side of the car many feet away and fell—unnoticed in the frenzy. He ran toward the house, but her magic seized his legs, bringing him to the ground. She was upon him in an instant, holding him, shouting his name, though he didn't hear her.

"Astara!" Bran called again, as if it would somehow erase what he had seen.

"Stop, Bran!" Adi hissed in his ear. "Stop this now before we're both arrested and we can't help her at all!"

Bran hadn't even realized there were tears in his eyes before he felt them, though no cries escaped from his lips. There were just tears: hot tears that fell down the side of his face and were dried by the grass as Adi kept him pinned. He saw white shoes running past: paramedics who would have no way of helping Astara anymore.

"She's gone," Bran said, his voice cracking.

"I saw it," Adi whispered, her voice filled with terror. Bran heard the medics hollering, trying to revive Astara and yelling into radios for backup.

He heard another siren, lights flashing from an ambulance. He fought Adi once more, trying to see Astara, but as the medics lifted her body, her arm fell limply at her side. They rushed past Bran, and he pressed his face against the grass, unable to hear himself weep.

Adi loosened her hold on him, and so he shoved her away, leaping to his feet and dashing toward the ambulance. The medics had already loaded her, and they slammed the door just as he caught a glimpse of her face: a breathing mask over her mouth and nose. He kept running, but the ambulance took off, roaring around the corner in the direction of the hospital.

"She's not dead," Bran said to himself. "If she were dead, they wouldn't even take her to the hospital." He sank to his knees on the pavement. It was the only thing he could believe. The only reason they would have taken her away was if they thought they might revive her. He told himself this over and over, rubbing his palms against his jeans as his hands shook.

Adi came up behind Bran and put her arms around him. The scene was still pandemonium; some of the crowd was still screaming, some were on cell phones, others leaned against one another for support. The officers were wielding their guns as if something might erupt from the darkness at any moment.

"Bran, get up," Adi said.

"No, leave me alone," Bran shouted, striking her arms away.

"Shut up, Bran!" Adi yelled—he had never heard her shout in that way before, and it caused him to shrink back. "Listen to me! Either you can sit here in the road or you can get up and get in my car and we can get down to Holdsben Hospital so Astara isn't all alone."

Bran couldn't say anything, but he let Adi pull him up and into her car. Through the front window, he saw the Wilomases gathered across the street, Balder and Baldretta crying into their parents' sides, while Sewey and Mabel just stared blankly. A pair of officers looked in the direction of Adi's car as she slammed the door, and turned to come after them, but Adi gunned the engine, roaring in a sharp circle. Bran looked out the back window and saw the wreckage of what had been their home: the windows reduced to jagged pieces of glass, the bushes and the grass bent out, a large hole in the roof through which Bran could see the attic and what was left of his bedroom. But his mind seemed to have no fear at all for his things or the place in which he had lived for so long—all that consumed his mind was Astara and her face of terror as she had been pulled toward the strange green glow.

He hadn't even realized that the tears had stopped, and he wiped his face with the back of his shirtsleeve. His head pounded, and his muscles were sore. His ears burned; every nerve in his body was calling out in pain.

"She's not dead, is she?" Bran asked. Adi didn't say anything, her hands gripping the wheel so tightly that her knuckles were white. Bran's senses were slowly coming back to him, and he realized that Adi had her foot flat against the floor of the car, weaving in and out between traffic and swerving around corners.

"Please, Adi, just tell me she's not dead," Bran said, his voice more of a whispered sob than a question.

"Just don't ask me that, Bran," Adi said, and Bran noticed that tears streamed down Adi's cheek as well. Whatever strength that had remained within him vanished immediately as he saw the answer written across Adi's face, and he slumped against the car door.

Adi slammed her car to a stop in front of the hospital. She threw her door open, and Bran stumbled out on his side. Someone yelled at Adi that she couldn't park her car in that spot, but she swore at him so angrily he left her alone, and she threw the automatic sliding doors apart because they didn't move fast enough for her to get inside.

"Excuse me!" the woman at the front desk protested as Adi stormed in. Adi simply rushed past her to the emergency center, but the thick doors slammed shut and locked. She spun on the woman at the desk, whose finger was still poised over a large red button.

"You can't go in there, miss," the woman said sharply.

"We have to see someone, she just got here a few minutes ago," Bran said desperately.

"Are you family?" the woman asked.

"No," he said after a moment of hesitation. "But we're—"

"Only family is allowed back there now," the woman said.

"But she doesn't have any family!" Bran said.

Adi looked as if she was about to fly into a rage, and for a moment Bran thought she might even use magic—but Adi curled her fingers into fists, then loosened them once more. She let her breath out slowly.

"All right," Adi said dejectedly, and Bran knew the fighting was over.

He fell into a chair, and sat in the lobby among all the others who wept for their loved ones. But Bran remembered nothing from the rest of that day, except for two words whispered to Adi from one of the doctors:

"She's dead."

Chapter 15

The Shadow of Her Memory

The feeling of numbness did not leave Bran in the hours that followed. It was as if his mind had built a wall to protect him from being hurt anymore. He heard voices, but he did not know who spoke; he saw faces, but he did not recognize who they were. Many doctors came and left, speaking to Adi and to him and to others, but the only word he seemed to catch was "Astara"—the name that had once been hers.

Things became a blur as the pain sank deeper into his soul. Adi forced him to eat, though every bite of food made him sick inside. When the Wilomases showed up at the hospital, he covered his face with the blanket and let Adi tell them he would be spending the night in the lobby with her. She had tried to convince him to go back with them, but he did not want to leave that chair.

His mind didn't believe that she was really gone, even when Adi finally got him out of the hospital and loaded him into the car. He stared out the window, saying nothing as Adi drove away. He didn't even know how much time had passed. As he watched the building disappear, he knew that somewhere inside was Astara's lifeless body.

"I hope they don't put her in a freezer," Bran said. "She doesn't like the cold."

His words made no sense—they just fell out. Adi didn't reply; she stared tearfully at the dark, rainy streets of Dunce.

Bran stayed at Adi's house and slept in the spare bedroom. He saw Polland once when he came inside, but Polland didn't say anything—or if he did, Bran didn't notice. He crawled into the bed and held tightly to a pillow at his side. He fell asleep and remembered nothing more.

His senses slowly began to come back as the numbness wore off, and he found himself days later standing outside with other people in suits and formal clothes. He realized that he was also in a suit, though he had no memory of putting it on, or the black tie either, or even riding in the car there. His eyes were trained on a deep hole in the ground. Beside it rested a dark, wooden casket with the lid already closed.

He slowly began to recognize the faces of those around him: Sewey and Mabel and the children standing across from him; Mr. Cringan, his rough face haggard and unshaven and his eyes red with tears; two other women Bran didn't recognize. They were all holding umbrellas to block out the light rain that drizzled down from the branches of the trees. He looked to his right and saw Adi standing beside him, holding an umbrella for the two of them.

His mind registered who was in the wooden casket, though it didn't quite wrap itself around the fact that it was Astara who was being buried. It felt wrong that he wasn't crying as he stared ahead in stony silence like the Wilomases, who were there simply because she had died in their home and it was the respectable thing to do.

Some men came forward to place the casket into the ground. Bran started.

"Wait," he whispered. "I didn't get to tell her good-bye."

"You did, Bran," Adi said, swallowing hard. "You don't remember."

"No, you need to stop them," Bran said desperately.

"Please, Bran," Adi said, her voice filled with pain. "You don't want to see her like this. I promise you."

Bran stood silently for the rest of the burial. When the men filled the hole in with dirt, everyone stood around for a few minutes before slowly drifting off. As the others walked away, Bran started to tell Astara how chilly and wet it was that morning, and how he hoped it didn't put Sewey in a bad mood, and how it sometimes made the brakes on his bike slippery, which was actually fun because it would make the tires skid—but he just shut his mouth again, because she just wasn't there.

Sewey came their way, and Bran ducked down so Sewey wouldn't notice him.

"Erm…" Sewey stammered, not sure what to say. "I'm… sorry, Bran. About your friend."

Bran didn't say anything.

"He's doing all right," Adi said to Sewey for him.

"And he's all right at your place?" Sewey said, his voice taking on a strange, foreign tone of sympathy. "Ours is in a bit of a…situation. We're sending the children off to relatives while things get fixed, and we can send Bran off as well."

"He's no trouble with me," Adi said. "I think he's better staying with me anyway."

"It'll be a few weeks," Sewey said.

"We'll be all right," Adi replied.

Sewey twisted his face up as he deliberated. "If you say so. I can take Bran back to the house to get what's left of his things from his room, and then you can pick him up this evening."

Adi agreed, and Sewey turned for the car. When he left, Adi looked down at Bran.

"Are you doing OK?" she asked. Bran didn't reply.

"Bran, I need to talk to you," she said. "It's very serious. I know you're hurt, but we have to talk. I need to know what happened back at your house."

"I don't know," he choked.

"Bran, it's the box, isn't it?" Adi said, her voice catching. "I knew something like this would happen. Whatever magic kept that box locked must have been unstable—it must have lost control or broken free. I'm sorry, Bran, I should never have let you keep it."

Bran pressed his face against her shoulder and let her hold him tightly.

"I'm going to get rid of it," Bran said. "I'm going to bury it."

"Bring it to me," Adi pressed. "I'll make sure it's gone for good."

"No," Bran said strongly. "I'm going to bury it. Whatever my mother left inside isn't worth it." He left her embrace and walked through the rain toward the Schweezer.

On the way home, Bran hardly heard a word, but he managed to pick up that Sewey had somehow convinced the police that the dramatic green lights were caused by radioactive paint reacting to fireworks that had exploded through the ceiling and windows. It was actually quite a grand excuse for Sewey, and Bran figured that it had taken all the Wilomases' brains put together to come up with it. The pandemonium of the whole event had rattled the officers so much they had either forgotten all about the Nigels' robbery, or were simply too frightened to go after Sewey.

When they reached Bolton Road, Bran paid little heed to the state their yard had been left in. A path had been cleared to the house through the mess of broken boards, but Bran's shoes still crunched against splinters and wood chips.

He paused at the door for a moment, reminded that Astara had died in that very spot. Bran had to step around the fallen table and chairs. He made his way upstairs and climbed up the ladder to his room but didn't have good footing and slipped and hit his head.

His vision was filled with bursts of stars for a second, and he fell again, dizzy with pain. It seemed to break him out of the stupor he had been in for so many days, so that he blinked and realized that he was back in his room. He managed to look up and saw that part of the roof had broken inward, so that many of the boards were scattered about and some hung precariously from the ceiling by weak, bent nails.

He climbed up again and felt his way, the only guiding light coming from the hole in his ceiling. Everything was very wet from the rain, and the wind from outside was cold on his face as he looked at what remained of his things.

His chair was there, as was his bed, though they were covered in boards and nails and a sludgy dust. His pillow was in shreds, having taken a nail-covered board through the middle. His drawings were partially protected by a fallen piece of plywood. They were not completely destroyed. The desk was untouched. Every item that had sat on the desk was scattered on the floor—all except for one object, which still sat in its center, uncovered once more like a phantom that had chosen to show its face.

"The box..." Bran said aloud. But from the box there came no reply. It just sat there, as if by consuming Astara, its voice and hunger had been placated.

In a moment, Bran was seized with a fiery rage. He leapt to the box as if it were his enemy, throwing it to the floor so that its contents rattled abruptly. The box did not give nor break, as he greatly wished it to. It gave no defense of itself, even as he lifted it again and threw it against the wall, where it smashed in one of the broken boards but fell to the floor unscratched. If it had had a voice, it might have laughed in his face at the tears that fell down his cheeks.

Bran had no strength remaining, so he fell upon his bed, getting his suit covered in splinters. He stared through the giant hole in his ceiling at the gray cloudy sky encircled by broken nails and splintered bits of wood. He had no answers—he only knew Astara was gone and that somehow the box was at fault.

"What do you want from me?" Bran asked, staring at it from across the room. He watched it for a long while, and the anger began to boil within him even hotter, so that he leapt up again and took hold of the box. He clattered down the ladder and toward the front door in bitter silence, holding the box tightly to his side.

"Wait, Bran," Sewey commanded, coming from the dining room. "You need to pack your things and be ready in—"

"Shut up for once, Sewey," Bran hissed, and his voice was so sharp that Sewey took a step back and obeyed. Bran went outside and grabbed his bike from the yard—still in the same spot the officers had dropped it—and started to pedal down the street.

He was still in his suit and tie, but he hardly noticed. He stared straight ahead until he finally came to the bridge he crossed on his way to the Third Bank of Dunce. He stopped his bike half-way across and dropped it against the side, going to the edge and looking over.

The water gushed beneath the bridge, flowing harshly because of the recent rain. Bran could hear it crashing against the rocks and the pillars that held up the bridge, and as he stared down into the water he breathed in the misty air.

He looked at the box, now cradled in his arm, and he realized that just before Astara had died, she had suggested that they bury it. Remembering their last evening together on the water tower sent pain racing through Bran's heart, but it was such a familiar pain that it almost didn't affect him. He remembered convincing her that they should go on fighting and should try to open the box

"But I'm done with you," Bran said under his breath. "I've done nothing but try to help you, and you've done nothing but hurt me. So I'm finished."

He took the box with both hands and, with a mixture of anger and heartbreak, threw it over the edge as hard as he could, so that it plummeted down to the water. He pressed himself against the edge of the bridge, looking down until he saw its shape splash against the surface. He watched until it was dragged underneath the waves.

He thought that as it disappeared, he should have felt a

weight lift from his shoulders. But instead he only felt more lost than before, and he trudged alone and bitter back to his bike and started home.

Chapter 16

A Place under the Bridge

Three days passed, though Bran remembered little of it. He slept in the spare room at Adi's house, which only reminded him of Astara since she had been staying there. Adi and Polland had thoughtfully moved all of Astara's things into the hall closet so that Bran didn't have to look at her records and CDs and tapes and think of her. But even if he had been in a blank, empty room with no color on the walls and no doors or windows, he would still think of her every morning.

The Specters did not haunt his dreams nor visit him, though he kept expecting to see some sign or message. He didn't leave the room much at all, and Adi would bring him meals at different times of the day just to make him sit up from the bed. It wasn't until the third day that he awoke on his own and looked out the window behind the headboard. It faced out into Hadnet Lane, and the sun was burning brightly through the opened curtains, spilling golden light across the lawns and the cars parked down the street. Bran took a deep breath and dragged himself out of bed and down the stairs.

"Bran?" He heard Adi's voice as he came down. She was in the kitchen, pouring some milk into a bowl of cereal. Bran nodded at her.

"Feeling any better?" she asked. He didn't answer. She looked deeply saddened as well, though her eyes were not red anymore. She pushed some food at him, and he ate just because it was there.

Afterward, he decided he wanted to head home for a bit, just to get out of that house. So he went outside and got his bike and took a deep breath of the outside air. It didn't feel right for it to seem so fresh.

Bolton Road was strangely a welcome sight for him after so many days of being gone: just something familiar, passing the same houses he had been seeing all his life. Mabel was downstairs when he came through the door, with a giant glass hat like a fishbowl over her head, covering everything down to her shoulders with a rubber seal around her neck and a grille for her to breathe through.

"What are you doing here?" she asked, though it was hard to understand through the glass.

"I'm picking up some of my stuff from my room," Bran told her.

"Where's your mask?" she demanded, tapping the glass hat.

"I haven't got one," Bran said.

"Well, if you end up getting the Bee Flu from all these protosynthisites," Mabel said, "don't say I didn't warn you."

She carried on about how all Bran's future children would have wings and stingers, but Bran wasn't at all in the mood for it, so he left her at the bottom of the stairs mid-rant. He could still hear her talking to herself when he got to the top.

This time, Bran was careful to avoid the broken beams as he climbed the ladder to his room, though it was admittedly far easier now that sunlight was shining through the hole. The entire attic was lit up in a spectacular manner, so that he could see into corners he had never gazed into before. When he walked forward, his steps threw dust into the air, and it swirled around in the sunlight like tiny floating monsters riding around the room.

He sat upon the edge of his bed, and the rain-drenched mattress squished inward disgustingly. Still, as he let his eyes survey his room and he saw again what a miserable mess it had become, he didn't really care how dirty his bed was and only felt like lying back against it and staring across the room and trying to forget everything that had happened there.

Suddenly, he heard a familiar sound and turned his head in its direction.

"Nim?" he said, but no answer came. His eyes scanned the remains of his room, but the only things that moved were the papers and the dust. He listened intently but only heard Sewey grumbling into a telephone about replacement windows and warranties. He sighed and lay down, looking back toward the hole in the ceiling. Suddenly he sat up straight again.

"Nim?" he said in an excited whisper. He squinted in the bright sunlight, and then he could see her, standing up on one of the jagged boards, looking down at him with her large, blinking green eyes filled with curiosity.

"Come down here!" Bran said, and she leapt off the beam and danced through the air toward him, spinning around his head as she did before. He turned in a full circle, trying to catch her.

"Stop, now!" Bran hissed sharply, and she did, darting down to the front of his shirt and crawling up it. Bran seized her immediately, and she crumpled over into his hand.

"How in the world did you get away?" he demanded, not sure

if he was happy to see her. He could hardly believe his own eyes as she struggled to her feet.

"Nim," she said to him, in her melodic voice that made his heart leap. His hands were shaking so much that she fell over again and quickly leapt back to his shirt. He looked up to the hole in his ceiling and then around the room again, struggling to understand what was happening.

"How did you escape Thomas?" he asked. But she didn't seem to hear him. She began to tug on his shirt, pulling him toward the ladder. He was startled for a minute, but she flew up to his face and started to point frantically down toward it.

"You want me to leave?" Bran asked. She pulled on the front of his shirt again and pointed down the ladder.

"We're going somewhere?" he asked, and she nodded quickly. She was very insistent, which made Bran wary, but he followed her instruction outside to where his bike lay against the bricks.

"Are we going far?" Bran asked, and she nodded quickly, so he grabbed his bike and started moving. She darted away, and Bran pedaled hard to keep up.

"Where are we going?" he asked, though there was really no point in it because she couldn't respond. He was so frustrated that he couldn't understand her, he considered trying some Comsar magic to get into her mind, but she was too far away for him to get her attention.

She took him a long way from his house, and he lost all track of where he was. *Am I really following Nim somewhere?* His good sense came roaring back, and he slammed on the brakes of his bike, causing the tires to skid on the dirty pavement. Nim immediately spiraled back to him, pulling frantically on his shirt.

"Wait," Bran commanded, and she stopped but stared pleadingly into his eyes.

"I want to go back," Bran said, picking up his bike and turning it around. Nim immediately followed his face, waving her arms and pointing down a road that led farther into the woods that bordered it. Bran looked up and down the street, which only had a few cars coming from either direction.

"No, I'm not going down that way," Bran said. "This is getting weird. How did you even escape Thomas?"

Nim just kept blinking at him. It made him wonder if she even knew what transpired while she was under the strange control of the music box. Nim only shook her head and begged him with her eyes to go on a little farther. It went against every instinct that told him to head back home, but finally, he turned his bike around again and started off down the side road. Nim stayed closer to him until they got to a low concrete bridge that crossed over a tiny creek, where she stopped. Bran slowed his bike halfway across.

"Is this it?" he asked, setting his foot down and looking around. There was no one there. He let his senses go free, trying to detect if Thomas or anyone else was there and he had been led into a trap, but he couldn't feel any danger nearby at all. It surprised him that she had led him to this empty place, and even as he peered over the bridge, he saw that it was mostly dry, and only a thin trickle of water still flowed down that way. It was wet and muddy along the bank, however, so he knew the rainwater had filled it recently.

"See anything special?" he asked, turning to Nim. She was standing on the railing of the bridge, peering over into the little bit of water, looking around quickly before leaping up and crossing to the other side of the bridge. She came back to him and pulled on his shirt again.

"All right, all right," Bran said, getting off his bike. She led him off the road and down toward the water bank.

It wasn't far, but it was steep. He caught hold of gnarly tree limbs as he slid down, keeping his balance against the side of the bridge. They kept going until they were at the bottom. The bridge was quite solid, except for a large tunnel that let the water pass through. The sides of it sloped inward and were made of solid concrete. Nim left him behind and shot into the tunnel. Bran followed, still trying to catch his breath. He cautiously stepped into the shade of the bridge but remained outside, leaning against it.

The sunlight kept him from seeing well through the tunnel, but he heard Nim clambering about inside, every noise echoing. He took deep breaths and hesitantly stepped through, careful for spiders or whatever else might be lurking under the bridge.

"This is nice," he said, unable to think of a reason why Nim would bring him there. She was acting odd and darting from one side of the tunnel to the next. Bran let his eyes adjust, looked about, and saw that the roof was covered in chalk drawings and names: kids from the schools and from camps, scribbling out notes and hearts and messages years old. He had to bend over just a little so that he didn't hit his head. Nim came back to him again, insisting that he go in farther.

"No, Nim, I think I'm fine here," he said, a bit fearful of going in deeper. He cautiously sat down against the side slope of the tunnel and let the quiet sink in around him. It was very peaceful for a change, even as Nim tried to get his attention.

"No, really, it's very nice here," he said to her, but that didn't appease her at all, because she shot away from him to the other side of the tunnel. Something was there, washed up on the side of the concrete where the water had been flowing days before. Nim landed on it, and it scraped down a few inches under her. Bran started and almost fell over.

"What—" he gasped out, the moment he recognized what Nim had found. He stumbled to his feet and hit his head on the roof. Doubled over in pain, Bran shuffled across the tunnel toward Nim.

"The box!" he said. Nim leapt from it, and Bran could see the emblem of the moon on the top, just as dark and deep as it had been before. It didn't even seem wet or the slightest bit damaged: it just sat there, waiting.

Bran didn't know how he should approach the box, for he was afraid to touch it and yet he was in a shocked state of awe that, despite his efforts, it had turned up yet again. It made hot tears spring into his eyes once more, so that as he fell toward it he felt the energy drain from him as all the pain came rushing back. He cursed himself for coming out there, and he cursed the box as well.

"I didn't want to see this again!" he seethed, spinning on Nim, but she darted out of the way in terror. He wanted the box to go away and never return, because simply seeing it there caused the strength he had built over the past days to crumble until he collapsed, sobbing into his knees as he hugged them close to his body.

"What do you want from me?" he asked aloud, and Nim came to comfort him, but he hit her away. She spun against the side of the tunnel and dashed away in fear again, hiding behind the box. Bran clenched his fingers into fists, hardly able to look at the box even though it seemed to silently call to him.

"Why won't you go away?" Bran asked. As always, there came no reply. He wanted to throw it back into the water or throw it deep into the woods, but he knew it would make no difference.

"You've got to tell me something!" he screamed, anger and frustration boiling over. He took hold of the box and set it in front of him, gripping the sides of it tightly.

"Why did you kill her?" he demanded of it. "Why did you have to take her? Why didn't you take me instead? Isn't it me that you wanted?"

Taking Astara had to have been a grave mistake. He was the one whose mother had been a criminal. Astara was just a girl. It seized him, wishing to know why, so that his senses broke free at once and he felt magic reaching through his hands, toward the box in a way he had not done before. He knew immediately that it was the Comsar side of his subconscious trying to communicate with the box as if it were a sentient being—and though he pulled his untamed powers back, it momentarily scraped against whatever inhabited the box. Just that one, simple scratch sent a start through Bran, as if he had connected with something for an instant, and it caused him to drop the box with a crash that echoed throughout the tunnel.

"What…?" he whispered, and everything was silent again, and he realized there had been a noise or a voice in his mind. It was as if someone had tried to speak but had been cut off.

He grabbed the box again, squeezing it between his hands and reached for his powers once more, driving them into the box with such fervor they leapt from his palms. The feeling returned with an overwhelming flash of green light that surrounded him, throwing the tunnel and Nim and everything around him aside as if they had become water.

He gripped the box and refused to let go, even as the light forced him to close his eyes. He felt wind on his face: a strong gust of hurricane force that should have knocked him over if not for the strange strength that kept him rooted in place. It was oddly exhilarating, a blast of pitch-black darkness and then green light again, and suddenly he was somewhere else.

Chapter 17

A Voice from the Grave

Even though Bran's eyes were shut, he could see flashes of light and bursts of strange colors; it felt like he was being plunged into another world, although he could still feel the concrete of the tunnel beneath his feet. His heart leapt when he caught a glimpse of an image: a face, one he recognized.

"Astara!" he said, but the face disappeared, and he wasn't sure if he had really seen her or if it had been imagined. But then she was back, dressed the same as just before she died. She was stumbling toward him, and the world around him materialized. It was Bolton Road, the street shining violently in the green light that pulsated from behind him, police cars and people fanned out on the street. He was somewhere different than he had been that night—standing now in the doorway of the house, looking out at everything. Astara was struggling toward him with blank eyes. Every scream and shout was silenced by a roaring, rushing wind, and everything was blurry except for him, the house, and Astara.

She was as clear as he remembered, her gaze staring straight into his. It caused him to grimace, because it hurt to see her again when his mind knew she was dead. But he couldn't look away. He stared straight into her eyes once more.

"Come," he found himself whispering against his will, though the softness was magnified as if through a thousand loudspeakers. Astara seemed to fade, to mold and morph, until it was not Astara anymore but an image of Bran himself, stumbling in his own direction. Then it changed again to Astara.

"Become one of us," Bran said, his lips moving on their own. Astara was just inches away, and then she stopped. His arms opened, wanting to reach out and pull her close, so that he might drag her from this horrific world—and as if she saw his invitation, she opened her arms as well and stepped forward to embrace him softly.

The instant they touched everything vanished into a smoky haze, turning to dust. He wanted to scream but was yanked backward, hitting against something hard. He opened his eyes and found himself in the tunnel under the bridge, his back striking against the wall.

He rolled over, coughing for breath. The box had fallen to the side, and he struggled to get up.

"Bran!" he heard a soft voice, and Bran froze in recognition. He looked up and saw that he was not alone in the tunnel: there was a girl standing at the end, her hand against the wall.

"Astara?" Bran said, his voice breaking

"Are you even real?" he asked, thinking that perhaps he was still trapped in the vision. She didn't answer.

"You've got to help," she said, her voice desperate, and he noticed her normally bright eyes were dull and empty. Bran got to his feet.

"Take the box," she said, so he did, and then he started toward her to make sure she was real. She stepped backward.

"Wait," Bran said, but she just walked away. Bran didn't care if she was real or not and dashed after her. He stumbled outside and saw that it had grown dark—the magic he had done, which had seemed like it had taken minutes, must have actually taken hours. The woods and water were covered in blue, shaded light.

"No, wait, Astara!" Bran said, but she was already walking briskly down the bank. He ran after her as fast as he could. She moved tirelessly, and he began to pant for breath as he followed her into the darkened woods.

He called after her, but she didn't respond, darting through the trees but always staying within sight even as the woods grew thicker. The canopy kept out what little light remained, so that Bran stumbled over branches and sticks as he tried to keep up.

She drew him in deeper and turned down a side path, stopping in a small clearing. He slowed, trying to catch his breath, and she stared at him, not speaking. Bran just stood there as well, not quite able to move closer and yet not wanting whatever magic was at work to end. He wondered if it was just an illusion triggered by magic and his imagination. But then he looked down and realized exactly where they were.

He remembered the place, even though his mind had tried so hard to forget—Astara's grave site. The dirt was freshly covered over, and he could still see the indentations in the ground from the casket. He looked back up to Astara again, his eyes wide with fear and confusion. She looked at him intently and then pointed down to the place where she was buried.

Unable to hold himself back any longer, Bran stepped toward her, but the moment he moved, Astara's feet began to sink, as if her body was losing substance and seeping into the ground.

Bran stopped in his tracks, but then he leapt forward, dropping the box and grasping for Astara as her form began to disappear, sinking through the surface. She disappeared before he could reach her, and he fell, kneeling over her grave.

He looked around, hoping that she would reappear somewhere else. But she was nowhere to be found, and the woods had gone deathly still. He stood up quickly, cursing himself for being led so far into the woods. He looked down at the grave.

"You're trying to tell me something…" he said under his breath, stepping around the grave, letting his shoes sink into the fresh dirt. Nim had caught up and flew about the clearing, knocking leaves down and scrambling against branches, as if she could feel something happening. Bran kept staring down at the grave, and he could feel Astara calling to him again.

"Are you still alive down there?" he asked, feeling near madness for even thinking it. He kept telling himself to leave that place and go home—but seeing Astara again, even for those few fleeting minutes, had broken forth a magic he could not reign in.

He almost restrained his powers, but his hands wrenched outward, and magic flowed down his arms toward the place where Astara had disappeared. The dirt blew up from the ground as if being struck by an invisible palm, spewing away as tendrils of roots curled toward it like fingers, ripping the ground apart. He was calling on so much magic he couldn't even discern what kind: Netora powers tearing at the ground, Archon magics calling forth plants. The ground tore and split, fueled by Bran's anger and frustration. Nim flew about, throwing dust and dirt into a whirlwind around him.

The ground seemed to erupt, coughing out a large, wooden box. Dirt and rocks fell from the sides of it as it burst out, and Bran let his powers go. The roots slithered back into the ground like a thousand tongues being drawn back into their mouths. He didn't move, breathing hard as the echoes of the furious magic resounded in the woods. Nim flickered to his side, catching hold of his shirt and crawling up to his shoulder cautiously.

Bran said nothing, and slowly it began to sink in exactly what he had done. Astara's casket stood before him, dirty and scratched on all sides. He clenched his teeth together until the woods fell silent. After hesitating, he finally inched closer, placing his hands on the side.

The wood was cold to the touch, and his fingers left imprints in the dust. *Do I really want to see this?* What if he opened the casket and found her body, having already lain in the ground for days? It made him sick even thinking of it, but something within him forced him to go on, forced his fingers to undo the clasp. His arms slowly pushed open the lid, the hinges creaking.

His gaze stared into the coffin. His hands and arms began to tremble, eyes searching the box. But he could not deny what he saw. The casket was empty, as if no one had ever been in it at all. There were no bones, no markings, nothing. Astara had simply vanished.

"The Specters took her," Bran said with realization, as Nim sat shivering and silent on his shoulder.

Chapter 18

The Box Is Opened

Somehow, even in the dark, Bran was able to find his way back to his bike, pedaling madly until he reached Hadnet Lane. He skidded to a stop in front of Adi's house, pounding furiously on the door until the porch light came on and the door was thrown open. Adi stood there with a look of terror on her face, which only deepened the moment she saw him.

"Astara isn't dead," Bran gasped at her. A minute later, she and Bran were in her car, Polland in the back seat as they roared down the road, headlights showing the way through the darkness. Adi drove wildly until they pulled off to the side of the road, and Bran leapt out and led them through the woods.

He pulled Adi around the bends of the path, Polland struggling to keep up as Nim flew unnoticed in the trees above them. Finally, they reached the spot, and Adi gasped when she saw the wreckage Bran had caused.

"Bran, what have you done?" she choked, stumbling toward the casket. Bran threw the lid open, and she gasped again. Her trembling hands stroked the interior, not believing her own eyes.

"They took her, Adi," Bran said, his voice filled with anger and bitterness. "The Specters. Somehow, they took her, and I don't know why."

"How did you find this?" she demanded, turning to Bran. He seized the box from where he had dropped it before and told her exactly what he had done and how he had seen the vision of Astara.

"Comsar..." Polland whispered. "I wouldn't have dared suggest such a thing. The danger of communicating with whatever is inside is boundless."

"It doesn't matter; it's done," Bran said. "What does this mean, Adi? Where is Astara's body?"

Bran dropped the box from his hands into the small mound of dirt in front of him and sat, fatigue taking over. His body wanted to scream, but his mind was filled with a fire of determination.

"It's the Specters, whoever they are," Adi said. "It's haunted or filled with something evil that wants you."

"That's just it," Bran said. "It wants me, not Astara. Why didn't the Specters take me instead?"

Adi just shook her head, Polland's flashlight casting dark shadows under her features. Bran absently turned the box over, the moon emblem facing up. Seeing the shape, he reached under his shirt and drew his mother's necklace out. He took it off and found a beam of moonlight that broke through the trees above them. The word HAMBRIC flared on the necklace's surface, lighting the woods a bit more so that Adi and Polland could see the box as they examined its edges.

"Light up the top of the box again, Bran," Adi said, so Bran set the necklace on the lid, letting its white glow fall upon its surface. The three of them stared at it silently, for none of them could see a way of opening it.

"Your mother must have liked that shape," Adi said, nodding at the similar emblems.

"Look, it's even the same size too," Polland noticed, reaching forward to align the pendant on top of the shape to compare them. It fit seamlessly, covering the mark on the box completely.

"It does," Bran said, perking up at Polland's discovery. "Almost like it was—"

He froze. Right before their eyes, the moon pendant sank into the surface of the box, as if the wood had turned to quicksand. It stopped with the top of the necklace still standing out of the box's surface. The glow of the name Hambric flickered and then flared with the same white and blue glow, rushing around the letters like fire before it disappeared again.

The necklace seemed to have merged with the lid of the box, standing out like a glassy ornament. Then Bran heard a click. The lid gave a tiny pop, and the box opened.

For a few moments, none of them could move, even as Bran's fingers fell against the opening that had split the separate pieces of wood.

"I can't believe it..." Adi breathed out. Bran had been holding the key the whole time.

He broke free of his shock and carefully swung the lid up without the slightest sound from the thick hinges.

Even with the smell of the woods he could perceive the box's musty odor. Polland leaned closer so that the flashlight beam was trained on the two lonely objects inside.

Lying diagonally, fitting the box corner to corner, was a thin, black wand. It bore little decoration, unlike Adi or Polland's complicated designs. It was simply a long rod that narrowed at the end, and Bran immediately pulled it out of the box. Adi drew in a sharp breath but was in too much shock to stop him. On the wide end closest to his wrist, a large, glimmering diamond threw sparkles onto all of them. He quickly covered it and saw that the wand had thin, almost unperceivable markings, going all down its sides toward the end point. When he turned the wand, the tiny lines shone and then disappeared as light hit them. Engraved at the bottom, where his hand would grip the wand, was the tiny indention of a moon, just like his mother's necklace.

"A wand..." Adi whispered. Bran held it tightly in his fist; it seemed to sway before him, and only then he realized that his hands were shaking. He restrained himself from letting his magic touch the wand, afraid of what it might do. Polland lowered his flashlight, and Bran lifted the wand higher, into the light of the moon, and just as with his necklace, the moonlight caused the thin lines to glow in a bluish white light, swirling toward the tip like water running over diamonds. It was startling and beautiful and strangely dark at the same time. The marking of the moon on its handle had begun to glow as well, softly pulsing like a calm heartbeat until his hand covered it and drowned the light.

Bran realized that the others were watching him, and he looked up quickly to meet their eyes.

"Your mother's wand, perhaps?" Adi said. Bran could feel power within it, enchantments that his mother had placed in that wand—he couldn't feel whether they were good or bad magic, just powers beneath its surface.

"Maybe she left it to me before she died?" Bran wondered aloud.

"No mage would part with a wand easily," Adi said. "Especially not for all the time it would take her to hide it in Dunce."

"She could have sent it with me," Bran said. "When she put

me in the trunk, in the alley. Astara said she saw her put me in there. Perhaps it was in the trunk as well when she sent me?"

"Or," Adi said, straightening with realization, "perhaps it was part of the magic, Bran! When she used Netora powers to send you to the bank, your mother needed something to focus on as the destination. Maybe the safe deposit that you found this box in was the object your mother's magic used to put you in the vault!"

The thought had never occurred to Bran before. He hadn't even thought about the magic his mother had done to send him away. But it made sense: it was the only real way that his mother could have sent him to the vault. And then the safe deposit box must have gone unnoticed all those years.

Simply holding the wand made him shudder. He knew what immense power it wielded. Had it been chance that he was sent to the bank? Or had it been planned by his mother all along?

As he looked into the box, he saw something else was there: a small package, wrapped in black paper. He set his mother's wand down beside him and gently undid the wrapping, and a large skeleton key fell into his hands.

The key appeared to be made of a dark gray silver, the metal surface still shining as if just from the mold. The bit of the key was simple, only two curving rods. The key felt heavy, and it had deep markings along its cylindrical shaft. However, in the center of its curved handle was its most distinguishing feature: a solid, shining green gem.

Bran recognized the green color instantly. It was the same shade and hue as the beam of light that had destroyed the Wilomases' house many nights before.

"What is that?" Adi asked. The key made a high-pitched sound as Bran ran his fingers across its surface, like the ringing of a bell.

"It's warm," Bran said. Adi reached forward to take it so she could examine it closer.

The moment her finger touched the key's surface, there was a mighty, trembling explosion of green light, and Adi screamed. It threw her hand back like an electrical shock, and Bran dropped the key in fright, where it slammed into the ground and threw up dust. All three of them jerked from it, and Adi was breathing hard, her hand shaking with terror.

"Are you all right?" Bran gasped.

"That burns," Adi said, shaking her hand. "It's got magic on it, that's for sure."

"But it didn't give me any trouble," Bran said, and to prove it he picked the key up again, and nothing happened. Polland curiously touched the key, and again, it burst forward like green fire, throwing his hand back and knocking him back a step.

"Blasted burning!" Polland yelped, sucking on his finger. "That's probably it then. All this while, that key's been the cause. You can pick it up but we can't?"

"Then your mother meant for you to get that key," Adi realized. "Why else would she put that magic on it?"

"But what is it?" Bran stammered. There was something more to the key, something beneath the surface that was pulsing with power and yet sedated and quiet at that moment. He understood that the box itself had never been cursed, for as it lay next to his knee all power seemed to have vanished from it. He knew there was something inside this key, some deep magic that hissed in his ear every time he looked at it.

"I just don't know what to do anymore," Bran said. He set the key down, and they stared at it. He felt as if he had taken a step forward only to be thrown ten steps back. But he wondered just how lost he really was.

"There's a door, somewhere," Bran said, "and this key fits its lock. That door has something to do with the Specters or where they're trapped or something."

He shook his head. "Whatever it is, I've got to find out. What if I could speak to them, do something to convince them to give Astara back? Shouldn't I have some way with them, since it was my mother who had power over them?"

"Bran, you don't even know if they can give her back," Adi said quietly. "This is deep, dark magic here. The vision you saw might have not even have been Astara—it could have been your imagination or these Specters simply using her to lead you to them so they can take you as well. Even going any nearer to them could mean your death, with little hope at all of finding her."

"But it's all I have to hold on to," Bran said. "I can't just give up now. It's my only chance of getting her back. And if I don't do it, I'll never be able to forgive myself for not going after her—because she would have gone after me."

He looked at Adi, wishing to convince her. "Is there anyone who can help me, Adi?" Bran pleaded. "I just don't know the magic, I haven't learned enough. But there's got to be someone who knows about this."

She couldn't meet his eyes for more than a moment, looking torn between two parts of herself that argued for and against letting him go on. She looked at Polland, but he only shifted his gaze down. Finally, one part of her seemed to win out.

"All right, then," she whispered. "If you want to go on, I know someone who can find the door that matches that key."

Part II

Chapter 19

A Flight to East Dinsmore

Before dawn the next morning, Adi shook Bran awake.

"It's time to go," she told him, and he got out of bed without a word and got dressed. His hands shook as he zipped up the front of his jacket; it was still mid-August, but Adi had told him he would need it where he was heading. He carried his bag down the stairs. The strange key and his mother's wand were both in its front pocket, so they were close at hand.

Adi pulled out of the driveway and headed off toward Deeper Dunce, which was what many Duncelanders called the bustling and busy downtown region. It was misty and cool that morning, and the sky cast a dreary atmosphere over the city.

"He's my brother," Adi finally said, breaking the silence. "He lives off the coast of East Dinsmore, in a place called Elsie Island. It's a short flight from here, and you'll have a driver take you from the city to his house."

"And does he have experience with things like this?" Bran asked. Adi smiled halfway.

"With keys?" she said, seeming amused. "Bran, I don't think there is anyone on this planet who is better suited to solving your dilemma than Gary."

Gary, Bran repeated the name in his head. He hadn't known that Adi had a brother.

"Is he a mage?" Bran asked.

"He is," Adi replied. "And a far more powerful one than I will ever be."

"You never told me about him."

"I haven't spoken to him in many years," Adi said, with a sigh. "In fact, he's been entirely cut off from the outside world for over fifteen years now."

"Fifteen years?" Bran said with dismay, as Adi switched lanes. "He does know I'm coming though?"

Adi shook her head, and Bran laughed. When Adi did not laugh back, he realized that she was actually being serious.

"No, really?" Bran asked.

"No, really," Adi said with a strong nod.

"How do you even know he still lives there then?" Bran said with panic.

"Don't worry, Bran," Adi said. "He wouldn't have left that house. He will be there when you arrive. And he will surely help you when he reads my letter."

At this, Adi removed from the pocket of her door an oversized red envelope with a thick, silver seal on the back holding it closed.

"What's in it?" Bran asked.

"Just a few things Gary needs to know about you and the key," Adi said quickly.

"Can I read it?" Bran questioned. Adi shook her head.

"It's just something for my brother—there's no need for you to pry into it. The seal is magic too, only Gary can open it," she said, and the tone of her voice only made Bran all the more curious.

"But trust me," she went on, "he'll take you in when he reads it."

Her words were meant to reassure him, but to Bran they sounded foreboding and made the envelope seem heavier when he took it. The seal bore a faint image of a crow with its wings outstretched as if about to take flight.

"You'll also need this," Adi said, cautiously handing him something else. It was a business card but unlike any normal business card Bran had seen. In fact, though it was on very plain, solid black card stock, there were no words or contact information on either side. However, in the center of the card was a silver, embossed image of a crow. Bran softly touched the raised image, and the crow faded to black so that it was invisible, and behind it the gray image of a large key, spanning the card, appeared, as well as the single word: Gary.

Bran removed his thumb, and the image returned to normal.

"Do not lose that card," Adi said. "It is your passage to, and into, his house, and without it there could be very dire consequences."

Bran didn't really know how to reply to that. Adi exited the highway at a sign that pointed them toward the Hintons O'Guincy Airport, and a bustle of cabs and buses surrounded them, even so early in the morning. Adi instructed Bran to go through lane three in security and to quietly tell the woman working there that he had spiders in his bag—which, obviously, was some type of code to this security officer, a secret cohort sympathetic to the Mages Underground.

"She's helped us before, getting in and out," Adi said.

"She'll make sure you don't get caught up there with anything you're carrying. If there's any trouble at all, have her call me."

Bran nodded, and Adi seemed to hesitate, even as Bran slid out of the car and set his bag on the sidewalk. She stood across from him, trying to gather her words.

"You know Astara means much to me as well," Adi finally whispered, her voice unheeded by the passerby.

"I know," Bran nodded.

"I'd go with you if I could," Adi said, with a tinge of guilt. "I really would. But if I leave this town suddenly, especially after what happened on Bolton Road, it won't just be the police who might notice, but the Mages Council—and I think it best we keep them out of this for now."

"Don't feel bad," Bran replied. "I've got to do this myself."

"But if you don't get anywhere, Bran," Adi said, "I don't want you to feel bad either. We don't even know if there is any chance of you getting Astara back, you know."

Bran shrugged. "But if I don't try at all, I'll regret it the rest of my life."

His words quieted Adi, so that she said nothing more but only gave him a hug and got back into the car, leaving him to go on alone.

Bran made it through the airport with no trouble, going into the correct lane as instructed. He made it to his plane just as the final group was boarding.

His seat was the farthest in the back of the plane, and he began to feel a bit nervous as he walked down the aisle, and the walls seemed to curve in a bit too closely over his head. At least it wasn't as tight as a dumbwaiter compartment, but Bran still couldn't help his minor claustrophobia. To his relief, he found that no one would be sitting beside him. He placed his bag under the seat in front of him and then unzipped the top pocket carefully. Nim was inside, in a small glass jar with no lid just to keep his things from accidentally crushing her, and she looked up at him excitedly when his face appeared.

"All right?" he whispered at her, and she nodded.

"Takeoff is soon," he said. "We'll be on our way."

He heard someone cough loudly and looked up to see two men in ripped shirts across the aisle from him staring in his direction. Both had muscles so big that their arms looked like strips of skin with baseballs stuffed underneath, and they had matching bleached hair and coppery artificial tans.

"Do you have someone in your bag?" the nearest man asked, twisting his face up.

"Um, no," Bran said. Both men blinked.

"Where you heading?" the other asked.

"Elsie Island?" Bran stammered, not sure he remembered right. Both of them laughed.

"Oh really?" the first said with a snort. "Elsie Island? Good luck getting there, buddy."

"What's wrong with it?" Bran returned, already disliking these fellows. They chuckled.

"You can't get to Elsie Island," the second man said. "It's got rocks all up and down the sides. What boat are you going to take to get down there? No one'll do it."

Bran blinked, for he had no idea. Adi had simply told him that someone would be waiting for him at the airport when he landed.

"See, he's stupid," the first man said, jabbing a thumb toward Bran. "Talking to his bag, and doesn't even know where he's going."

Both of them started to laugh as if this was the funniest thing they had ever heard, and Bran chose that moment to zip Nim back into the bag while they were distracted.

It was still so dark outside that when the pilot turned off the overhead lights, everything was immediately engulfed in darkness save for a few night lamps. As the plane taxied to the runway, they started playing one of the propaganda videos the mayor had created specifically for flights originating in Dunce: the one about how gnomes could get into the engine, put ice on the controls, and subsequently down the plane. It was followed by an assurance that the Dunce Airway Patrol was always on the lookout but that if any citizens saw a red isosceles triangle during the flight, they should report it to the flight attendant, as opposed to firing off a volley of bullets in its general direction.

As the plane climbed into the sky, Bran watched the city of Dunce disappear below. It was a breathtaking sight to behold. He watched all the sparkling lights from each little house and streetlamp. For a few moments, he was able to spot one of the larger streets that he took often to get to the bank, and he shifted his gaze and caught the Givvyng Tree, towering on the landscape below like a point on a map. A few minutes later, the pilot announced they had crossed the border of Dunce, and immediately two midgets who had been riding a few rows ahead flipped off their jacket hoods and popped on a pair of red, conical hats they had been hiding in their bags. They clapped their hands and chuckled at their clever escape from the city, while still making their Sevvenyears—the custom that required every gnome to visit the Givvyng Tree within the walls of Dunce every seventh year of their lives.

The two men across the aisle from Bran were jointly furious.

"Hucksters!" Bran heard one grumble lowly. Bran turned to look.

"Hucksters, the whole lot," he grumbled at Bran. "I knew they were gnomes! Sneaking into our city and then just waltzing out! Hucksters, all of them."

"Well, you don't have to call them that," Bran said. "I mean there are probably kids on this plane who can hear you."

"So?" the other man said, his lips twitching up. "They're still hucksters whether the children hear it or not. Hucksters!"

"Excuse me, sir," the flight attendant came around the corner from the back kitchen. "Please watch your language."

Both men only became more incited by this and even more bent on using the derogatory term for gnomes as loudly as they could. "How can you let those vile hucksters on the same plane as us?" the first protested. "Don't we have laws against this?"

"We aren't in Dunce anymore," Bran hissed at him, trying his best not to cause a scene, though the men were doing very good jobs of it all by themselves.

"Well, I don't like this plane!" the other man whined at the attendant. "All these hucksters. I can't even breathe without smelling huckster! I demand you let me off this instant!"

"Well, I think the emergency exit is that way," Bran pointed, feeling angrier. "Make sure you hold on to your seat cushion."

They glared at Bran for a minute, but Bran was not about to relent and had to restrain himself from doing something rash. They finally gave up, grumbling and muttering low enough so that Bran couldn't decipher their words.

Bran was finally able to settle back into his seat and saw that the two gnomes ahead of him had been watching, and they sent a little wave his way in thanks. One was a man, who had the usual beard, and the other was a woman, who had dark red and brown hair and a thick book in her hands.

He made himself rest and awoke later with no real sense of how long he had been asleep. The plane had become colder, and he reached to take his jacket out of his backpack to use as a blanket. He found a sleeve and pulled it out—but as he did, something else came with it and fell right into his lap.

It was a little, black ball that looked like one of Balder's toys. He studied it in confusion, and as he turned it over, he saw that the surface of the ball was broken by a small, thick antenna sticking out like a miniature sail.

"What...?" Bran said aloud. He hadn't put that in his bag. He turned it over again but still didn't recognize it.

"It's a GPS tracking device," he heard a sharp whisper to his left. There was an elderly businessman in a suit across the aisle and one seat ahead from him, with a pair of headphones in his ears and a pillow against his neck.

"A what?" Bran whispered back. The man nodded.

"That ball there," he said. "It's connected to a computer somewhere on the ground. It uses satellites to tell them where you are."

Bran jerked his gaze back to the ball immediately, feeling his breath torn away. Someone was following him! But how? He couldn't even fathom a single instant where anyone would have had a chance to place something in his bag since the night before.

"I have one just like it, in my car," the man went on. "If it gets stolen, all I have to do is go on a computer, and it tells me exactly where it is."

"But why…?" Bran said with confusion. The man shrugged.

"Maybe your parents want to keep up with your whereabouts," he said, leaning back and closing his eyes again. Bran was nearly petrified in shock. Sewey? Mabel? Wanting to know where he was going?

Realization hit him before his previous thought had even finished: It wasn't the Wilomases. It was Thomas.

Chapter 20

Oswald and His Cab

The thought was so sudden and startling that Bran could only stare at the device. He shook his head. Thomas had left him there at the Nigels. His father didn't want to see him. Why in the world would he put a tracking device into his bag?

The answer came to Bran, so obvious that he knew he should have guessed it before. Back at the hotel, Thomas had only been acting like Bran didn't matter to throw him off. Thomas was still following him.

He's got something planned... Bran realized, and a slight amount of anger rose up within him as he thought about it. Was his own father going to use him as bait yet again? He immediately felt as if he had been betrayed another time, and it caused him to despise the very thought of Thomas even more.

He wasn't about to let him get away with it, though, and now that he knew what was happening, he was intent on doing anything in his power to foil Thomas's plans. Holding the tracking ball in his fist, he looked about for someplace to discard it on the plane. As if on cue, one of the rude men in the row across gave an enormous, plane-rattling snore. Bran checked the other passengers quickly, making sure no one was watching, and then deftly tossed the ball into the man's open bag. Bran silently hoped the men were transferring flights to some faraway island and would lead Thomas on a wild chase across the world.

He had gotten rid of the tracker just in time, for the pilot announced over the speakers that they were about to land in East Dinsmore. The plane rattled, and the rude man fell over, coming to in a fit of swearing. He glared at Bran, then glared at the other passengers, and then glared in the general direction of every other person in the world.

"Sleep well?" Bran asked cheerily, thinking of the even grander annoyance the man was about to get when Thomas finally caught up with him.

They landed, and Bran made his way with the other passengers into the bustling airport. The crowds were so varied and different, with red gnome caps poking out intermittently. It reminded Bran of Farfield, where he had first seen gnomes in public, though even here he could see a very obvious separation between the peoples: the humans kept three or four empty seats between them and the groups of gnomes. As he walked down the busy terminal, he saw that many of the restaurants had special sections set aside for people and gnomes, with signs pointing out which was which.

There was a giant sign that read Welcome Ye to East Dinsmore over the escalator. There was a long row of people in sharp suits and ties waiting at the bottom, holding signs with names of executives they were there to pick up in their sedans. They all looked alike—except one. In fact, he didn't appear to be human at all. His skin was entirely gray in a sickly manner and hung off him in blobs of blubbery fat, poking out from under his dingy shirt, which was far too small to even cover his waist.

He had the head of a man, though, with wild rolls of fat surrounding his neck, but where his arms should have been, he had six thin tentacles, three on each side of his body. The lower two sets were crossed impatiently, and the upper pair held a sign that read: Barn Ha'brick.

"Oh no..." Bran said to himself. One of the creature's tentacles snaked around his back to lift up his pants, which kept falling down. Bran swallowed hard and approached him.

"I think you're my...driver?" Bran said aloud. The squat man looked up at Bran.

"Eh?" he said, bending out an ear. "You Barn?"

"Bran," he stammered in reply.

"Bran?" the creature said. "Eh. Oswald."

One of the tentacles moved toward him, and Bran guessed that he was supposed to shake it. So he did with only a bit of hesitation, and it felt as if he was shaking hands with a balloon.

"Car's out this way," Oswald said in a nasally, snorting voice, folding the sign and waddling ahead toward the doors. "Got any bags on th' wheel?"

"Not besides these," Bran said, and Oswald took the heavier one right out of Bran's grasp, lifting it onto his shoulder as he ambled along, the legs of his faded jeans swishing against the tile floor.

"Don't plan on stayin' here long then I suppose, eh?" Oswald said. "Not too much to be packed in 'er."

"Hopefully just a day or two," Bran said.

"Really?" Oswald replied, shooting Bran a strange glance. "And you're visitin' Gary down there? Would have thought you'd stay at least some, bein's no one's gone in so long."

"No, just a short time," Bran said, and Oswald dropped the subject as they went outside, where it was windy and cold. They crossed two lanes of bus and taxi traffic and came to the parking garage. Oswald led Bran down a way and stopped at his cab.

It was perhaps the most battered piece of machinery Bran had seen, and that was after years of suffering through Sewey's Schweezer. The trunk lid was white and had the number 314 painted on it like a race car, and the hood was a slightly different shade of yellow than the body. The door on the driver's side was purple, and attached to the back of the car appeared to be a large propeller from a boat engine. There were at least four antennae attached to the back, one nearly scraping the ceiling of the parking garage.

"Had Shirley here for nineteen years," Oswald said proudly as he popped the trunk open. "There ain't no cab in all of West and East Dinsmore that'll take you where you need to be this morning."

"And you drive this…for a living?" Bran said.

"Every day," Oswald replied, slamming the lid with Bran's bag inside. "Let's head off before traffic gets bad."

The tears in the seats scratched against Bran's jeans, as did the holes in the carpet which were not quite being held down by the duct tape stretched across its tatters. There was a single, orange curtain on the far window, drawn aside on its rod so that Bran could see out.

Oswald was an adept driver, swerving around every car on the road, never staying in the same lane for more than ten seconds. There were at least fifteen times that Bran was certain they were about to run someone over, but the other drivers always got out of his way, as if they were very accustomed to this. Bran imagined Sewey and Oswald would make a perfect race car team.

The city sprawled out with skyscrapers and businesses all about, even busier than two or three Deeper Dunces put together. Oswald navigated it all by memory, heading across the city and never once having to stop for a red light.

When the buildings ceased to block Bran's view, he saw to the west a giant bridge with at least twelve lanes of traffic going back and forth. It was painted bright yellow and crossed a wide, rushing river far below. The bridge separated East Dinsmore from West Dinsmore—but Oswald was not heading in that direction at all. He was pointed straight ahead toward a long, wooden dock, which poked out far ahead into the seemingly endless ocean. In the distance there was an island, and on the island was a lighthouse.

"There's Elsie Island," Oswald said, nodding. "I'll have you there soon enough."

"There's a ferry?" Bran asked as Oswald roared around a corner so he could get to the pier. Oswald didn't seem to hear him, because he didn't reply. Bran looked ahead but could not see any large ferries docked there, and very few boats even.

"Is this the right place?" Bran asked.

"Eh?" Oswald replied. "Of course it is. Can't you see Elsie right out there?"

Bran could not argue with this, but then the tires of the car met with the beginning of the dock, and the land disappeared behind them.

"What are you doing?" Bran shouted, but they were going so

fast it came out as a garbled and embarrassing scream. Oswald looked in the rearview mirror.

"Eh?" he said. "What's that now?"

"Look where you're bloody going!" Bran roared, and Oswald obeyed, swerving back into the middle of the pier.

"What's the matter?" he said. "We'll be on our way in no time. Here's it now."

He waved one of his free tentacles toward the front window, though they were going so fast Bran could not see anything except for the end of the dock.

"Are we getting on a ferry?" Bran shouted.

"Eh?" Oswald replied.

"A ferry!" Bran said even louder. "Are we going to wait for a ferry?"

"No ferries here," Oswald said. "What do we need a ferry for?"

"Because we're surrounded by water!" Bran nearly screamed. Oswald shook his head, disregarding Bran entirely as they raced across the pier, the boards threatening to pop beneath them. The car just went rumbling on as the end got closer and closer with each second—until there was no pier left. The car left the ground and went soaring through the air. For a moment, Bran felt weightless, and he couldn't draw in enough breath for a shout. They seemed to float there for a second, sailing like a glider, as Oswald calmly turned his radio dial to 88.1 FM and turned the volume all the way up.

The moment the radio was tuned, classical music blared out from the speakers in a fiery flash of pianos and trumpets, and at the same time, something happened to the outside of the car. There was a whoosh, and something invisible sealed the outside so that the air felt different; as the car tilted forward, Bran saw the water coming right at them and the hood break the surface and go diving down into the waters below.

It all seemed to happen in slow motion, but the moment they were under the water, time rushed back. The car dove so smoothly that it seemed it was far more accustomed to being below the water than above, and its motion was so effortless that if it had had a mouth and eyes, Bran felt the car itself might have been smiling with glee, as the violins and the horns and the flutes continued in victorious song.

Two men stood, shivering and yet sweating with terror, in a narrow alley of East Dinsmore, their hands bent behind their shoulders as if attached to the brick wall. Both had perfectly smooth, tanned faces, with bleached hair. But their faces were bloodied now as Joris stood before them, wielding his pistol as they tried to quiet their pained moans.

Elspeth appeared from the shadows with a look of calm annoyance on her face. She paid no heed to Joris.

"Look at me," she hissed to the men, and they struggled to lift their heads in their painful, bent positions. They whimpered, breathing harshly as she looked upon them with disdain—the same gaze she had held when she had shoved them into the van at the airport, then pushed them into the alley, and then slammed their skulls and bodies against the bricks.

"I really, really want to kill both of you," Elspeth said, her voice never rising. "I want to torch each of your bodies so no one even knows who you are anymore, then I want to put your remains into a dumpster where no one can tell the difference between you and the garbage."

The men trembled.

"But that is so tiresome," she said, putting one of her hands under each of the men's jaws and lifting their faces. "I've got so many better things to do. And I would love to be distracted by them instead of having to entertain myself with you."

She let their heads drop and lifted something in front of their eyes.

"How did this get into your bag?" she said. She held a small black ball with a miniature antenna. The men blinked at it, shaking their heads in denial.

"N-never seen it before," the first man said shakily, sweat pouring down his face.

"You didn't take it from someone?" Elspeth asked. "Not a boy, about fifteen years old?"

"No!" the man choked, his breath going in and out in quick gasps.

"Just kill them," Elspeth hissed at Joris, and the men screamed terribly until the other man shouted.

"Wait, wait!" he said. "I do remember a boy though! He was on our plane!"

Elspeth turned to him. "What did he look like?"

"Brown hair," the man stammered. "He was right across from us."

"You know where he was going?" Elspeth pressed.

"Yeah," the man wheezed. "He was heading off to Elsie Island. And we told him he couldn't get there, but he said he was still going that way."

Elspeth shifted, turning the man's head higher so she could stare deeper into his eyes. He seemed to bend under the pressure of her gaze.

"But nobody ever goes out that far toward Elsie Island," he went on, "because of the undertow and the rocks: it drowns divers and wrecks the ships."

"And the ghosts," the other man said. "The island's haunted, they say. There's light under the water there, you can see from far off on really dark nights."

He nodded his head painfully toward the open end of the alley, where the outline of the Elsie Island lighthouse could be seen towering out of the mist, its bulb turning across the waters.

"It's off limits, on account of the lighthouse," the first man rasped. "They say there's a man who lives there who keeps it runnin', but he's got special order to be let alone."

The man whimpered, fear in his damp eyes. "I-I don't know anything more."

Elspeth gently stroked his cheek.

"Of course you don't," she said gently, and she gave a smile as if to reassure him that she was done. She turned to walk away. Joris lifted his pistol and shot twice, the sound of it silenced. The moment Joris finished, the gruner leapt at the head of the first man, ripping his body from the wall and tearing into his flesh with its teeth.

"How do we know they were telling the truth?" Joris asked Elspeth, moving to follow her as the alley filled with snapping and thrashings from the gruner as it fed. Elspeth did not answer him but stood at the end of the alley and stared, as if her piercing eyes might discover where Bran was hiding.

"He was," she assured him after a few moments.

"How do we get over there then?" Joris pressed. Elspeth shook her head.

"Don't worry," she replied. "We won't need to. Bran will come to us."

"How?" Joris said.

"Thomas will make him," Elspeth said. "And he will return with the missing piece."

She looked to Joris. "Thomas has this going exactly according to plan."

Joris didn't like to hear her speak of Thomas in this way, with reluctant admiration. After a few moments, the gruner gave a low growling purr and slid against Elspeth's leg, but she continued to stare into the waters, her eyes never leaving the waves as they crashed against the rocky walls of Elsie Island.

Chapter 21

The Lights beneath the Water

Bran could neither move nor speak as the taxicab plunged through the water, the speed of its descent slowing the deeper they got, until the walls of the cab were buffeted gently by tall grasses. They rocked side to side a bit until the car hit the bottom with a soft bump.

Oswald turned the radio down, and all was silent within the car. It was very dark deep under the surface—Bran was frozen in his seat, waiting for the walls of the car to break and let the water consume them.

"Aye there, mate," Oswald said from up front. "Doing all right, eh?"

He snorted loudly and flipped a switch on the dash, and the headlights flashed on, illuminating the world outside. A school of silver, glimmering fish rushed away from the light, swimming around the car. Oswald turned the ignition, and the car came to life again.

"How in the world is this working?" Bran asked.

"Eh?" Oswald replied, looking at him from the mirror. "My cab? I told you: 'tis the only cab in all of West and East Dinsmore that can take you to where you need to be. No doubting that, no sir."

And that was all Oswald would say on the matter. He shifted gears, and the car started forward, its tires throwing back a tiny spray of dirt behind them as they went. The car pushed through the water as if it was dry land and the floor was the road, carrying them over bumps and around reefs and grasses, parting schools of fish as they went.

Bran didn't think the six-tentacled Oswald would find a fairy odd, so Bran let Nim out of his bag. She flew up to the window and pressed against it, watching with wide eyes. He wished he had a camera—no words would ever be able to describe what he was seeing. He also wished that Astara might be there with him. The thought made his heart fall.

They drove on, Oswald steering them around wavering grasses and things sticking out of the ground, until they came over a hill and saw the tall form of Elsie Island poking out toward the surface. The island itself was shaped oddly—much like a rough stone pillar that had been placed into the ground, sloping out closer to the bottom. The house had been built into it, so that only part of the gray stone and the dirty glass windows stuck out from the rocky sides, age and water having caused the structure to go dull and washed out.

As they approached, Bran began to really see just how tall the inside of the house must be, the windows crawling all up the side of the mountain in odd, crooked places, curtains drawn over them so that he couldn't see in. At the bottom, lights glowed atop an encircling brick wall. Behind the wall, the water was somehow kept away, so that Bran could see the dimly lit forms of dead trees and moldy statues.

The cab pulled up to a large gated entrance, and on the

outside stood two towering, monstrous stone statues: the hideous forms of creatures, black with wings overshadowing the gate like a canopy, long tusks, and large eyes wide with rage. They seemed to watch Oswald and Bran as the cab approached. It felt like few had ever come this far toward that house in recent days, the wall so high that as they approached, it blocked the view of the garden entirely.

The gate was black and made of stone, solid and smooth save for the silver emblem of a giant crow in the center. Oswald didn't hesitate at the menacing statues, driving under their wings until water around them disappeared, and they were once again on dry land.

"Here we are now, to the gate," Oswald said, throwing his door open. The outside of the car was dripping with water. Oswald had Bran's bags out and was opening his door before Bran had fully come to his senses.

"That was amazing," Bran said, still in wonder.

"Aye," Oswald said, gesturing for him to slide out. Bran did, and Oswald moved to get back into his car.

"Wait!" Bran said. "What do I do?"

Oswald didn't turn back. "Well, I don't have a ticket in now, mate," he said gruffly, and the roughness of his voice seemed to be a disguise for his uneasiness. "Gots to be going before something terrible happens with no way to vouch for it. Good day."

He slammed the door of the cab, glancing nervously up toward the wings of the statues. He shifted gears and rocketed backward, and the moment he left the shadow of the wings, the car was again enveloped in water and started to float toward the surface. Bran was left alone, aghast.

It was eerily silent—the only sound Bran heard was the beating of his heart. Nim blinked at him and the gates before them.

"Well, we've got to get in somehow," Bran said, leaving his bags and stepping closer to the gate. The second he moved, however, a great rumbling sound made him turn. The heads of the black statues moved, and Bran backed away until he stood trembling against the gate.

"Have you an invitation?" The lips of the statue on the right parted, revealing solid, black teeth and an endless stone mouth. The second statue pulled its head closer, its nose nearly touching Bran as its eyes studied him.

"I-I'm here to see Gary," Bran stammered, not sure what to say.

"No one has approached this gate in many a day," the second statue said, its voice hissing. "We are to be left alone. The house is to remain untouched. You are not welcome."

"But I was sent here," Bran protested. "By Adi Copplestone, his sister."

"Gary's sister has no authority here," the first statue replied. "Even she must have an invitation or suffer the consequences."

"But she sent me to see her brother," Bran stammered. The statues were not impressed, their heads edging closer to him as if they might snap his head off.

"Have you any sign or proof of your invitation?" the second statue asked, narrowing its eyes upon him hungrily. Bran's fingers shook as he dug about in his pockets, but the letter from Adi was in his luggage, sitting far away, with the creatures' heads in between. His hand touched the business card Adi had given him, and he drew it out quickly.

"This!" he said, and both heads snapped to look at what he

held. He shoved it outward so that they could see the crow embossed on the card's surface. Both creatures pushed their heads closer, studying it, sniffing at the card.

"This invitation shall suffice," the first creature said, and then both heads drew back, hardening into stone once more. Before Bran could say anything, there came a great heaving and creaking, and the gate parted, scratching loudly against the stone as it swung inward, revealing the mansion.

Nim leapt from Bran's shoulder and started forward, so Bran had to follow her, grabbing his bags as he did—though not before taking Adi's letter and placing it in his pocket, in case there were more guards. He shuffled through, and the gate closed behind them the moment they had cleared it. They were left in the darkness of the garden.

It was not a very large place, for he could see the walls clearly encircling them even through the sparse trees and bushes scattered about in an unkempt manner. There were statues: gray, hulking things, just as monstrous as the two outside, with hideous faces of fear, locked in battle with one another. Order seemed to have no place. Straight ahead, between them and the mansion, was a long pool of water with a black fence encircling it and tendrils of vines and plants growing up through the bars of its short gate.

"Such a cheery place, isn't it?" Bran said, looking about. Far above his head, the water seemed to appear again, though he could see no line of magic or glass where it began and ended. There was a shimmering where the surface of the water was, far above their heads, and he could see the shadowy shapes of fish swimming by.

He wondered how the plants and things grew there, so far from the sun, but he guessed it was some type of strange magic. There was little grass besides small pockets where it dared to grow, and the ground seemed to shimmer slightly from the broken light through the water above their heads. Bran looked to the house.

"Let's go that way," he said. "We'll knock and see who answers."

He had an uneasy feeling, one born not just from the surroundings. There was a pathway of rough stones through the garden, and he followed it. When they came to the pool, he slipped a glance through the bars. The water came up to the edge of the pool, its surface unbroken by wind or motion, the water so dark and dreary that anything might have hidden beneath the surface.

When he came closer to the house, he saw a porch built into the bottom, so that it was inset in the side of the rock and cast a deep, dark shadow over the doorway. It was supported by six tall, black columns, high and foreboding, and he passed them briskly, coming to the door. There were no windows on either side, and those that were nearest to him were too high for Bran to see any shadows or movement. He hesitated but then reached forward to knock.

It echoed deeply, the door bearing no evidence of age. There was no answer, so Bran shrugged and knocked again. He searched for a doorbell, but there was none, and after minutes of trying, still no one came.

He wasn't about to just leave after coming all that way, and he also realized that he couldn't leave anyway, because there was no way for him to get back to the surface. So he sat there on top of his luggage for nearly five minutes, hoping that someone would come.

"He's probably in there now, but the house is so big he can't even hear me," Bran said to Nim. He was feeling very impatient, for every moment that he sat there waiting was another moment lost when he could be finding Astara. Using that as an excuse, he reached his hand out and quietly said, "Onpe likoca," and the door gave a click, swinging open. He stuck his head around the edge to see in.

Bran expected a great room or a wide foyer; instead he was greeted with a narrow, darkened hallway. The walls were richly decorated, however, with fiery red and orange and yellow paintings. A long row of stone columns supported the ceiling, and at their tops flickered yellow light, as if there were candles there that he could not see. Bran took an unsteady step through the door.

"Hello?" Bran asked, his voice echoing lightly in the hallway. Nim skittered to his shoulder again, looking around.

"Gary?" Bran called out, taking his bags and closing the door behind him without taking his eyes off the hall. No one replied. The walls were dusty, and as he looked closer, he thought that he could see forms and faces in the outlines of the paint, though they appeared to have been brushed over and smudged away. He walked down the hall, and the corridor curved off a bit to the right up ahead so that he couldn't see around it. There were dark, wooden doors with black metal hinges and keyholes and curved tops that fit into the stone walls tightly. Bran's steps continued around the bend.

"He's not one for cheery lighting, that's for sure," Bran told Nim, just to hear his voice in that dreary place. It smelled of stone and water in a strange way, and the columns on either side continued down, every step lit by the flickering candles above his head. He checked almost every door that he passed, but each was locked tight and wouldn't budge. He considered using magic on them as well but thought better of it—he'd broken into the house, and it'd be hard to come up with an excuse for sneaking in any further.

He passed nearly eight doors when the hallway split. At the center there was a great painting that was nearly half as tall as Bran, hanging above a simple wooden table. The painting was of a giant golden key with red and orange flames bursting out from its sides, making the key seem to be afire itself. Bran thought the picture was stunning but a bit absurd.

"A key?" Bran said, and Nim jumped from his shoulder to look at it closer. "Now there's an obsession to have. Where do you even buy paintings of keys?"

The diverging hallways were covered with a rich red carpet, and the walls were papered with a red and dark yellow design. The columns ended and were replaced with candles attached to the walls. Bran started toward the hall at the right without really even thinking, and Nim followed.

He almost called Gary's name again but couldn't bring himself to speak as he went down the hallway. It started to curve up and around, like a circular ramp going higher into the house. The walls began to be neatly decorated with inset glass displays. Behind the glass were keys in various shapes and sizes: polished, some gold and others brass, and some with gems and others with rich designs and markings. Bran put his hand in his pocket, feeling the key there once more, burning to his touch.

The hallway continued around until he found himself at a kind of crossroads; the hallway straight ahead went back down in a full circle. But there was another hall proceeding straight away to the left, which he followed. There were more key displays there, lit by soft lights he could not see. The hall began to lead upward again, and as he came to the end, he saw something looming in the darkness before him.

The thin hallway opened into a grand, circular room like an amphitheater, with the hallway carpet continuing around it to the left. Stepping forward, Bran saw that the hallway spiraled around the great room, like a balcony ramp that went up and around, higher and higher until it met the ceiling, too far above for Bran to see if not for the candles that continued up its walls.

However, Bran paid little heed to these things, for his gaze was riveted on the middle of the room where a towering wooden ship was floating in midair as if magically free of gravity, held to the floor by heavy black cables that were anchored with giant bolts. It was the type of ship that a pirate might have sailed in, the wood broken in many places, rusty cannons sticking out of portholes, the sails tattered and ripped to shreds. It was very old, and one of the masts was missing entirely, but its fierce power was still as intimidating as if Bran had seen it on the sea.

Bran looked around the giant room but saw no sign of anyone. He drew closer to the giant ship, running his eyes across its side and studying its materials. It seemed to get larger the closer he got, until it hovered above his head. Every sail was triangular, which struck Bran as odd; he was no expert on sailing, but he knew a triangular sail was probably a waste of wind power. The sails were layered, however, so that they seemed to cover one another.

He suddenly noticed a small pedestal with a metal plaque in the shadow of the ship. The words were hard to read in the dark, so he drew out his mother's wand.

"*Obro litighe*," he said, and from the end of the wand came a tiny glowing orb of light, detaching and floating in front of Bran's head. It cast a dim white glow across the words on the plaque, and Bran read:

The Ship of Pythagorus Fearum

"Fearum?" Bran said, giving a small laugh.

At that sound there came a deep, rumbling noise, breaking his concentration on the glowing orb so that it vanished. He was again engulfed in the shadow of the ship, and the noise stopped, though it echoed up the giant room. Bran could not move, the sound having shaken the very floor itself, and he looked up to the ship again, feeling that it had come from its direction.

He started to slide away slowly, and he heard another sound. The ship seemed to rock slightly, then stop again.

The noises seemed to have come from a gaping hole in the side of the ship far above his head. There were many holes in the ship on that side, all so dark that he could not see within. Still, Bran's curiosity got the better of him, so he moved a cautious step closer, trying to peer deeper into the dark.

"Hello?" Bran said. "Is that you, Gary?"

He heard another soft rumble that died out once more. Bran started to take slow paces backward, getting a very bad feeling under his skin. He heard something moving about inside the ship, and it began to shake and tremble slightly against the cords. Bran took another step, not letting his eyes leave it.

"I can come back later," Bran said quickly, and he was turning to dash for the hall when there came a giant roar that filled the room. From every hole in the ship burst forth black tentacles, shooting out toward Bran. He shouted and started to run, but the tentacles caught him by the leg, grabbing him and pulling back. He dropped the wand when he was slammed against the hard floor. Then the tentacle lifted him high into the air, and the room filled with the violent roar of a beast.

Chapter 22

The Revdoora

Nim saw Bran being lifted by the tentacles, and she bit the creature, but it swatted her away angrily, and she tumbled across the room and out of sight.

"Nim!" Bran shouted as he flew through the air, the tentacles snaking around his waist and neck and arms, slinging him toward the ship. Through the high, gaping hole he saw a giant, black, dripping mouth and behind it a dozen glassy black eyes filled with hunger. There were no teeth in the mouth, just a gaping throat from which came another startling roar that blew his hair like wind.

"Feiro!" Bran shouted, fire launching from his palm toward the mouth of the beast. The fire sprayed into its mouth, but the beast shook Bran so that the magic was broken and roared again in pain and anger. The tentacles of the beast tightened so that Bran could barely breathe.

Nim came back again, trying to find a place to attack but spiraling as she was pushed away. The beast pulled Bran closer, and Bran struggled to regain his senses, to do anything to fight as he saw its mouth gaping before him.

"What's all this noise?" came the roaring voice of a man. In an instant, the creature stopped its movement, so that Bran was held high above the ground in its grasp. Bran managed to open his eyes and saw that someone was standing at eye level with him on one of the balconies, holding a glowing lantern.

The man appeared to be in his late thirties, with short, dark hair and a few days' stubble on his chin, already going gray. His nose was broken slightly, but Bran might not have noticed except for the lantern throwing such deep shadows on his face. Being so far under water, one might have expected the man's skin to be pale, but he appeared healthy, despite the circles under his eyes and the wrinkles around the edges of his face.

"Who are you?" he demanded, gesturing at Bran with the lantern. Bran coughed; he couldn't draw in enough air to breathe, much less answer. The man narrowed his eyes.

"Answer me!" he shouted.

"Wait," Bran said, breathing hard. "I was sent here to meet Gary."

"Well, that's me," the man with the lantern said. "But you should know visitors are unwelcome here."

The tentacles of the beast tightened even further at Gary's words, as if in anticipation.

"No, please," Bran said. "I've got a note from Adi. Look, it's in my pocket."

"My sister?" Gary replied, lifting the lantern higher. "What of her?"

"The note," Bran said, sliding one arm free and drawing it out of his pocket. He held it out in Gary's direction.

"Open it yourself," Gary commanded. "Read it to me."

"I can't, the seal can only be broken by you," Bran said, insisting with the letter. Gary seemed unsure, but finally he beckoned the creature closer. Gary snatched the letter and drew back a few steps from Bran, opening the seal effortlessly and unfolding the paper.

He began to read it with anger in his eyes, but as he scanned down the page, his expression changed. Before he had even reached the bottom, his hands began to tremble. Bran didn't know whether to read Gary's reaction as fear or anger.

"Oh no," Gary whispered, turning the page to read the back. "Oh no, no, no. No, Adi."

He looked up at Bran again. His face had changed so drastically that Bran was shocked. Gary's eyes had become filled with such agony, it was like he had been stabbed through the heart with a knife. He studied Bran's face and shakily folded the letter, returning it to the envelope.

"It can't be," Gary's voice cracked once. "You're Emry and Thomas's son." If the room had been deathly still before, the silence had dropped even deeper, so that even the creature made no sound.

"I am," Bran replied. "I'm Bran Hambric."

Gary flinched at this but tried to hide it.

"Put him down," he ordered the creature. The creature hesitated, and Gary straightened up.

"Put the boy down this *very instant!*" he shouted, so filled with rage that the end came out as a mad scream. The beast immediately deposited Bran over the railing and onto the balcony at Gary's feet, and Bran rolled over dizzily. Gary stood over him, nervously holding the lantern out and extending his hand.

"I'm Gary," he said. "I apologize so sincerely, Bran. I really do. Maven has lived in that ship since I got it, and I can't get her out without wrecking the whole thing."

"I'm all right," Bran said, getting to his feet. Nim was at his side in an instant, clinging to his shirt in fear. Bran went to the balcony edge and, spotting the wand, held his hand out, and it flashed through the air into his palm.

"I thought I was gone for sure," Bran said. Gary shook his head.

"You're alive at least," he replied. "I haven't welcomed a visitor here in a great time. And even you, Bran…even you, being the first after so long?" Gary shook his head. "I never thought my sister would do such a thing to me."

Bran did not understand what Gary was talking about, so he just nodded.

"She told you about the key, then?" Bran said. Gary looked up at him.

"Some," he said. "Not very much. I still don't understand why she would send you to me, considering our circumstances."

Gary gestured around the room, as if Bran should know something. Gary glanced at Nim for a second and then pointed ahead with the lantern.

"No matter, we can speak of this in my office," he muttered. He started up the balcony, and Bran followed with Nim on his shoulder, their steps taking them higher up. The beast drew back into the ship dejectedly, its tentacles slithering inward once more until it had disappeared entirely and gave a low grumble in disgust at losing a good meal.

As they continued up, lit by the candles and Gary's lantern, Bran saw that these halls had no glass displays but instead had hooks spaced evenly every few inches. On each hook was a different key: car keys, house keys, skeleton keys; keys that were worn and keys that had been polished; some worth nothing and others inset with tiny jewels. They passed so many keys that Bran felt it would have taken a lifetime to amass them all, and yet every space seemed to be filled.

Gary led Bran through another long, carpeted hallway, with more keys on those walls as well. The house seemed to continue off in winding directions, like tunnels through an old hill. It had to have taken years to build, and Bran realized with amazement that he was still actually under the water, and far above his head somewhere was an island.

Many doors later, the hallway opened into a larger, circular room. It wasn't very wide in circumference, but the ceiling domed high above Bran's head. Messy furniture spread across the floor in a disorganized manner in front of a great, wooden desk at the end of the room. There was a gigantic brick fireplace to Bran's right that crackled with flames, its mantle the shape of stone beasts like the ones at the gate. Bookshelves lined the walls around and above the doorway. But the most startling feature was behind the desk: a wall made entirely of glass.

The candlelight reflected in it, but Bran could see tiny glimpses of fish swimming by and little glimmers of color. It took his breath away, and again, he thought that Astara would have loved it. Thinking of her brought him back to reality, and he saw that Gary was watching him from behind the desk.

"Sit down?" Gary offered, his voice shaking. Bran nodded, and Gary rubbed his hands together nervously and then sat himself. He got up again, though, and went to a side table and began to pour two glasses of water. Bran noticed there was a small, open bird cage hanging to the left of the desk. Inside was a crow, with the darkest black feathers and the harshest expression its face, standing still and stately, its beak a solid, reflective silver that caught light. The bird sat in the exact center of his tiny cage, head held high as if looking down upon Bran for being such a loathsome mortal that was hardly worthy of being in his presence. The bird's eyes narrowed.

"Escrow!" it shrieked suddenly, in the loudest, shrillest of voices, making Bran jump.

"Quiet down," Gary ordered, pouring the water. "He's an honored guest."

"Unwelcome!" it said, louder. "Unwelcome here!"

It spread its wings and flapped at Bran, as if to shoo him away.

"Hush, Escrow!" Gary hissed, waving his hand. "He has an invitation."

"Lies!" Escrow screamed. "Salty, salty lies!"

Escrow went on mumbling to himself and glaring at Bran, turning disgustedly until he was facing the window.

"Here, have something," Gary said, returning with the cups. "You've probably been traveling a while, I suppose?"

"I have," Bran said, drinking it down. "It's been a long trip."

"Hopefully I can make it worth your time," Gary said. "I haven't had visitors in a very long while. Even my sister...you know, I have no contact with the outside. The fact that she would send you here, of all places, still confuses me."

"She said you could help me," Bran said. "That you were the only person who might know how to find the door this key goes to."

"Well, I do know a thing or two about keys," Gary said, and for the first time he gave a smile, though it was wry, and he seemed to be amused at something entirely different. Bran drew out the key and placed it gently onto the desk between them, and Gary's smile disappeared.

"Oh," he said. "This key."

He seemed to say it as if he recognized the key, which was very surprising as it had been locked in the bank vault for years. He figured that Gary had seen so many keys in his life that he had to have come across one like it before.

"Do you mind if I...?" Gary said, reaching forward.

"Wait, I wouldn't—" Bran tried to warn him, but Gary had already touched the key, which spit out a green shock.

"As I expected," Gary said, unfazed. "Very smart. Can you hand it to me then?"

"What?" Bran said, blinking.

"Just give it to me," Gary said. Bran did as he was told and cautiously held the key out, and Gary reached forward and took it right out of his hand.

"It didn't hurt you," Bran said.

"Of course," Gary replied, turned the key over in his hands and studying the markings on its side. "It's enchanted, so that it can only be given from one person to another willingly. If I had forced you at gunpoint for example, it wouldn't have worked. It's quite a magnificent safeguard. And it means your mother obviously intended it to go to you next, since she left it with you in the bank vault, and it doesn't hurt you when you touch it."

"How do you know about the bank vault?" Bran asked. Gary said nothing in reply. He examined the gem in the handle and kept turning it over. Bran felt a strange nervousness now that he wasn't holding the key, as if there were danger in simply giving it to Gary. Gary put his mind to rest the next moment, however, when he passed it back.

"Fascinating," was all Gary would say. "But I still don't understand why you have come to me. It is very old. Finding the door to that key could be unwise—and could open something anew that is best left closed."

Bran then began to tell Gary exactly why he had come there. Gary seemed fixated on the bank vault and had Bran return to it many times, asking him about his past. He was very curious about the wooden box itself, which was very strange, but when Bran told him about Astara, Gary's eyes filled with tears.

"You poor boy," Gary said, interrupting him. "I'm so sorry you lost her."

"But I know she's got to be alive," Bran said. "She's trying to tell me something. But I don't even know where to begin, and I think finding the door to this key is the start."

"I don't think you want to find the door to this key, Bran," Gary replied. His words took Bran by surprise.

"No, I do," Bran insisted. "I've got to. I've come all this way—I have to find her."

"She could very well be gone, Bran." Gary shook his head. "This is dark magic, and a lot of it. You could get drawn into it just like she was."

"I don't really care now," Bran said forcefully. "I've already made my choice. I want to get her back."

Gary sighed. "Sometimes, Bran, it's better to just let her go."

"But I'm not going to," Bran said. He couldn't believe he was actually arguing this point with a man he had just met.

"I don't understand," Bran said. "Adi told me you could help.

All I need is for you to tell me the door this key goes to, and I'll be on my way. You'll never have to see me again."

Gary seemed to ponder this, folding his hands and looking across the desk at the key. His expression then turned darker, almost as if he had become angered and offended by some thought, and he sat up straighter.

"All right then," Gary said gruffly. "I'll do my part, and then you're on your way, and I never have to see you again."

"It's a deal," Bran said, arising. Gary's face returned to the stony, emotionless expression it had before as he pushed past Bran roughly, as if eager to be rid of him. Gary unlocked a door opposite the fireplace, and it opened to a thin hallway. Bran and Nim followed him through.

The hallway sloped up a bit and ended in a circular room far smaller than the office. It had no windows and was littered around the edges with bits of machinery and trash. When Gary moved out of the way, Bran saw that sitting in the center of this room was a strange device. It appeared to be a solid, red wooden door. It was just sitting there, held in a metal frame, as if it was waiting to be installed. Beside it was a solid pedestal with wires running back and forth from the door to it and a clear bowl of water on top.

"As keys are my obsession," Gary said, "I have created a great many inventions involving them. I assume this is the one my sister has sent you to make use of."

He touched the door. "This device is my Revdoora—the only one in the world, and its deeper workings are many years older than you or this house. If anyone else was in possession of this device, the powers that be would demand it be removed and placed in some Mages Council vault. But as those powers have a very wise fear of me, it has been let alone for my own purposes."

"What does it do?" Bran asked.

"Observe," Gary said, drawing an ordinary house key from the pedestal and placing it into the bowl of water, where it sank to the bottom. He then reached forward and pulled the door open. To Bran's surprise, the door opened to the entryway of a house he did not recognize. It was dark beyond the door, but he could see stairs and furniture and toys on the floor. He couldn't resist taking a step closer, but before he could do anything, Gary slammed the door shut again.

"You see, Bran," Gary said, "this device will turn this door into the entrance that the key belongs to. In this case," he pulled the key from the bowl of water, "it's the house of some family somewhere in the north, if I remember correctly. If I was to put a car key in, I'd step into someone's car. If I was to put in the key to the Morkhoml Bank Vault, I could be a very rich and untraceable villain."

"That is incredible," Bran stammered. Gary gestured toward the bowl.

"Just put your key in there, and you're off," he said impatiently. Bran didn't see a reason to waste any more time, so he dropped the key into the bowl and stepped back. His heart began to beat faster as he realized how close he was to finding Astara again. He rubbed his hands together nervously.

"Go on," Gary pressed, waving his hand at the door.

"It was nice meeting you, and thank you," Bran said, but Gary only nodded again, so Bran took a deep breath and reached for the handle. He hesitated and then pulled on the door.

A shattering explosion threw Bran back off his feet. It erupted in his ears and crawled up and down skin, filling his vision with green light until he was blinded by it. The noise was so loud that his eardrums popped, and he felt his head strike against the wall, and all went black.

Chapter 23

Escrow and the Letter

When Bran awoke, he couldn't remember how he had gotten into a bed, and his vision was so hazy that he wasn't able to tell where he was. He turned his head and blinked and was able to make out that he was in a small bedroom with furniture against the walls and a window that had thick curtains over it. The room was oddly shaped, every corner angled and crooked, and even when Bran blinked his eyes to make sure it wasn't an effect of the explosion, it still appeared crooked.

Bran tried to sit up, but an overwhelming pain burst from his left hand, and he lay back against the pillows. He winced and saw that his hand was entirely wrapped up in gauze.

"What?" he said with dismay, trying to move it but finding that even the slightest motion sent a fiery pain all through his wrist and arm. He slowly pushed himself up with his legs, which were under the heavy gray bed sheets. There was no television or telephone to be seen, and Bran became more and more uneasy.

He heard a noise outside the door, and Gary poked his head in.

"Good, you're awake now," he said, nodding in Bran's direction.

"How long have I been asleep?" Bran asked.

"Many hours, I would expect," Gary replied, entering and

moving toward Bran's bedside. "I haven't really kept track. Hit your head pretty hard in there."

"What happened?" Bran asked with horror. "Did I do something wrong?"

"No," Gary shook his head, with a hint of disgust. "Unless nearly destroying my device counts as something wrong. Then yes, you did."

He glared at Bran. "Your key blasted the device into pieces, and I barely made it out of that room without injuries myself!"

Bran was left in shock, unable to even speak an apology, but then Gary's expression reversed, and he began to laugh loudly.

"Oh come on, Bran, it's only old machinery," Gary said. "What's important is you're alive, and I've discovered my device isn't quite as perfect as it seemed. I think what I need now is to begin work immediately on repairs for Revdoora version 2.0."

He laughed and then pushed something at Bran. "Drink this."

Bran swallowed it, though he was still confused at how happy Gary seemed.

"I am sorry, though," Bran said.

"Don't worry!" Gary laughed. "It might be a good thing you've got to stay with me a few extra days, on account of you being hurt."

He leaned over the bed to look closer at Bran's injured hand. "You hurt that side the worst I would say. Can't tell if it's broken or what, but it wasn't in good shape."

"I can't move it," Bran said, wincing again as he tried to. "You don't have a doctor I could go see? That might be best."

Gary shook his head. "Not down here I don't. And I don't

think you're in much condition to make it all the way back to the mainland by yourself."

"You don't have a way of getting me there?" Bran asked.

"Unfortunately," Gary replied, "I cannot leave this house for any reason. You would be on your own."

"But—" Bran protested, struggling to get his legs free of the sheets. "What about Astara? I've got to find the door to that key somehow!"

"Well, be patient," Gary said. "You can't go anywhere in that condition—and no matter how great your magic powers may be, I know for certain that an untrained mage such as you attempting to heal that injury will almost assuredly make it worse."

"But I can't stay here!" Bran said with desperation. "I have to go. I'm wasting time just lying here in bed!"

At hearing those words, Gary looked hurt.

"Well..." Gary began, but he couldn't finish what he was going to say.

"I mean, it's just important I help Astara," Bran said, trying to calm himself. "Nothing against you."

"I-I understand," Gary stammered. "But...you're hurt, and you're welcome here, and I'd hate to see you leave so fast—it doesn't have to be a bad thing you're stuck here. I could take a look at that key for you some more, you know."

"You have more devices?" Bran asked.

"Oh yes, plenty," Gary quickly returned. "I've got gobs of things I could do to study that key. I am an expert on keys you know, and I'm sure I'd find something."

He seemed to be grabbing anything just to make Bran stay, and it was very odd, because Bran had thought that Gary didn't want him there. But Gary was obviously eager to help, and Bran really needed him.

"All right then, I guess staying a bit won't hurt," Bran said with reluctance, and Gary's face lit up.

"That's splendid!" he said, rubbing his hands together. "You won't find a finer place than this one. And you and I will find a way to get your friend back, I promise."

It was just peculiar how excited Gary was all of a sudden. Bran hoped that it was perhaps nervousness or seeing another human after being alone so long.

"What happened to the key?" Bran asked.

"It's over there in the bowl of water," Gary said, gesturing to Bran's bedside table. "It seems it's got a way of keeping itself from harm. The bowl and the pillar are the only things that weren't wrecked in that room."

Bran slid closer and drew the key out with his good hand, shaking it so the water fell off. As he sat back down, his necklace slid out from under his shirt. Gary drew back and gasped, stumbling as if his heart had stopped. Bran, afraid at first the key had done something, moved away as well, but then he saw that Gary's gaze was on the necklace.

"Are you all right?" Bran said, looking down and then back to Gary.

"Yes, yes," Gary stammered. "Quite all right, Bran. It's just...I hadn't expected to ever see that necklace again."

"You've seen it before?" Bran said with surprise.

"Oh yes," Gary nodded, regaining control of himself. "I just thought for sure she would have...gotten rid of it, a long time ago."

"My mother?" Bran said with shock, reaching to touch the

necklace and feeling oddly as if he should hide it from Gary's gaze. "You knew her?"

A silence fell over the room as Gary hesitated.

"I did," he said simply. "Once. A long, long time ago."

His face became forlorn, and he moved like he was about to say something else, even holding his hand out toward the necklace. But he stopped himself, and stepping back through the door, he disappeared.

Bran froze in shock but pushed the sheets off his legs and hurried to the door.

"How did you—" he began, but Gary was already gone. The hallway beyond split off in two directions. He looked down each but saw no trace of Gary in either. The candles lining the walls seemed to have dimmed on their own. It made the red and gold wallpaper and the dark carpet appear sinister. Bran listened for Gary, and he heard a sound straight ahead, so he started off.

"Gary?" he called, trying to get his attention, but he found that the end of the hall met with another, which he took, passing many doors and displays of keys. He came to the end of the hall rather quickly and found that it opened into the main room at the balcony, the ship hovering many levels below his feet and the gentle rumblings of the sleeping creature within causing the floor to buzz.

At first, Bran didn't catch any trace of Gary, but then he saw a shadow two levels higher, disappearing through a door that closed quietly. Bran hurried around the balcony, winding up until he reached the level where the shadow had been, finding that he was back at the door to Gary's office. He almost knocked, but his eagerness got the best of him, so he simply burst through.

The room was shrouded in total darkness. The dim light from behind him sliced through it, a beam falling across Gary's desk, Bran's silhouette framed across the room. No one was there.

"Gary?" he said softly, but there came no reply. He was sure he had seen him go into this room. He gently closed the door behind him, and the only light came through the giant window behind the desk and from the low coals in the fireplace. Bran was suddenly able to see through the glass clearly: the fish that swam by, the debris that carelessly floated there.

Bran was about to leave, afraid he might wake Escrow and be caught snooping, but he spotted something sitting on Gary's desk. It was Adi's letter. He glanced around the room one more time, but he didn't sense anyone watching, so he crept closer to take a look.

There were various odds and ends strewn across Gary's desk, and Bran was careful not to knock anything aside. Bran stole one more glance at the door before he picked the pages up from the unsealed envelope, opening them and squinting to read. It was too dark, so he bent them toward the light.

A great shriek split the air, and the letter was jerked from Bran's grasp. He spun, but in the darkness he only heard the scream of Escrow.

"Unwelcome!" the bird called. "Unwelcome here!"

"Hush!" Bran demanded in a hoarse whisper, but he heard the sound of papers being torn, and he spun to see Escrow viciously shredding the letter with his beak. Bran dashed across the room, but the bird cried out again, dodging to the desk and tearing it up with his talons, until in mere seconds it was nothing but worthless confetti.

"Unwelcome!" Escrow said, and he hissed and spread his wings. The bird scratched the shreds of the letter behind him and snapped at Bran's hand when he tried to grab them.

"You've made a mess!" Bran said angrily, but as he had only one usable hand, there wasn't much he could do to fight the bird. Escrow nipped at his fingers, and Bran jerked back.

"Stop that!" Bran ordered.

"Unwelcome!" Escrow retorted, snapping his beak to keep Bran back.

"I was just going to look at it," Bran said, trying to keep his voice down.

"Lies!" the bird's voice came. "Salty, salty lies!"

"Quiet!" Bran said, snapping his fingers around the bird's beak and forcing him to be silent. "You've already destroyed it, so I can't read it anyway."

The bird wiggled his head free and waddled around on the desk, glaring at Bran until he finally left the room in disgust.

Chapter 24

A Lullaby for Lost Love

As there was no television, Bran sank down into the pillows of the bed and stared at the ceiling. He felt that he should be doing something, and yet he was trapped where he was, and twice he considered using magic to attempt to heal his injury. Bran finally drifted away into slumber, but he was given no rest. His mind was filled with a repeat of what he had seen under the bridge in Dunce, following Astara's ghostly form through the woods to her grave. His dream was so vivid it was as if he was there again, the magic tearing at the ground and pulling her coffin back to the surface. But this time, her body was there beneath the wooden shell. Her eyes were already open, staring back up at him as she huddled in the corner, buried alive.

He reached to pull her out, but his hands went straight through her. Her ghostly body washed away into a green mist. She blew upward, swirling freely out of the coffin and into the air. He chased her body as it glowed, flying through the trees, but as it went, it slowly dissipated until there was no light left.

His subconscious told him to look down, and he saw that he was holding something tightly. The green gem in the key's handle glowed into his face, the same color as Astara's smoky form. It was blinding, and Bran moved his hand to cover it, but then the gem itself became a mist and drifted out of the key, leaving the woods around Bran black.

Bran awoke, rolling over, twisting his legs in the bedsheet. He winced as he leaned on his injured hand and swung over to the other side, finding that he was covered in sweat though the room was cold. He managed to sit up, unable to recall why he was out of breath until he remembered the dream. He reached up to wipe his forehead with his good hand and nearly knocked himself in the eye with the key, which had somehow made its way into his fist.

He stared at it, though the room was dark, and unlike in his dream, no light came from the gem. He set it on the table next to the bed and wiped his face with the edge of his sheets, which were soaked in his own sweat. The dream was hard to clear from his mind, and it had left his body so weak and sore that he had to lean against the chair when he stood. He dug some fresh clothes out of his bag and managed to get them on with his good hand.

He didn't see Nim at first until he spotted her asleep across the room on a long string of fat cotton balls that had been placed on the dresser. It felt odd knowing that Gary must have come into his room, though Bran could not complain, for there was also a glass of water and a silver tray of food beside the bed.

There was a bowl under the lid of some type of soup with vegetables and garlic and tiny bits of fish. It tasted so fresh, though Bran couldn't tell what was in it. He sipped it down with the spoon, and as he ate, he slowly began to feel a little bit better and more alert. He glanced over at Nim again, but he didn't want to wake her, so he set his spoon quietly to the side and left the room.

He wandered down the hallways, and presently he heard

clanking noises and a hammer coming from around a bend. He followed the sounds until he reached the balcony and saw Gary far below, working on the giant ship. He was suspended by a system of pulleys and ropes so that he was hanging against the side of the hull, hammering a board down over a rotted opening.

Bran almost called down to him but thought better of it and walked down the circular hall until he finally reached the bottom.

"That's a big ship," Bran said, trying to start conversation. Gary glanced at him.

"Good morning," he said. He wasn't as cheerful as he had been before.

"What's it doing all the way down here?" Bran pressed. "I can't even imagine how you got it inside this place."

Gary didn't seem very willing to stop his work, but he finally did, setting the hammer down onto the plank of wood.

"This ship," he said, wiping his hands, "was once sailed by the great pirate Pythagorus Fearum."

"A pirate?" Bran asked. "Then why have you got the ship down here?"

Gary grinned at that.

"Well, there's a lot of history behind this ship," he replied. "Keys aren't my only obsession." He lightly tapped the wood. "I've got many of Fearum's personal items. I suppose you would say I collect them. I'm probably one of few who know his true legend."

"And what's his story?" Bran said, trying to keep Gary talking.

"Well, I shan't tell you the whole legend of Fearum," Gary said, "but suffice it to say that Pythagorus was perhaps one of the nastiest, and least spoken of, pirates in his day."

Gary shook his head. "He committed a great many crimes, including the one against a monastery of the Ancients which sealed his doom. The Ancients cursed Pythagorus and all of his descendants to suffer their deaths by fire."

"How many descendants does a pirate usually have?" Bran asked.

"More than you want to know about," Gary replied, and he slowly began to lower himself down with the pulley until his feet touched the ground.

"Pythagorus was thankfully more reckless on the open seas than he was on land," Gary said. "He had only one son, who in turn had only one son, who also had only one son."

"And did he really die by fire?" Bran asked.

"Tragically, yes," Gary said. "As every descendant has after him. His son was said to have been burned at the stake; his grandson died when his burning house fell on him. It is difficult to find the true history of the other generations, as few public records are kept on it."

Gary nodded at the ship.

"I fancy myself the world's only true expert on Pythagorus Fearum," he said with a grin. "Legend has it that after Pythagorus's death, his loyal first mate Skully Crossbones wrote the only existing record of his life, and that Skully still wanders the world, awaiting his final leave from Pythagorus so that he can die."

Gary gestured upward. "And the triangular sails were his sign, colored green and black, so that all ships that came within sight would know to turn about rather than risk the wrath of the pirate named Fearum."

"You seem to know quite a bit about him," Bran said. Gary looked up at the giant ship with an affectionate gaze.

"Perhaps I have a weakness for obsessions," he said. And at that, Gary began to wheel himself back up with the pulley. Gary started to hammer again, but Bran gathered up his courage and started again.

"I went looking for you last night," Bran said. "But I couldn't find you in your office."

The hammer did not stop.

"I wanted to ask you about my mother," Bran pressed.

"What of her?" Gary said, his voice cool.

"Well, last night you told me you'd met her before," Bran said.

"I did," the man nodded.

"But I don't remember anything about her," Bran said. "You're one of the few people I've found who does."

"There were many of us who knew Emry before she died," Gary said, and he stared straight ahead at his work, as if ignoring Bran would make him disappear.

"You can't tell me anything about what she was like?" Bran said. Gary stopped the hammer suddenly, its head hovering an inch from the nail.

"Did Adi send you here for this?" Gary snapped. It took Bran by surprise.

"N-no," he said, confused. "Adi didn't even tell me you'd known my mother."

"She didn't, did she?" Gary responded. "She didn't tell you anything about the Project?"

"You mean the Farfield Curse?" Bran asked. The speed of his reply caught Gary unawares. He looked down at Bran quickly with anger in his eyes.

"Adi failed to mention you knew of it," Gary said. "I only

knew it as the Project until it was twisted into that deplorable thing you know as the Curse."

"You worked on the Farfield Curse?" Bran said with alarm. Gary seemed to take offense at those words, because he started to wheel himself down until he was just above Bran's head.

"How about I tell you a little story," Gary said, his eyes narrowing. "Many years before you were born, someone stumbled upon a cave, and in this cave was the corpse of a man whose arms were clutching a box of ancient scrolls. The Mages Council, wishing to decipher these scrolls, commissioned a secret group of mages to decode them. At its head was a man by the name of Baslyn."

Bran blinked at this, and Gary caught his reaction to the name.

"You have heard of him as well," Gary said. "No matter, this story is not Baslyn's. It is actually the story of a young man—one who knew entirely too much about a pirate by the name of Pythagorus Fearum. When Baslyn discovers that the corpse that had held these scrolls was none other than that of the legendary pirate himself, he brings this expert onto his research team—along with others, including a man named Thomas and a woman named Emry.

"Along the way," Gary went on, "this man, Baslyn, discovers that these scrolls spoke of a magical power beyond anything in his wildest imagination: of another place, of creatures, of dark magics no one had seen even in their nightmares. And feeling that he might find a way to use these for his own advantage, he proposes to his group of researchers the outline for a plot.

"Being young and under this man's influence, his group sides with him—all save one, the young man who knew so much of the pirate Fearum. He alone decides to stand against them but unwisely chooses to ignore them rather than alert the Council of their true plans. So he is forced to leave."

"And so Baslyn," Gary said, "and his followers, with the man named Thomas and the woman named Emry, continued their horrific work, and I think both you and I know the end."

Gary shook his head sadly.

"So yes, Bran," he finished, "I do know much about the Farfield Curse and how your mother was brought to her end."

Bran opened his mouth to reply, but Gary only wheeled himself up the side of the ship again.

"She changed before she died, you know," Bran called up, in what little defense of her name he could muster.

"But her end was hardly when it was meant to be," he heard Gary say.

"Well, you were just a friend of hers," Bran called back. "She was my mother. So you can hardly act like it affected you more than it did me."

Disgusted, Bran spun around to leave the room before he became angrier.

"Where are you going?" came Gary's voice.

"I don't know," Bran said sharply. His voice carried the bitterness that had washed over his heart. Time was being wasted with every moment he was stuck there.

"It might do you well to rest, Bran," Gary said, with unexpected concern.

"I can't sleep anymore," Bran replied over his shoulder. "I've been having the worst of nightmares."

He heard Gary's pulley begin to creak once more until he reached the ground.

"Come now," Gary said, cleaning his hands in a towel. "Let me help you."

"I don't want any help sleeping," Bran hissed. "I want to find my friend!"

"You won't have any luck there until you're well again," Gary said, though his voice carried no anger. He tossed the towel back onto the table, passing Bran for the hall.

Though Bran did not feel like doing anything that Gary said, he reluctantly followed until they had come to the office. Gary gestured Bran to the couch, the fireplace crackling warmly as Gary sat in a large leather chair across from him. There was a square wooden table beside him with two drawers, and he reached for the brass pull of the top.

"I think that a bit of music might help you," he said. He drew a long, slender box from the drawer and opened it gently. Within it was a perfectly polished silver flute with black etchings around its surface.

"Just rest," Gary insisted. "I'm a Netora, if you haven't figured it out by now. Music is one of my many passions."

"My friend is a Netora as well," Bran said. Gary looked up at him.

"As was your mother," he said softly, "before she fell for that which was her end."

Bran did not know how to take Gary's words, because they only built new monuments upon the mysteries he had already constructed.

"But don't think of her for now," Gary whispered, as if he could feel Bran's uncertainty. "How many nights has her memory haunted both you and me?"

Bran did as Gary had told him and lay back, as much as he wished to do otherwise. The couch was comfortable, and he realized that though he had rested the night before, the nightmares had left him even more tired. His heart was weary as well, and each thought of Astara pained him all the more.

"Close your eyes," Gary said. "You'll feel better after a while, Bran."

Gary began to play. The song started slow at first, a few notes repeated like the droning sound of the flute awakening from its slumber. It surrounded Bran, opening like a new morning in another world. The notes flowed out effortlessly from the instrument, as if it was playing itself in the softest tones it knew. Bran's eyes had opened without him fully realizing it, and he saw that Gary's fingers were working the flute, his mouth pressed to the other end as he did. He nodded for Bran to close his eyes again, and so Bran obeyed and let the music wash over the room.

The song went on, repeating the first short verse once and then transforming into a lullaby, one that was so familiar that Bran had to force himself to keep his eyes closed. He knew he had heard it somewhere, but he could not place the sound. It seemed to be buried deep in the recesses of his mind.

The melody was unhurried and mournful, like the lament of a lost love, its notes seeming to fade into one another like the soft weeping of a man. It was odd how the music seemed to drift across Bran's mind like soothing incense, sweetly lulling him deeper against the couch, though he tried to fight it. His mind softened to its notes, the worry and the pain over losing Astara slowly wearing away, until its burden lightened from his shoulders.

He opened his eyes wearily to ask Gary the name of the song. But when he looked toward the chair, he saw that Gary's eyes were closed, and there were tears rolling down the man's cheeks, as he slowly continued to play the notes by memory.

The room became hazy, and notes washed over Bran like ghostly hands pushing his eyelids closed until he had fallen asleep.

Chapter 25

The Key and Its Map

Bran slept better that night than he had in weeks. He awoke in the crooked bedroom, and there was another tray of warm food beside his bed. He didn't feel like eating, but he made himself down everything that was there. He had no sense of the time, and though he didn't think he could sleep any more, he couldn't drag himself out of the bed. So he lay there and did nothing until he fell asleep again.

When Bran awoke again, he had gotten so much sleep that it hurt him to remain in bed, so he pulled himself up and struggled uneasily to his feet. Nim, who had restlessly moved from the dresser to the chair beside his bed, immediately leapt in front of him.

"There you are," Bran said to her. Nim seemed relieved that he was finally up and ready to move about. Bran saw the key was still sitting on the table beside his bed, where he had left it, so he absently picked it up.

He ran his fingers along the markings on the shaft, not really concentrating on what he was doing. His fingers kept going over the same shapes.

He held the key closer to his eyes, for the grooves were very small and hard to see. They didn't follow any real pattern, it seemed, because there was no start or end to the shapes, and they didn't make any form but seemed to spread in circles and straight, maze-like lines, until they met up at one thin, flat bit that ran all along the bottom.

He thought it would be interesting to show to Gary, as he was the obvious expert on keys, and perhaps there was a way of matching the design to where the door might be.

Bran and Nim left and wandered down the halls, looking for any sign of where Gary might be. Bran was still very curious after all that Gary had told him about working with his mother. There were so many questions in his head that he wanted to ask—questions that had plagued him for years. But even as important as they were to Bran, he could hardly think of them for more than a few minutes before his mind returned to Astara and his driving urge to find her.

He had made his way down the hall and found an open door, beyond which was a room with a low ceiling and a long desk in the center holding two lamps and some open books. It was a library, with three rows of shelves in the center of the floor, like miniature walls about an inch taller than Bran. "Hello?" Bran said, stepping in with Nim keeping close to him. There came no response. So he crossed the room to the desk, glancing from side to side as he passed the shelves.

There was something on the table that caught his attention. It was no longer than the length of his thumb, bright red and cone shaped; attached to its side was a small length of chain connecting to a ring on the other end. Bran picked it up and realized that it was a key ring.

"Well, that's random," Bran said, amused. Nim passed his

shoulder and landed on the desk, and Bran saw that she had found something else. It was an old, bent map, folded at the edges. It was opened to Elsie Island and West and East Dinsmore, with the blue water separating them and other small islands littering the area around. Elsie Island, curiously enough, was marked with a red triangle, and as Bran looked closer, the red marking was actually glowing slightly, though hardly perceivable under the lamplight.

"Good morning." Bran heard Gary's cheerful voice behind him suddenly, and he spun, which he regretted because it made him appear guilty. Gary was standing just over Bran's shoulder with a smile.

"I was looking for you," Bran said quickly. "The door was open."

"No worries," Gary said. His eyes shifted to the key ring in Bran's grasp. Bran quickly set it onto the table, though Gary picked it right back up.

"I'm glad you found this," Gary said, tossing the gnome-hat key ring into the air and catching it again.

"It's one of my own inventions," he said, eager to show it off. "I don't usually get to show this stuff off to anyone. You see, it is connected with the map here. Wherever this key ring is," he touched the red triangle on the map, "this symbol points to it."

"What do you use it for if you never leave?" Bran asked. Gary seemed puzzled by this.

"You have a good point," he replied. He looked at the key ring and then tossed it to Bran.

"You should keep it," he said. "I obviously have little use for it. It'll be a souvenir from your visit here."

Bran turned the simple device over in his hands. He didn't

have much use for it either but didn't want to turn down Gary's gift. Finding he didn't have anywhere to place it, and not wanting to put it in his pocket for fear of stabbing himself in the leg, he settled with attaching it to the zipper of his jacket. "You've got the key again, I see," Gary noted as he went to the other side of the desk and started closing the books and placing them back on the shelf.

"I noticed something that I wanted you to take a look at," Bran said. "It could be nothing, but it seemed a bit odd."

Gary leaned over the desk and took the key. When Bran had pointed him toward the markings, Gary drew a magnifying glass from a drawer, looking closer at them.

"See?" Bran said. "It doesn't follow any real pattern, like decoration usually might. I don't know if you can tell who made it or maybe what country it might be from because of that. Maybe like a marking certain keysmiths might use?"

It sound rather far-fetched, but Bran wasn't about to leave any chance behind. Gary turned the key over and actually seemed to be curious about what Bran had found.

"That's strange," Gary said after a few moments. But he wasn't looking at the design Bran had pointed to; his attention was on the oddly shaped handle. He turned the key around again, and then his eyes lit up.

"Look at what I found," he said, squeezing the handle. Inside the grip, Gary's fingers pressed two tiny buttons that Bran had not seen before, as they blended into the key's design. Gary grasped the key at both ends and began to twist it. Bran jumped, fearing that he was going to break it between his fists, but suddenly there was a click.

The bit and the handle, which had been lined up perfectly, were suddenly uneven, and Bran thought the metal had been bent. But Gary continued to turn the key slowly, and Bran saw that the key itself was actually made of two twisting pieces, and as they turned, the bit folded inward mechanically, tiny hidden gears creaking until the metal disappeared entirely, leaving behind nothing but the handle and a straight, metal rod covered in the markings.

"What is that?" Bran asked with a gasp, reaching forward instinctively to take it.

"Wait a moment, Bran," Gary stopped him in a hushed tone, and he dug about in the desk drawer again, finally pulling out a thin black box no larger than his palm. He opened it, and Bran saw that it was an ink pad. Before Bran could react, Gary had pressed the shaft of the key against the ink.

"What are you doing?" Bran protested, but Gary pressed the straight end of the key upon a piece of paper. He began to roll it, gently pushing down as he turned the key, and the ink left behind a stamp of sorts. Gary returned the key to Bran without taking his eyes from the paper and drew the magnifying glass over it. To Bran's surprise, he saw that the markings formed a map.

It was so plain in front of them that Bran wondered why he hadn't noticed it before. The markings were so small that he wouldn't have been able to see them if not for the magnifying glass. As Gary focused it more, Bran perceived a tiny series of arrows pointing a way through a complicated maze, with symbols all around the edges in a language he had never seen before. Gary moved the glass to the end, and Bran saw that the directional arrow was incomplete.

"There's a missing part," Bran said, touching the blank end of the paper.

"Of course, he would have taken it," Gary said under his breath.

"Who?" Bran asked. "You know who has the other piece?"

The magnifying glass flew across the room, and Bran jumped back as he heard it crash and shatter.

"Yes, I know who has it!" Gary spat his reply. His eyes were filled with rage.

"But it's not worth it," Gary said. "Look at what's happened! Haven't you seen where all this has gotten you?"

Bran put his hands up to calm Gary but was cut off.

"Your friend is dead," Gary went on. "Emry is dead. Do you want more people to die while you try to make things right?"

"I'm just trying to help her!" Bran burst, anger welling up within him. Gary drew back at this and started out the door.

Bran heard Gary's angry footsteps getting further away and, seized with anger, started after him. Nim struggled to keep up, and Bran followed Gary, calling after him. When he got to his office, Gary slammed the door in Bran's face.

He balled his fingers into fists and almost left, but then he grabbed the door handle, only to find that Gary had locked it. "*Onpe likoca!*" he commanded, and he threw the door open.

"Gary!" Bran hissed, but he stopped. Gary was not in the room. Everything was still and untouched, as if Gary had gone through the door and disappeared entirely, yet again.

"Gary?" Bran demanded again, though his voice held little power. He and Nim were by themselves again, except for Escrow sitting in his cage. Even the bird, however, only rocked back and forth wordlessly. Bran closed the door, the room still lit by the light in the fireplace. He crossed the room slowly to Gary's desk and peered over in case the man had stupidly hidden there.

"How does he just disappear like that?" Bran said angrily, striking the desk with his fist. Escrow croaked irritably at the noise.

"Lies, lies," the bird murmured. "Salty, salty."

"Shut up," Bran said to it. "You know where he's gone, but of course you won't tell me, because you're a stuck-up bird."

Escrow turned his back on Bran.

"Gary!" Bran yelled, filled with frustration. Bran seized the glass of water on Gary's desk and threw it with all his might into the fireplace, screaming Gary's name once more so loudly his voice pained him, and Nim dove out of sight.

However, Bran's outburst brought him back to his senses. Bran was scared at just how angry he had become. But beyond that, another sound captured his attention—he heard the water glass clatter into the distance.

He turned to the fireplace and stared at the flames. His curiosity drew him forward slowly until he was standing on the rug in front of the grand fire, and he peered deeply into the flames. It might have been his imagination, but for a second, as the flames wavered among one another, he thought that he could see a deep darkness behind them that went somewhere else.

It was hardly something he considered before, but seeing it sent a start through him. He looked all across the mantle for some way of turning off the fire. There was a hidden hole on the right side where a key might have fit. He was in such a rush that he wasn't even thinking straight, so he opened his palm toward the fire and shouted, "*Wirate!*"

A blast of water spewed from his hand like the bursting of a fire hydrant. It drenched the fireplace until Bran closed his hand so the water ceased its gushing. For a second, nothing remained but blackened coals—but the fire burst up again, roaring even more powerfully than before and with such heat that Bran was forced to step away.

"Of course you're hiding something back there," Bran hissed, and he rapidly searched the room with his eyes for anything that might help him. He looked down at the rug, and an idea came to him—one he might not have even considered if he had been in a sane state.

But he was desperate. In a second he had lifted the rug, and Nim dove at him as if she might stop him, but he only grabbed her and pushed her into his pocket. He took one deep breath of air and started to run directly at the fireplace. The fire roared as if in welcome, the heat burning his face, until Bran was at the mantle. Lifting the rug in front of his body, he threw it into the flames.

Bran burst forward with a shout, and he tumbled and tripped over the rug. The flames consumed it in a second so that his knees brushed the white-hot coals, and he felt every inch of him beginning to burn. He pushed himself ahead, his lungs filling up with smoke. And though his mind screamed at him that he would slam against the back of the fireplace and be trapped, he tumbled ahead, until his face felt cool air once more.

Chapter 26

The Room beyond the Fire

Bran's chest struck hard against the floor beyond, and he rolled once, wincing as his head slammed against something wooden. He looked up quickly and saw that he had fallen straight through the fireplace and found himself to be in another room.

The fireplace was double-sided, and flames lit this side as well in a flashing, crackling light that sent shadows up the walls as it consumed the tattered remains of the rug. Bran sat up, blinking as he looked around. There was furniture, mostly couches, strewn about messily, everything in disarray from old lamps falling against the walls to bird cages and tables on their sides. It looked like a storage room, but as Bran turned his head to soak it all in, he saw a distinctive feature. The winding walls that circled high above his head were covered with picture frames. In the frames were photographs of a familiar person: his mother.

No matter which way he turned his head, Bran was greeted with the face of his mother. Pictures of her smiling, laughing, sitting down, and standing; one of her in front of a building and another of her in a red jacket. He stood and turned in a circle; there were more images of his mother than he had seen in his entire life.

Behind him, Bran heard a flute playing the last few notes of the heartrending song Bran had heard before. He turned quickly and saw Gary lying on one of the couches, his eyes closed and the flute pressed to his lips. The pieces finally fit together, and Bran recognized the melody. He had heard this song before, played in Nigel Ten on the music box that had held Nim. The music stopped.

"So, Bran," Gary said. "You have stumbled upon my room of misery." And his voice was filled with such desolation that Bran felt a pain go through his own heart.

"How did you get these?" Bran asked. Gary did not reply, and Bran's eyes continued up to the pictures on the opposite wall. As his eyesight adjusted, he saw another familiar face in the images: it was Gary, and he was standing beside Bran's mother in every single one.

"You didn't just know her," Bran said. "You loved her."

"That I did, Bran," Gary said. "And it was that love that led to my downfall."

He pressed the flute to his lips once more, but he only managed to draw forth two notes before he began to weep. Gary sat up slowly, burying his face in his hands.

"It's the song I wrote for her, before she left," he said, his voice intermingled with sobs. "I made it into a music box and gave it to her, so she could hear it anytime she wanted. But it wasn't enough."

Gary shook his head with grief. "I met your mother while we worked on the Project. It was good, I promise you Bran, the Project was good—or at least I was fooled into thinking we had good intentions. Perhaps Baslyn was far more influential than I realized, even after I separated myself from his group."

Gary wiped his eyes quickly. "Your mother captivated me the first day I worked with them, simply captivated me—I had never met someone like her before, with that smile and those eyes and her laugh that would bring joy on the dullest and darkest of days. We worked so closely that it was mere months before we were together. Everyone knew of it. Even Baslyn. And even...Thomas."

Gary spat Bran's father's name out with contempt. "When I found out Baslyn's true motives and told them that I was leaving, I thought that Emry would go with me. But I had gravely miscalculated Baslyn's control over them."

He sobbed again. "It was almost a cult, Bran. Baslyn had done something to Emry, he had changed her somehow. Whatever Baslyn ordered, they carried out. When I told Baslyn I was leaving, Emry didn't come with me, she left me. And she came to be with Thomas, the man who stayed behind with her and the Project."

"And they just let you go?" Bran whispered. Gary nodded.

"They couldn't kill me," he said. "They knew that much. And Baslyn knew that with Emry still there, I would never turn them in. So I simply left."

Gary's face was filled with tears again. "But I still loved that girl—your mother. I loved her more than life itself, more than anything in the world. I would have done anything to get her back. I would have paid anything, Bran—but sometimes there is nothing you can do." Gary shook his head sadly.

"You never got over her," Bran said. Gary shook his head, glancing around at the photos.

"Most people move on from ones they love and lose," Gary said. "But I haven't. I have gone forward in solitude. I feel as if

Emry died without ever giving my heart back. And these photos are all I have left of her, Bran."

Gary sniffed, his expression turning bitter. "And Thomas—with me gone, your mother clung to him. I began to wonder if I had made a mistake by leaving them, if I had lost the one thing I truly cared about. I had to watch them, your father and the woman I loved together, because I had refused to take part in their Project."

Gary sighed. "Perhaps I am simply an addict to pain, Bran. Because every second I saw her happy with your father, I wanted to tear my own heart out just to make it stop; at the same time, I could not stop watching them, just to make sure she was all right. And even now, after she's been dead for all these years, I cannot stop watching her. She haunts my dreams—dreams of us together, of how things could have been; dreams that turn to nightmares when I awaken. And seeing her necklace..."

Gary gestured toward Bran. "You wear it now, don't you? She gave it to you before she died?"

Bran hesitated, but then he drew it out from under his shirt, so that the silver of it glimmered in the light. Gary looked at it, but then turned his head away.

"That necklace was my gift to her," he said. "It was...very special to me, something that had been mine for a long time. I thought for sure she would give it back, but she never did."

"Maybe she kept it as a memory of you, Gary," Bran whispered.

"I can't hope for that much," Gary said quickly. "She hardly loved me when she died. Why would she want to keep it as a memory?"

"Perhaps she realized she had made a mistake," Bran said, his voice lowering even further. Gary said nothing but only sat staring at the wall. He seemed deep in thought, and the tears continued down his face, drying on his cheeks.

"Perhaps that is why she wore it close to her heart," Bran said. "Maybe she realized that if she had stayed with you, then none of this would have happened; she never would have created the Curse and wouldn't have lost everything she loved."

Gary bent forward, hiding his face in his hands. "You might have been my son, Bran," Gary said. "I might have been your father if she had chosen differently—if fate had only led me and her together."

Bran could say nothing. Would things have been better had it happened that way? Would his mother still be alive, and would she and Gary and Bran be living somewhere together, happy? The thought tortured Bran, so that he felt lost, as if that crossing of paths, and her decision, had changed everything from what might have been into what it was now.

"Perhaps that was not our fate," Bran said. It was all he could say. Gary did not move.

"What is fate?" Gary asked. "How can one believe in fate when it has betrayed me so much?"

"Because it means that it has all happened for a reason," Bran said.

"That is foolish."

"And it's all we have," Bran replied. "Maybe it was fate that you would lose her and all these terrible things would happen. Maybe it was fate that Astara would be gone and I would come here and meet you. Maybe this is simply one tiny piece in a grand fate that all of us are set to fulfill—and even though my mother's choice changed everything, I'm still here, and maybe I can make it right again."

Gary mulled over this, saying nothing for a long time.

"You don't think I wish our fates had been different?" Bran whispered. "I've only been here for a few days. And you, Gary, are far closer to a father than my real one ever was."

No other words in the entire world might have warmed Gary more. He closed his eyes.

"I've been such a horrible person, Bran," Gary said, wiping his eyes. "All of this has been a lie. I knew from the moment I saw the Key where you were headed. I just couldn't bear to watch you go after your friend, when she might very well be dead and you might go on searching for ways to save her all your life and become just as heartbroken as me."

"I'd do anything to get back the people I love," Bran said. "It would hurt me far more to leave my friend to die and know there was a chance I might have done something."

"I loved your mother the same," Gary said. "More than anyone ever did or ever will." He wiped his eyes. "I know what love is. I have felt it. I have suffered from it. And you damn well better go after your friend before the same curse that took your mother from me also takes Astara from you."

His words held bitterness and pain but also the strongest resolve. Gary then held both of his hands out and took Bran's hurt wrist between his own, drawing him closer. He had something in a bottle next to the couch, and he unwrapped the gauze around Bran's injury, pouring the liquid over it. Bran jumped because it stung at first, but a second later his whole arm felt different, and he realized that whatever Gary had poured on him had healed it.

"You had that all along?" Bran said with shock, turning his hand in circles.

"I thought I might convince you to stay," Gary said. "But I see now that you will not be deterred in freeing those bound by the Specter Key's power."

"You know of the Specters?" Bran said.

"Yes," Gary nodded. "You know much of your mother's crimes. Think to her greatest: the stealing of those innocents in the desert, those souls she used for the Curse. That Key binds the lock that holds their spirits imprisoned, and he who holds it holds the power of their souls."

"Can't we destroy it?" Bran asked.

"It's protected by magic," Gary replied.

"Then why can't I simply set them free?"

"There is only one place for that to be done," Gary said. "The door to their prison. I do not know how to get there, but the map from the Key will guide you through."

"I don't have all the pieces," Bran pointed out.

"You will have two now, though." Gary picked up his flute again and unscrewed the mouthpiece. What was left was a metal rod with intricate markings, and Bran knew what it was: for the other piece of the map.

"This map," Gary said, after putting ink on the flute and imprinting it onto paper, "is many centuries old and separated into four pieces so that only those deemed worthy might enter the ground. It was not done this way by anyone who was part of the Project but by those who built the place to which it leads."

He slid the paper into Bran's fingers in a slow but deliberate motion. "A piece was hidden on the Key, another on the flute. I don't know where the others ended up after the police discovered Baslyn's plan, but I assume they are with those few who escaped. You must find your father, and he will take you and the Key to its door."

Bran looked down at the piece of the map in his hands and then back up at Gary.

"Come with me," Bran said, but Gary only shook his head.

"I have not left this island since before your mother's death," he said. "I don't have the strength to leave it now."

"Just come with me," Bran said fervently. "You'll be better once you are over her."

"Not yet," Gary said. "But the day will come."

Bran took a deep breath. It pained him to see Gary's eyes fill with tears again.

"You should be off," Gary said.

"Thank you," Bran replied. Gary only nodded. And Bran left him behind with the photos of Emry and set off to save Astara.

Part III

CHAPTER 27

A DEAL AT THE ROADSIDE

OSWALD WAS WAITING FOR Bran when he stepped through the gates.

"I got Gary's signal," he said. The trip to the mainland was quiet, with only the rumblings of the car and the sounds of the water rushing by outside. When the cab finally came to the surface and drove up an abandoned side of the mainland, Bran asked Oswald to leave him at the nearest pay phone.

They spotted one just a minute away, planted outside an old grocery store, and Bran bid Oswald farewell. He walked briskly to the phone, put his money in, and dialed the number for home.

It rang many times before he finally heard the other line pick up.

"Who's this?" came the irritated voice of Sewey, by way of greeting.

"Hello Sewey, it's Bran," he replied. "I'm going to the Jenkins Plaza Mall. I'll be in the food court."

"What the rot?" Sewey spluttered. "What are you even talking about?"

"The Jenkins Plaza Mall," Bran said again. "Probably in about an hour. I'll be sitting somewhere obvious, in the food court."

"Are you drunk, young man?" Sewey said with horror. "There isn't a Jenkins Plaza Mall anywhere in Dunce. What is all this absurdity?"

"The Jenkins Plaza Mall," Bran said a third time, speaking very clearly. "That's where I'm going. Good day, Sewey."

"The *rot?*" Sewey nearly screamed with confusion, but Bran hung the phone up before he could say anything else.

He managed to catch a bus and cross a few miles into downtown East Dinsmore, using up nearly all of the little cash he had left on him. He got off at the intersection he had written down before leaving Gary's house. From the corner he could see a sprawling parking lot covered with cars, and beyond that a great collection of buildings and shops. There was a sign at the entrance that read JENKINS PLAZA MALL.

He went under the concrete overpass that supported the highway crossing and walked across the lot to the entrance. People were strolling in and out of the mall in small crowds. It felt so odd being outside after being secluded in Gary's house, and seeing other humans actually felt strange too. Bran tried to act natural—he only wanted to attract the attention of one person in particular. Nim stayed hidden as he passed through the doors.

Two escalators and a towering map of the mall later, Bran found a seat in the food court, which was packed with children and their parents who were desperately trying to bribe them with food so they could shop in peace. Bran had gotten two sandwiches, resting one in front of the single, empty chair across from him. Both sat untouched as he stared off into the distance, waiting and watching.

"You're far smarter than you appear, Bran," came a familiar voice not ten minutes later. Nim, who had been on Bran's shoulder, was taken by surprise and fell, clinging to his shirt.

"I've had practice," Bran replied, not turning as Thomas passed him and slid into the seat across.

"Perhaps it's hereditary?" Thomas replied with his half-smile.

"Don't think so highly of yourself," Bran said coldly. "I figured if you were smart enough you'd have my home phone lines tapped, and you'd be somewhere nearby." Thomas's eyes moved from Bran to Nim, and she clung tighter to Bran, afraid that he was going to take her. But he merely glanced at her and returned his gaze to Bran. Thomas was wearing a dirty jacket and jeans, blending in well; his eyes scanned the crowd of people around them, silently studying each of their faces, but he masked any unease he might have meeting Bran there.

"I'm still curious as to why you would choose to bring me straight to you," Thomas said. "I mean, it is altogether dangerous, considering how little trust you have of me."

"I don't have any other choice," Bran said. "I want to make a deal with you."

Thomas turned so that he could meet Bran's eyes. "A deal, with me?"

"Yes," Bran said. "I know you want the Specter Key. I don't know what for, and I don't really care. But I'm willing to give it to you if you help me."

Thomas seemed only slightly shocked at Bran's words, but even that little bit was enough to confirm in Bran's mind that he had taken him by surprise.

"Just like that?" Thomas asked.

"Yes," Bran said. "Like I said, I don't have any other choice."

Bran reached into the front pocket of his luggage bag and slid both tiny pieces of the map toward Thomas.

"Ah, I see," Thomas said, and he smirked.

"Where does this point to?" Bran said. Thomas gently lifted the pieces of paper from the table and brought them closer, studying the markings even though they were still far too small to be read in that manner. He seemed to confirm whatever he was looking for, and he set it back again without comment.

"Is this for me?" Thomas gestured to the sandwich and drink. Bran nodded, and Thomas started to eat. His father seemed to be pondering something as he ate, not meeting Bran's eyes even once. He kept looking at Nim, and each time she moved to hide from his gaze, so that finally Bran moved her to his leg under the table and out of Thomas's sight.

"That map you have there," Thomas finally said, still chewing, "shows part of a labyrinth inside a temple. I've never been inside of it, but your mother was there, a long time ago."

He reached for his drink, but it was only a cover for him to study Bran's face for a reaction. Bran did not give him the satisfaction.

"There's a place in that temple," Thomas went on, "where that Key you've got fits. We found out about it while studying the Fearum scrolls. There's deep, ancient magic there, one of few places where such a power exists in this world. Your mother turned it into a prison for the souls."

He drew a slow drink through the straw. "The door has been secret for thousands of years: hence, the labyrinth and its traps and dead ends. You've got part of the map there. Each piece was kept in a different place."

"And who's got the rest?" Bran asked. Thomas swallowed his food.

"I've got it," he said simply. "One of the pieces, at least. The last is with Elspeth."

Bran could not keep himself from sinking back into his chair bleakly.

"Don't do that now," Thomas said. "You were doing well acting confident."

"I don't know how I could go through a labyrinth this big with only part of a map," Bran hissed, trying not to draw attention to them.

"You wouldn't stand a chance," Thomas replied.

"Then we'll need the other piece," Bran said.

"That's the only thing that really makes sense, isn't it?" Thomas said, and he seemed so at ease with the situation that Bran was irritated.

"Calm down," Thomas said, and his voice was low but held warning. "You don't want to bring attention to us."

"If we don't have the rest of the map, then there's no point in me making a deal with you," Bran said under his breath. "And you know very well you can't pry the Key from me."

"I have no intention to," Thomas replied. "If we need the other half of the map, then we're going to have to get it."

"Well, then," Bran said, crossing his arms. "I'd very much like to hear your plan."

Thomas looked up at him with an amused expression. "I think it's about time I give Elspeth a call."

Thomas chose to meet with Elspeth in the daylight, down a

long, empty highway that cut through the grassy land outside the city. When Bran saw a black van rumbling down the road, he stiffened as he felt her presence getting nearer.

"You're sure this is safe?" Bran asked. Thomas was leaning against the back of the car and had donned a hat. He didn't reply, as if that was enough to assure Bran, but turned and opened the trunk. From it he pulled the same music box that Bran had found in Nigel Ten.

Before Bran could react, Thomas began to turn the wheel, and Nim immediately dashed toward it. The familiar song was hurtful for Bran to hear now that he knew who had written it. Nim's eyes glowed green, and she looked to Thomas with a wild expression on her face.

"What are you doing?" Bran hissed, stalking forward.

"Wait, Bran," Thomas said, holding up his hand. "Trust me on this one."

"You can't just take her like that!" Bran said through clenched teeth, even as he heard the van door pop open.

"Does she belong to you or to me?" Thomas asked. "Do you want to have this argument right here, or do you want to look to Elspeth like we're a team?"

Bran's anger simmered. "I'm not on a team with you," Bran said.

"Then we're simply enemies forced to work together," Thomas said. "Whatever you want to call it, neither of us has a choice. And I know a bit of what I'm doing here."

Bran clenched his teeth together and stood silently, glancing at Nim.

Elspeth wore a dark, new jacket that was clean and zipped up the front, and her jet black hair was loose—a single white streak played in the wind. Her eyes were so blue that Bran could see their color even in the dusk sunlight. She was stunning, but Bran felt nothing but deep loathing for this was the woman who had killed his mother.

To Bran's greatest surprise, when Elspeth appeared, Thomas's fingers rolled up into fists before he relaxed them and returned to a calm pose. Nim rested on Thomas's shoulder, and Bran sneaked a glance at her, but she did not even recognize him.

"You presented me with an offer I could not refuse," Elspeth said, giving Bran a glance and then turning her attention Thomas.

"As are all my offers," Thomas replied, with equal lack of feeling.

"Then why waste time speaking more of it?" she said. "You know I want the Specter Key, and you know the only way I might obtain it."

"And you have something that we want," Thomas said.

"I do have it," Elspeth said. "An exchange, then? Mine for yours? Willingly."

She looked to Bran, and Bran nodded slowly, saying nothing as Thomas had instructed him.

"Still, I think it's only fair to ask for a bit of proof on your end," Thomas said. Elspeth reached into the hidden pocket of her jacket, drawing forth a single, tiny slip of withered paper. It was just as small as Bran's pieces were, though older and bent at the ends. She held it up flat between her fingers, and Nim flew from Thomas's shoulder, drawing closer so that she could examine it. Satisfied by whatever was there, she darted back to Thomas without a sound, and Elspeth hid the paper once more.

"Happy?" Elspeth said.

"Very," Thomas replied with a smile.

"I shall follow you to the location," Elspeth said. "When we arrive, the three of us will go down into the temple together, and I will provide my part when it is needed in the labyrinth. After we reach the end, and you know my piece bears no counterfeit, you will willingly hand over the Key."

"Agreed," Thomas said. And they were done. Elspeth said nothing more, turning and going back toward the van.

"That wasn't right," Bran whispered to Thomas as they started to walk. "I only agreed if Astara is freed first, then she would have the Key."

"Just get in the car," Thomas commanded under his breath. Bran obeyed, closing his door as Thomas smoothly started the engine. He checked the mirror to see if Elspeth was following and saw her still walking to her van. Thomas, however, did not wait, and began to roll forward.

"Hold the wheel for a moment, will you Bran?" he asked, so Bran reached across and held it straight.

"What are you doing?" Bran asked as Thomas reached around for something on the floor of the back. Bran managed to glance there and saw Thomas throw a blanket aside. Hidden underneath was the biggest gun Bran had ever seen. Before he could react, Thomas spun it over Bran's head and aimed it out the driver's side window.

Something launched from the end of the giant gun, speeding like a football toward the black van behind them, and Thomas slammed on the gas, with Bran being unable to do anything but hold the wheel straight as best he could as a rattling explosion shook the road beneath them.

Chapter 28

The Eyes of Nim

Thomas tossed the gun into the back seat and grabbed the wheel from Bran's grasp, swerving the car and speeding off.

"What in the world are you doing?" Bran demanded, his voice masked by the sound of the explosion still roaring around them.

"Be quiet for one minute, Bran—I can't see if she was hit or not," Thomas hissed, turning quickly to get a better look.

"See if she was hit?" Bran shouted. "She's got the other piece of the map!"

"Forget that for now," Thomas said, spinning to face the road again. "Looks like she's sent some trouble after us."

Bran spun to look out the back window, and he saw Elspeth's gruner launch out of the smoke and raining gravel of the van's wreckage. The creature had a hideous, slobbering look of rage, and it shot after them at a startling speed, its long claws scraping against the road.

"Speed up!" Bran shouted, and Thomas gunned the engine, which spluttered as it strained to speeds it was hardly meant to handle. Even then the gruner still sped after them, the hairs on its back bristling and its teeth bared in a roar.

"Hold the wheel again, Bran?" Thomas said.

"No!"

"Just hold it still," Thomas said and let go. Bran had no other choice but to grab it and right the car. Thomas reached down between the seats and produced a large handgun. He poked his head out the window again, taking shots at the gruner. He missed the first few because the car was swerving, but then the bullets began to strike the creature. It tripped and slid but was back on its feet in less than a second, even more incited and faster than before.

"Cars are coming!" Bran shouted, trying to hold the wheel.

"You're doing fine," Thomas said. "Just ease us a little more into our lane. They'll get out of the way."

"That's a bit difficult from this position!" Bran said. Thomas didn't seem to care. There was a collection of large freight trucks headed their way, and even though Bran was trying his hardest, from the passenger seat it was nearly impossible to even stay in the boundaries of the road.

The gruner, much to Bran's dismay, had actually caught up with them. Thomas had run out of bullets, so he tossed the empty gun into the back seat and reached across to Bran's side, pulling another gun from between his seat and the middle compartment.

"How many guns have you got in this car?" Bran demanded.

"Not nearly enough," Thomas replied, shooting three more times at the beast. It seemed entirely unperturbed, as if the bullets merely bounced off its hide. It leapt forward in the air, slamming against the car with its body like a wrecking ball, and the wheel jerked in Bran's grasp.

"He just dented the car!" Thomas roared.

The car sped onto a bridge, the gruner still right beside them. It slammed into the side again with a possessed roar, throwing the car against the railing and causing sparks to fly as metal brushed metal. Thomas tossed his useless gun and reached under his seat. He produced yet another gun, this one twice the size. The recoil of this one threw Thomas back against the wheel when he shot it, and Bran lost his hold. The car flew in and out of their lane dangerously. A truck had to swerve to avoid them as they rocketed over the bridge.

"Missed him again," Thomas said as the beast lunged ahead and reached the window of the car. Its face was right in line with them, seething for air as it kept in pace with them. It roared and jumped at the window, but Thomas drew back just in time. It once again rammed into the car, grinding them against the guard rail.

Bran was thrown about in his seat. He saw the beast leap forward, snapping at the window and nearly reaching Thomas's neck. Bran had had enough. Thomas was obviously getting nowhere, so with his free hand he reached behind the seat, pulling his mother's wand free from the front pocket of his luggage. He blasted magic out of its tip toward the gruner. The powers hit the creature, and it was thrown from the car and into the other lane, where it was struck head-on by a passing freight truck.

Thomas grabbed the wheel and slammed on the brakes. One final truck passed on the other side of the road, narrowly missing them and then swerving to miss the body of the gruner, which sat like a black, hairy mound in the middle of the bridge.

"What do you think you're doing, Bran?" Thomas roared. He slammed his fist into the wand so hard that it fell from Bran's grasp. Thomas then spun the car around in a U-turn, sliding into the other lane and rumbling to a stop in the middle of the road.

He leapt out, tearing the hat off his head and coming up to the creature. Bran jumped out the other side, the engine still running.

"That was magic!" Thomas shouted, stopping in the road and looking wildly at Bran. "You're never to use magic in this car!"

"But look, he's dead!" Bran shouted, gesturing to the creature. "He almost had us."

"No!" Thomas burst, and his eyes were filled with such rage that Bran drew back, ready to defend himself.

"Never use magic to kill, do you understand?" Thomas said. He spun again, as if he didn't even want to look at Bran's face any longer. He still held the gun in his hand, and he waved it at the gruner, blasting one shot at its body, and then a second and a third.

"Look, it's already dead!" Bran protested.

"It's not the first time that one's been dead, Bran," he said, but he stopped and turned to the car and wiped his brow with the sleeve of his shirt, putting the hat back on.

"Would you mind telling me what you're thinking?" Bran demanded, but his father just walked to the car, reaching inside and grabbing a bottle of water. He downed a gulp.

"I don't guess we're in a worse position now though," Thomas said, ignoring Bran. "Elsepth'll be heading this way soon enough, once she gets a hold of Joris." Thomas smiled. "And once he's on board, the real killing can begin."

"But now that you've completely broken our deal with them not ten minutes after making it," Bran burst, "how do you think we're going to get that piece of the map?"

He was beside himself with anger, and Thomas flashed a grin that made Bran even more irate. Nim appeared from the car at just that moment, unshaken by the ordeal in her present robotic state. Thomas nodded in her direction, and she flew to his side, and he said nothing as he went around to the back of the car and opened the trunk.

"You're not going to answer me, are you?" Bran asked. "You know if I don't get into the temple, you're not getting the Key."

"Oh really? I'd forgotten," Thomas replied in a snarl. "Perhaps remind me of it once or twice or fifty times more. Maybe I'll start to understand then."

He drew the music box out of the trunk and started to turn the wheel. Nim leapt toward it, and Thomas opened the lid so that she could go inside. He slammed it shut and then placed it at the bottom of the trunk and reached for his computer bag, drawing a laptop out and starting it up. Bran watched silently as Thomas pulled out a thin wire and wrapped its exposed end around the metal handle of the music box.

"Watch closely," Thomas said, and he pressed a few buttons on his computer. A program popped up, and Thomas punched a string of keys into it, bringing another window in front of the others. He clicked once, and it began to play a video. It was the very spot they had met Elspeth not fifteen minutes before.

"How did...?" he began, but whatever it was stopped as the window wavered a bit, and Thomas pressed another key. It began to fast forward through Elspeth getting out of her car and then speaking in a garbled noise.

"This was all filmed from Nim's eyes!" Bran burst with realization. Thomas nodded. Nim's eyes had recorded everything he had done since getting her, allowing Thomas to following his every move.

"Isn't that magic?" Bran managed to gasp out, because he could hardly say anything more coherent.

"Not in the slightest," Thomas said. "It is entirely mechanical. The box reads the sensors connected to Nim's eyes and brain, and these wires transfer those signals to my computer. No magic needed at all."

"I might have been able to Comsar with her faster," Bran returned.

"But your magic would have fallen short," Thomas replied. "Even Comsar powers could not match with the ability of my sensors to do this…"

He struck a key, and the image froze. Thomas pressed two keys, and the image blew up larger until it filled the screen, and there was a precise and sharp image of Elspeth's piece of the map.

"See?" Thomas said. "I had it figured out from the beginning. But were you about to listen to me? Of course not."

He tapped a few keys, saving the image while Bran could do little but stand there. Curiously, he had a small printer in his trunk as well as many other gadgets that Bran did not recognize, and he only had to slide away a pile of handguns and bullets to uncover it.

"Think about it," Thomas said as he worked. "What sort of deal were we making there? Give Elspeth the Key when we were down in the temple? She knows just as well as I do that once we're there, and once you free the Specters, there won't be any power left. Why would she even agree to something as stupid as that?"

"She was going to double-cross us," Bran realized.

"Right," Thomas replied. "It was too stupid of a deal for her to simply agree. Elspeth is far smarter than that. She had other plans, and I wasn't about to fall into her trap."

Bran felt a bit stupid for not thinking it through as much as his father had but consoled himself with the fact that Thomas had worked with Elspeth before. Still, even as Thomas closed the computer and opened the music box to set Nim free, Bran could not help feeling dejected.

"W-why are you doing this?" Bran stammered. Thomas looked at him.

"Doing what?"

"Helping me," Bran said. "What use do you even have for the Key?"

Thomas was silent as he slid the items in the trunk and closed the lid. He glanced at Bran, as if trying to see through his question.

"Imagine this, Bran, if you can fathom it," Thomas said, wiping his hands against each other. "I loved your mother, though others might have led you to believe that I'm some sort of monster who led her astray.

"I was led to think that if both of us followed orders and did as we were told, we would one day be able to live freely while those around us did not. However, I discovered many years later that it was all a scheme by Joris, who was using us to make himself great amounts of money—ruining Emry and causing her death."

Bran was dismayed by Thomas's words. "You're one to talk about ruining my mother, as if you had no part in it."

Thomas narrowed his eyes. "So you'll listen to Gary above

your own father? You think I'm the only person who played a part in ruining your mother?"

"I believe what Gary told me," Bran said.

"I did little corrupting of your mother besides taking her when Gary left," Thomas replied, his jaw tightening. He set his fist lightly upon the car. "It was magic that led your mother wrong. It was magic and the manipulation of Joris and Elspeth and Baslyn. It was magic that led us all astray."

He waved his hand. "We're cursed with it, Bran! Can't you see the death and destruction and evil that magic has caused? How many creatures have we killed with it? If not for magic, your mother would still be alive."

Bran drew a deep breath but said nothing in defense.

"But," Thomas said, calming himself slightly when Bran did not respond, "I can hardly wage war against something as invisible and formless as magic, so I am forced to wreak my vengeance upon more physical enemies: Elspeth and Joris. I cannot rest soundly until they have suffered the same fate that your mother did. If you had any honor within you, Bran, you would seek their murder just as deeply as I do."

"Murdering them would make me no different than they are," Bran said between his teeth.

"No matter," Thomas said. "Not all of us think in the same way. I, however, cannot feel any peace until I see both of them dead. I'm haunted by images of Emry and the great deception that was drawn over both of us."

Bran, as angry as he was, could not help but detect an unexpected emotion coming from Thomas. It seemed as if he were about to weep right there, though no tears shone in his eyes.

Thomas hid it well, but even that slight change caused Bran's anger to waver.

"You weren't the only person who lost her," Bran said, his voice coming out as a hiss. "I don't remember anything about her. Gary had to watch her leave because he stood for something right. So don't think for a minute that this has been hardest on you."

Thomas looked away at that, as if Bran had hit him, and said nothing in reply. Bran stared at him with sharp and angry eyes. Thomas shrank under the weight of Bran's words.

"Well, then," Thomas finally said. "I suppose we have little choice but to go on working with each other if we want to make anything good come of this."

"And what is it you propose?" Bran asked.

"A new deal," Thomas said. "Or the first one, altered slightly. Joris and Elspeth will inevitably follow us, and they know where we're headed. I have absolutely no intention of letting either of them claim that Key—or its powers—before you have freed the Specters and rendered it useless."

"And what's my part of it?" Bran asked.

"Very little you aren't already accustomed to," Thomas said.

"Just act as bait, for Joris and Elspeth?" Bran said. Thomas nodded.

"And that's all?" Bran pressed.

"Once we're at the temple, you can go in by yourself. I will wait outside and kill both of them when they arrive."

"And what if they overpower you?" Bran said. "One's a mage, and the other has gotten away from you before, I imagine. I don't think either of them will go down easily."

"Don't worry about that," Thomas said. "I can take care of them both."

"Then it's a deal," Bran said. "You bring me there, and I'll act as bait, and we never have to see each other again."

Thomas tilted his head to the side at Bran's last words, but he covered it with a nod toward the car.

"We've got a bit of driving ahead of us," he said. "We should be off."

Chapter 29

An Angel in the Desert

Thomas drove for two days, only stopping for a few hours of rest each night, pulling off the road and laying the seats back. He and Bran rarely spoke until the last evening.

"A few more miles, I would guess," Thomas said. The road had taken them far out of the city, into a desert-like place with rocks and cactus and great hills of sand that blocked most of what was beyond. The sun had started to set, so that Thomas had to turn on the headlights as they drove. Where the hills sloped down, Bran could see the faint glow of a city far off to the west.

"Dansby," Thomas said, when he saw Bran looking. "We're actually closer to Dunce than we were in East Dinsmore, in a roundabout way."

"Maybe I should stop by home," Bran said. "Grab some snacks."

"Or more bullets," Thomas suggested.

"You need more?" Bran asked.

"A man can never have too many bullets," Thomas declared. "Nor can he have too many firearms on his person at one time."

"You plan on starting a war?" Bran asked, raising an eyebrow.

"No," Thomas said. "But I'll be able to finish one, if need be."

"You think there'll be a war sometime soon?"

"There will be a war," Thomas replied after a deep breath, all sarcasm gone.

"And you know this for a fact?" Bran asked.

"Assuredly," Thomas nodded. "It will be a war unlike any this world has seen. All of nature seems to be preparing for it. And those like you, who rely on magic, will wish they had been as those like me, who rely on things not."

Bran did not know whether to take that as an insult or a warning, or just Thomas being less than serious, as he commonly seemed to be.

"And here we are," Thomas said, removing any chance Bran had of pressing him further. Bran looked out the window and saw that they had come to a dip in the road with rocky sides. The road cut straight through, but Thomas stopped before the stones and pulled off the road.

"A few miles off that way is where it'll be," he said.

"We're going to walk?" Bran asked.

"I'd prefer to call it hiking," Thomas replied. So Bran climbed out of the car with his backpack, and Thomas walked around to open the trunk. He first took out a backpack of his own and then heaved a large wooden crate out, setting it gently onto the ground. There were two long ropes attached in a loop to the sides of the box and small ski-like protrusions at the bottom so that it would slide easily. Thomas put his pack on, wrapped the ropes over his shoulder, and started to drag the crate behind him.

"This way," he said as he slammed the trunk. And so Bran and his father started off into the sands, toward the light of the setting sun.

The day had worn on; the air around them cooler than Bran expected. He didn't think that this place could actually be considered a desert, more a very rocky and sandy place, which is very close to the definition of a desert anyway. Bran debated with himself on whether it was a desert or not until he felt silly. The sand and the rocks got old and boring very quickly, especially when both got into his shoes.

They trudged ahead with Thomas leading the way. Bran was thankful that his backpack held so few things, because Thomas's seemed to be rather full, though the man showed no sign of complaint. The crate slid lightly over the sand like a sled.

"What's in the crate?" Bran asked.

"My sins," replied the man amusedly, as the weight of it dragged behind him.

"Is that why it's so heavy?" Bran asked. Thomas regarded Bran with a raised eyebrow.

"Unbearably so." He heaved it forward. They stepped over rocks and came to high pillars of dark gray stone, made rough from sandstorms and wind. Thomas navigated around them, leading them straight on toward the sun, which was now only a tiny line on the horizon. Nim flittered back and forth until her curiosity about every lizard and fly was satisfied.

"Will you know the way when the sun goes down?" Bran said.

"No, we'll be hopelessly lost," Thomas replied. "And perhaps eaten by desert ronchins."

"But I hear they prefer to eat adults over teenagers," Bran said, having no clue what a desert ronchin was, but his father's sarcasm was beginning to annoy him.

"Actually, they eat sand," Thomas said, pulling the crate

forward. "Suck it up through their snout like water through a straw. Such a curiosity."

"Are you just making this up as you go along?" Bran said skeptically.

"Why would I make up a thing like that?" Thomas said, faking hurt.

"I don't know," Bran said, trudging along. "I can't ever tell when you're lying or telling the truth."

"Oh, my poor aching heart," Thomas said, putting his fist to his chest as if he were holding a knife. "You always think the worst of me."

"Give me a reason to think otherwise," Bran said.

"You're here, aren't you?" Thomas said plainly. "I could have shot and killed you a thousand times already in that car. Or I could have mixed in some uldiah leaf with your food and watched you burn up from the inside until you went mad."

"Would you actually do that?" Bran asked.

"Would you do it to me?" Thomas replied.

"You thought about poisoning your own son?"

"Twice," Thomas replied bluntly.

"Why in the world would any sane human even think to do that?" Bran said, astonished.

"Consider that ending your life might be showing you a bit of mercy from the things to come. You also have an uncanny ability to stay alive in places no one else would last for minutes, despite you being rather naïve."

"If by naïve you mean 'never once considering shooting and poisoning your father,'" Bran said, "then by all counts I am guilty. Though I'm slowly reconsidering."

"I shall get you a sin crate, then," Thomas said. "You can start filling it."

They said no more to each other. They had come to a hill where the ground became very rocky, and the crate kept getting caught on stones. They pushed on over the bumpy way until they could see down into the vast valley below. It was dotted by cactus that threw long shadows from the tiny prick of sun that still remained. There was a large cleared area straight below them—and in the middle of the sand rested statue.

Bran's eyes almost passed over it entirely, because it blended in with the rocks. It was an angel, its outspread wings carved with incredible detail, its eyes cast up toward the sky. The statue's arms stretched high above its head, its hands clenching a long sword, as if in victory over an enemy. Thomas did not stop his pace, and as they approached, Bran saw that the worn statue was nearly double his height and that the base of it was buried in a solid stone foundation.

"And there it is," Thomas said, wiping his brow and gesturing ahead. "They called him Iro."

"Who called him that?" Bran asked.

"The Ancients," Thomas replied. "He'd come alive and talk to them."

Bran looked at Thomas.

"All right, I made that part up," Thomas relented. "I'm not sure what he is, besides being called Iro."

Bran waved toward it. "Well, we have a statue. Where's the temple?"

"That's it," Thomas replied.

"That small?" Bran said. "Were the Ancients related to ants?"

Thomas shook his head and moved for the wooden crate.

He fished around in his backpack and dug out a long crowbar, placing its flat edge between the lid and the box and heaving against it.

"Letting them out to air?" Bran said.

"Sins do get a bit musty after a while," Thomas replied. The lid cracked off and fell into the sand, exposing the box's contents: long rows of packages wrapped in black paper.

"Take two and go set them over there in the sand," Thomas said. "Not close to the statue though."

"Over here?" Bran asked, a few feet away from the statue.

"Goodness, no," Thomas said. "Way out there. No point in ruining it."

"Ruin it?" Bran said. "What is this stuff?"

"They're bombs," Thomas said. Bran nearly dropped them right out of his arms.

"Bombs?!" he exclaimed.

"Don't worry," Thomas called to him. "You're perfectly safe cradling them close to vital body parts and limbs. They're disarmed, I think."

"You think?" Bran said, and he held the devices out a bit from himself, until he had walked about twenty paces from the statue. Thomas, carrying three of the devices, trudged past, and Bran followed until they were far from it.

"Here's the spot," he said, lining the devices up in a circle and then adjusting them so that they were in line with the pointed shadow from the statue's sword. "Now move back over behind those rocks there. I've got to put the wires all together to the remote, and sometimes they go off randomly."

Bran did not need any more urging to get out of the way, and he stepped behind the rocks to watch as Thomas connected the explosives together. He then trudged toward Bran, a small remote in his hands.

"And what's the point of blowing up the sand?" Bran asked.

"It's in the way," Thomas said. "Messy stuff. We can work far easier without it."

"But isn't the temple over there?" Bran said with irritation, pointing toward the statue. Without warning, Thomas pressed the button, and a giant explosion rocked the desert, throwing Bran against the ground. Sand and dirt burst into the air, mixed with smoke and a blast of flame and heat. It was over in seconds, but the debris continued to rain, so that Bran covered his head with his hands while his ears rang.

"What are you thinking?!" Bran shouted, but he couldn't even hear himself.

"Sorry, Bran," Thomas said. "My finger must have slipped around the time you started getting snarky. Apologies."

Thomas tossed the remote into his backpack, unaffected by the blast that had illuminated the now darkened skies. All the sound and smoke drifted away quickly, though the dust was reluctant to settle. Thomas waved it out of his face as he started toward where the explosives had been placed, so Bran drew the top of his jacket over his mouth and followed him.

"Careful," Thomas said. "It's still crumbling."

He gestured ahead, and through the dust Bran saw a gaping, black hole. The surrounding sand poured into the hole like water. Bran peered closer and saw that around the hole were the jagged edges of flat, white stone, entirely in contrast to the rest of the desert.

"Is that a door?" Bran said.

"A roof," Thomas replied. "The roof of the temple, over which you are now standing. At some point in time it was above ground. But that was many years ago. It has since been buried beneath these sands."

"And the statue?" Bran asked.

"It stands on the edge of the temple roof," Thomas replied. "Do you have your map?"

Bran, still so dazed from Thomas's revelations, drew the two pieces out with no hesitation. Thomas took both of them and arranged them with his and the one they had gotten from Elspeth to show the full map together. He took out a magnifying glass and clicked on his flashlight.

"Now, here's something you need to know about this map," Thomas said. "These arrows are the ones you want to follow. But the maze doesn't really look like it does here, because, see these?"—he gestured to the red dots—"Those are transora."

"And what's that?" Bran asked.

"I'm not quite sure how to explain transora," Thomas said, looking into the sky and scratching his head. "Just be careful, when you're following this map, to only step on the dots with the arrows. Because, as you can see, there are many others here to which the arrows do not point. I assume those are traps and will perhaps lead to your body colliding at rapid speed into a stone wall, splattering your bones and internal organs across some tunnel."

"It might be fun to become wall art," Bran said as Thomas and he moved for the hole.

"Save that for when you're home," Thomas replied, giving

him the pieces of the map and the magnifying glass. "And after I've killed two individuals assuredly heading this way."

Bran turned to look toward the gaping crack in the ground.

"You still up to going?" Thomas asked.

"Haven't got a choice," Bran replied, cautiously stepping closer to the edge.

"Then take my flashlight," Thomas offered, holding it out. "Least you can do is see."

Bran smiled but reached into his backpack instead and drew out his mother's wand.

"Suit yourself," Thomas said. And Bran turned from him to the hole and leapt through into the dark.

Chapter 30

The Labyrinth of the Temple

Bran's feet touched softly on the ground, his powers cushioning him as he landed in a crouch at the bottom. He was surrounded by darkness so black that he couldn't see his own hands in front of him. He felt Nim still holding tight to his jacket, and he held out his mother's wand, pushing his powers through it for light. The grooves in the wand began to shine with a pulsing white glow; his magic was washing along and filling the recesses. The darkness that surrounded him was vanquished, so that he could see the vast, towering hall he had entered.

As he looked up he couldn't help but feel dizzy as he peered through the opening in the ceiling and saw the world far above his head. He tore his gaze from the ceiling and looked again at the room. It was made entirely of white stone with eleven giant pillars supporting the ceiling—five on each side and the eleventh in the center of the room at the back. The floor was stone as well, white against the walls but then changing to a deep blue that ran like a carpet from the center of the room where Bran stood toward the front of the temple.

Bran pushed more power into the wand so that the light increased and he could see where the blue floor led. At the far end of the room, towering so high that it nearly scraped the domed ceiling, was an enormous statue. It was of a human—Bran could not tell its gender—made of white marble, leaning forward precariously so that it loomed over the room. Out of its back were giant wings like that of an angel that touched the walls on both sides of the room and covered the front of the hall like a shield. It was so smooth and cut to such perfection that he could see the very ridges of the statue's robes, and its eyes were staring down at Bran with a serene gaze of comfort.

It was difficult for Bran to look away from the eyes of the statue, and although cut from stone, the face was enthralling. Bran's eyes slid down the robes of the statue to the base where the image became a solid and smooth stone foundation, and there, embedded in the bottom, was an open passageway.

He had been rooted in the same spot since he had leapt through the roof, and now as he stepped forward he found it difficult at first, and he kept glancing at the face high above his head. It seemed that no matter how many steps he took, the eyes still seemed to be gazing at him with a peaceful expression.

As Bran came closer, the floor beneath him began to glimmer with tiny inset crystals. It was rather dazzling to see them light up in the dark, and the closer he got to the door, the more densely gathered the crystals became, so that the ground sparkled blue and white with every step he took. The air did not seem stuffy at all but felt cold and fresh. Bran looked up as he walked in silence, at the stone wings that formed an arch over his head.

"That must have taken someone years of work," he said to Nim, partially because the absolute silence was beginning to make him uneasy. Nim, who had been clinging to his shoulder, hovered away a few inches, looking around with a mixture of curiosity and fear as her wings beat softly. Bran wondered what the purpose of the temple was as there didn't appear to be any altar nor any sign of religious worship, only the floor that pointed to the statue, which protected the door. As he came up to the opening, he held the wand outward hesitantly to light whatever was beyond.

It was even darker through the opening than it was in the hall. The entrance went straight about three paces and then dropped down into a narrow, stone stairway. Bran stood at the top and counted eleven steps exactly, and at the bottom he saw a scarlet cloth hanging from the ceiling, covering whatever was beyond.

The cloth looked new and had a thick border of some tougher, yellow material that held it straight. Bran could not help feeling afraid as he saw the cramped stairway, but he also realized that he was stepping somewhere that few had entered in decades—perhaps even millennia. He looked down to the pieces of paper he clutched in his hand, and though he saw no marking on it of the temple or the door, he knew that he must pass through this curtain.

His steps down were slow and careful, though each time his foot struck against a lower step, he felt a deepening sensation of tranquility he could not explain. By the time he reached the bottom, a strange confidence filled him.

Thus, when he reached the curtain, he had no hesitation in brushing it aside. As his hand touched it, he saw that there were words inset in the design that he had not seen before. He held his light out so that he could read them.

THOUGH PURE OF SOUL SHALL FEEL AT PEACE,
IN WICKED HEARTS SHALL FEARS INCREASE.

Bran pondered the words and why they might have been placed there, though he did not let them disturb him and stepped through.

He found himself in a circular room that domed above his head like an inverted bowl. The ceiling here was low and covered with yellow chalk and there were markings all around the wall. The chalk images had faded and become blurry. In the center of the room was a single hanging lamp with a chain that held it suspended at the level of Bran's waist, with a wick and oil.

"*Feiro*," Bran commanded absently, waving his hand at the light, and it began to burn. Its light was very dim, however, so Bran did not extinguish the wand but was free to hold it lower as he looked around the room.

The floor was decorated with a set of three circles, each inside a larger one. It resembled a galaxy: the outermost circle was dotted with white stars against a blue background, the next looked like the moon, and the innermost was a fiery yellow and red sun. The lamp hung in the center of the sun, with five branching arms each holding an unlit candle in one of the missiv colors of red, purple, green, blue, and finally solid black. A small stone was suspended above each by a thin wire, matching the color of each candle. Inky symbols he could not read circled on the ground below it. At the far end of the room, spread out evenly, were six doors that drew Bran's immediate attention.

He lifted the papers in his hand again, and Nim came closer as he held them toward the lamp and studied the tiny marks.

He could not see them at all, so he brought the magnifying glass out and looked closer. And there, at the beginning of the map, he saw marks for six doors and the first arrow pointing to the third door.

"This way," he said to Nim, though she had already followed his eyes and flew ahead. Bran grabbed her from the air, noticing that the arrow pointed straight to a red dot.

"Stay here with me," he whispered. "I don't know what this thing'll do once I step in it."

Nim understood, because she crawled into his jacket pocket and held on. When Bran looked down at her, he saw the gnome-hat key ring still dangling from the zipper of his jacket, and he thought about what Gary might be doing then—but it was a sad thought, and he pushed it from his mind. He approached the third door and held the wand up into the dark.

His shoes made scraping noises as he shuffled forward slowly in case there were more stairs. He pushed more power into the wand again to feed its fading glow, and he saw that the passage went on farther than he could see, widening the moment he passed through the doorway into some type of tunnel that curled up at an angle. It was very rocky and rough there, as if the builders had simply stopped and left the stones as they were. However, he noticed a solid red chalk circle.

"Here we go, Nim," Bran said, taking a deep breath as he looked down at the circle an inch from his shoe. He stepped onto it, and the moment his foot touched the circle, he was wrenched from his feet and thrown through the air.

Bran shouted in alarm. The rocky tunnel wound in circles, up and down and in every direction possible, so that Bran was thrown tumbling uncontrollably until he couldn't tell what was up and what was down anymore. He shouted as his body twisted and turned, unable to fight the force that pulled him magically through the passage at a dizzying speed. He managed to right himself so he was facing forward as he flew. His heart leapt every time the forces seemed to bring him dangerously close to the rock walls, until suddenly he was deposited onto the ground.

His body slowed the split second before his landing so he wasn't squashed against the rocks. He tumbled forward but sprang to his feet, grabbing the wand from where he had dropped it.

"Drop me a bit harder next time," he grumbled back at the tunnel. "You didn't manage to break any bones."

He checked to make sure Nim was in one piece. She was, though dizzy.

"You're all right," Bran consoled her, turning so that the wand could light up the new location. It was hardly more than a small, enclosed room underground, like a tiny pocket of a cave deep below the surface. There were three openings carved out of this place, and Bran's light revealed that there were also three corresponding red dots on the map.

"We're headed the right way," Bran said, feeling excitement begin to rise inside him. He felt as if he were getting close to Astara, so close to everything he had worked toward. He looked at his map, and though it did not mark the length of the previous transora—showing it as merely a straight tunnel, which was hardly accurate as he had discovered—he saw the arrows pointing to the right-most tunnel passage. So he moved for it and again was lifted off his feet.

He was ready for it this time and was able to keep his body from turning as the forces seized him and launched him forward like a rocket. He had no sense of distance as he flew through the rugged tunnels, although it felt like nearly a mile or more, winding and twisting up and then down, taking him far from where he had started. He didn't consider how he might get back; all his thoughts were focused on how close he was to reaching the Specters.

He got to the end of that transora and found himself in yet another room, just as rocky as the previous. He had no trouble finding the correct passage through this one and again was sent flying through the tunnel. He did this three more times, following the map closely, until finally, passing through the last, he was dropped through the air and hit the hard floor of the final room at the map's end.

When he struck the ground, his grip on the wand was lost, so that it clattered beside him and the light went out. He rolled over, searching for it with his hands, which were lit with a soft, green light. Grasping his mother's wand, Bran slowly turned his gaze.

He was sitting in the middle of a cave that was larger and higher than he had ever thought possible. It seemed to go for hundreds if not thousands of feet in every direction from him, with stalagmites and stalactites so tall and wide that they might have been great redwood trees, some nearly connecting the floor to the ceiling like supports. The stone floor stretched ahead of him, stopping at a giant pool of water that separated Bran from the other end. The green light emanated from the other side of that pool—a glow so dim and yet so prevailing that despite the vastness of the place, Bran could see everything.

A wall made entirely made of crystal, like a towering stained-glass window, loomed before him. Its green light reflected on the water like a mirror, but what startled Bran the most was beyond the wall. For there, held captive behind its translucent surface, were the faces of thousands of people looking back at him.

Chapter 31

A Vision of What Was

THE FACES GAZED DOWN at Bran, all eyes locked on the boy who had appeared before them. The green of the wall cast a strange shade across them so that the faces were misty, like looking through the steamy wall of a shower. He could see many pressed against the rock, though there were others behind them who were only smoky shadows, the motion of which revealed thousands of people stretching behind the wall.

Bran could only stare at them with wide eyes. Their mournful gazes flicked back and forth between his face and his bag. So without taking his eyes off the ghostly faces, he pulled his bag off, reached inside, and drew out the Key.

The forms dashed themselves against the green wall in a wild frenzy, pushing one another out of the way. Their mouths opened in shouts though he could hear no voices save for those his mind imagined for them.

"Wait!" Bran said, holding his hand up, as they continued to scratch and claw against their prison, their empty eyes rolling in pain.

"I'm here to help," he said, his voice echoing through the empty cavern, but they paid him no heed.

He looked around the cave again and saw that before him

was a bridge. It was made entirely of flat stone and partly buried in the water, with barely an inch poking above the surface. It stopped a few feet from the other side. At the end was a circular platform, and in the center was a pillar of black stone.

He turned his gaze back to the Specters, who fought and struggled to get to the Key, and then he started toward the bridge. The water on both sides was so still that when his shoes struck the stone, even that tiny impact caused little ripples. His pace quickened as he got closer to the pillar, even as the Specters' fighting began to slow as their energies faded.

The pillar was flat on all sides and solid like deep black concrete. It nearly reached his shoulders, and the top was engraved with markings that mirrored those he had seen in the room beyond the temple stairway: stars on the outside, then the moon, and the sun in the middle. In the center of the sun was a hole, inset with metal. It was a lock.

"It's for the Key," he said aloud to Nim, realizing a second later that Nim was not there.

"Nim?" he said, turning but finding that she had vanished. He hadn't noticed her disappearance and couldn't remember when he had last seen her. He knew she had come through the transora with him, but she was nowhere to be found.

"Nim!" he called her again, louder, spinning and searching the cave for anywhere she might have flown off to. The cave was full of things that might have drawn her curiosity, but he felt for sure if she had gotten hurt or trapped somewhere she would have at least called for him.

Looking up, Bran saw the Specters had quieted, their fighting had ceased, and they stared down at him, almost motionless. And then, right in their midst, for a fleeting second, he saw Astara.

It was so quick that it was like the passing of her shadow. Unlike the others, her eyes were closed, and then she vanished once more.

"Astara!" Bran shouted her name, and the Specters began to move once more. Bran was so startled at seeing Astara that he wasn't entirely thinking straight, and jumping forward, he thrust the Key down into the lock like a sword.

He clenched his teeth together, and he gripped the curved end of the Key, turning it with all his strength. It slid effortlessly in the lock, until it stopped and gave a click that resounded throughout the tunnel.

The green gem in the Key glimmered, flashing once like a diamond in the sun, then fading. In that same moment, the glow of the crystalline wall that held the Specters vanished, so that he was left in darkness. The black was so complete that he could see nothing but the gentle glow of the Key, which stood atop the pillar like a candle, until it too faded. The pace of his heartbeat quickened as he felt magic begin to stir in the room.

Then, as if Bran had been sleeping before and had simply opened his eyes to find himself back in a place that was all too familiar, the smothering dark gave way, and Bran was standing in the middle of Bolton Road. Flashing lights from police cruisers cast strange shadows up and down the house before him.

It was like Bran had been plunged back in time, to the night Astara had died. This time, however, all the other people had disappeared.

Then, as if she had been there all the time, and Bran had

simply not noticed, Astara was standing before him. She was in the doorway of the house, staring at Bran, and she was so real, and it was so startling to see her again, that he could do little but stare back.

"Astara…" he whispered.

"Bran," she replied, in that same soft voice he had longed to hear.

"You're here," Bran said. "I've actually found you!"

He started for her but found that his feet could not move from the spot. He looked back up at her with dismay, and her eyes were filled with sadness.

"What's the matter?" Bran asked. Astara looked as if she was about to cry.

"You can't save me, Bran," she said. She did not move, only lifted her hand, and he saw that she was also rooted in the same spot in the doorway where she had died.

"What do you mean?" Bran said with desperation. "I've come to free you and the Specters. They'll give you back."

"No, Bran," Astara shook her head sadly, and her hair fell over her shoulders. "You've been misled. Everything has been a lie."

There was so much torment in her voice that Bran felt his heart drop, and a stone seemed to form in his throat.

"Don't say that," Bran choked. "I'm here for you. I'm going to free them. Then they'll let you go."

"It won't be enough," Astara said. "The Key controls the Specters' souls: whoever holds it holds power over them and the powers of their souls. Only the person who holds it can set them free."

It was strange how Astara spoke; it was layered as if her voice were mixed with others. When she spoke of "their souls," he heard other voices replace it with "our souls," as if while she was speaking, the Specters were as well.

"But I have the Key," Bran said. "I've brought it."

"Yes," Astara said. "You can free them with it."

There was a catch in her voice that rendered Bran unable to speak.

"And if you set them free," Astara said, "my soul will be freed with theirs."

Her words confused Bran for a few moments, so that he could not understand exactly what she was trying to say. But then, it sank in. If Bran freed the Specters, then he would free Astara as well, and if she were freed, then she would pass with them.

"How do you know this for sure?" Bran stammered, trying to fight against the surety with which she spoke her words.

"I know nothing, Bran," Astara said, and he saw the tears begin to roll down the side of her face. "I don't even know what has happened here. But I am their prisoner."

She is our prisoner, the echo of the Specters' voices resounded within Bran's head, even when Astara's lips had stopped moving.

"Then I can't do it," Bran said. "I'll find another way. I'll find somehow—"

"You have to set them free, Bran," Astara said. "You know you must."

"But I can't let you die," Bran said, and he began to sob softly, his eyes filling with tears as she tried to reach for him.

"I can't go back home if you're not there," Bran said, choking on his words. "It just won't be right. I can never just go back home and feel the same."

"But you've got to make the right choice," Astara said. "You know what you have to do, Bran. You can't let me get in the way of that. You must set them free."

"I can't just—" Bran started to say, but then a dash of blackness, like smoke drawing across his vision, blotted the world out from around him. As if he had fallen through a trap door, Bran found himself back in the cave underground, knocked to the side and hitting his head against the stone.

"Mind if I interrupt, Bran?" he heard a sharp voice say, and he looked up. Standing over him, with one hand still clutching the Key she had removed from the stone, was Elspeth.

Chapter 32

A Betrayal

Startled, Bran wasn't even sure that he was back in reality once more until he saw Elspeth's wand pointed down at him. And then Bran saw, standing not three feet behind Elspeth, holding a pistol ready to kill him if he made a wrong move, his own father.

"How did you get here?" was all Bran could muster to say.

"Is that the first thing you wonder, Bran?" Elspeth said. She waved her hand at Thomas.

"You've seen the fairy," she said. "You know what she can do. It was her powers that made you believe you had gotten away with stealing my part of the map."

Elspeth laughed lightly. "You didn't once think that she might be leading Thomas and me here?"

Bran was aghast, and he looked past Elspeth at Thomas, whose eyes showed neither regret nor shame for what he had done.

"How could you betray me after all this?" Bran said. Thomas's face still held no sign of remorse.

"Was it all just an act?" Bran asked.

"Unfortunately, it was," Thomas replied. "I'm quite ashamed of you. Obviously you did not inherit my sense of judgment, for I fooled you easily."

Bran thought he had set up every defense against this man,

but it felt as if his heart had been torn from his chest and split into pieces. Turning his head so he wouldn't have to look at his father, he noticed that Elspeth was holding the Key.

"No, you can't—" he shouted, jumping to his feet and diving for her, but her wand was faster, flinging him up and throwing him against the stone bridge. He caught himself, but his mother's wand went clattering down the bridge and rolled so that its tip was hanging precariously over the edge.

"You didn't think for once, Bran," Elspeth said, "that all of this has been part of a great plan? You didn't think at all that your father and I have been in league with each other, leading you along so you might get the piece of the map from Gary and put them all together and come here?"

She smirked. "You've trusted far too many people, and believed too many lies. Putting this Key into the lock does not free the Specters. It merely removes the Key's protections."

She looked down at it in her hands and smiled. Bran got up again to fight her, raising his hand to seize the Key with magic, but she barely had to flick the wand in her wrist to send him back again.

"You can't take the Key!" Bran shouted. "You have no idea what it does!"

"Yes, I do, Bran," she replied, in her low hiss. "I know full well whom this Key commands and how powerful are the ones controlled by it. Was I not part of the very Curse that enslaved them?"

She drew her wand upward, and Bran was lifted from his knees, lurching forward through the air with his arms bent behind his back, until he was hovering inches from her face, clenching his jaw in pain.

"It is you who does not understand their powers or their worth," she hissed. Then she laughed. "You cannot free the Specters. If you hold the Key, you cannot command them to be freed, for your very command only extends your dominion over them."

"My mother left the Key for me to free them," Bran hissed through clenched teeth. "She would not have done that if there was no way."

"If that was her intention," Elspeth replied. "But if the bearer of the Key controls the Specters, why did she not free them herself?"

Her words sank into Bran's mind slowly, until he realized just how true they rang. He had placed the Key in the lock, and nothing had changed. It was shocking to think that Elspeth might be right and all his efforts had been in vain.

"And you and my father have been working together all this time," Bran gasped.

"You might have thought that was the case," Elspeth said and spun from Bran with her wand out. Thomas—who had crept up behind Elspeth while she was distracted and aimed a pistol at her back—flew through the air, slamming into the black pillar. His gun fell away, and two tiny bursts of black substance flew from Elspeth's wand, striking against each of Thomas's wrists. In a second, he was bound to the pillar, his hands pulled back and stuck.

"Should I be diverted enough to leave you to your own devices?" Elspeth mocked, as she looked at him, his eyes squeezed shut in pain.

"All in your pursuit of ending Joris's life?" she said. "Perhaps I should guess that my life is also on your list of vengeances?"

"I'll kill you both yet," Thomas said, and his voice filled with scorn and hatred. Bran realized that Thomas had had his own plans all along, to kill Elspeth there.

"I swore to hunt you both until you were dead at my feet," Thomas seethed, his face going red with rage as he fought the bonds to no avail.

"Well, unfortunately for you," Elspeth said, "I shall be leaving you here to die in a cave."

She smiled again. "Does such a death ring familiar?"

Bran, seeing Elspeth distracted, leapt to his feet.

"*Bilali feiro!*" he shouted, the first magic that came to his mind. But Elspeth spun around, throwing him back once more and deflecting the ball of fire into the water, where it fizzled in sparks and disappeared.

"You're just as foolish as Emry was," Elspeth said. "Both of you."

Bran crawled up again, so desperate to stop her that he continued to fight, throwing another magic her way—a bright yellow beam of energy from his palm. She was startled for a second but lifted her hand and deflected it into the wall of rock, so that it crumbled bits of stone that fell into the water.

"Do you dare fight me?" she said, stepping toward Bran. "Is this some type of game, so that I might be forced to kill you quickly?"

Bran rolled over, ready to do whatever he must to keep fighting her, seeing amusement in her eyes that he continued to struggle when her skills with magic could overcome his powers due to his lack of experience. But while her eyes were trained on him, Bran noticed a small motion from Thomas. His father had bent his head down and worked the buttoned flap of his shirt pocket open with his teeth. He then managed to pull something out of it and drop it gently upon the bridge.

It was a flower.

Bran wasn't sure what was happening but came to his feet, and bringing both hands together he was able to combine powers, drawing air and dust from all around the room, launching them at Elspeth like an arrow. It was such a puny and unfocused move that Elspeth laughed and waved her wand in front of her face, chopping Bran's magic so that it fell apart.

"These magics are an embarrassment for one of your power," she said. Bran was able to glance past her again and saw Nim sprout from the flower. Nim flapped her wings in determination, and though her eyes were free of the green glow, she crawled across Thomas's arms like a bee and began to bite at the black paste that held him.

She was so small that she could do very little at a time, biting some away and spitting it out, slowly nibbling her way though his bonds. Bran held his breath and quickly darted his eyes back to Elspeth before she noticed his preoccupation.

"Will you fight me more?" Elspeth asked in arrogant invitation. "I took so much joy in killing your mother. Perhaps the son will provide more amusement?"

"Or perhaps you'll be killed by him," Bran said to taunt her, trying to keep her attention on him.

"I doubt that very much," Elspeth said as she slowly approached him, wand out and ready for whatever he tried next. So he launched another pitiful magic at her, attempting to pull her feet out from under her. She stumbled for barely a step but caught herself and swung her arm, flinging Bran to the side, a loud slap across his body like a hand striking him. He shouted in pain and rolled to his back, his left side burning.

"Another!" Elspeth taunted him. Bran saw one of Thomas's hands come free, but Thomas held it against the stone as if it was still bound, as Nim started on the other side. Thomas's eyes met with Bran's for a moment, and his were filled with helpless fury, catching Bran by surprise. Thomas had showed little care for him before. Bran's heartbeat quickened, sure that at any moment Elspeth would realize what was happening behind her back. So from the ground, he attacked her again, and she slapped him harder this time so that his face rolled over the edge of the bridge, and he was looking into the water.

Pain screamed from his face, but he could see no bruise nor marking in his reflection. It felt as if Elspeth had struck him with the back of her hand.

"Will you continue?" Elspeth said with another cruel laugh. Bran could not get to his feet, but he rolled over painfully. He saw Nim working furiously, and Bran's palms were sweating.

Nim finally bit her way through the other side and swirled up into the air. Thomas's hands were free, but Elspeth spun with realization, slamming him back into the pillar again. Nim shot through the air like a bullet, diving at Elspeth and screaming in a monstrous hiss. She bared her teeth and sank them into Elspeth's exposed neck.

Elspeth shouted, but Nim bit harder, and Elspeth's fingers wrenched open in pain, the Key and her wand clattering to the bridge as she stumbled backward. She flailed, sending Nim flying, but Nim flew back, hissing in Elspeth's face.

Bran saw the Key as it struck the ground, and he dove for it, sliding across the hard stone and seizing it in his grasp. Elspeth threw Nim aside and dove for him, grabbing her wand as she moved and slinging it out. Bran got to his feet, and he stood on the opposite edge of the circular platform, clutching the Key as strongly as he could.

"Give me the Key!" she commanded, her voice hoarse, wand outstretched.

"I won't," Bran seethed. He stepped back again and found his shoe touching the edge of the platform. His hands had begun to shake as his fist clenched the Key, and he saw the Specters moving about so that they might see what was happening below. They were staring at him with a look of fear.

"Give it to me," Elspeth hissed. Bran looked at her and clenched his teeth together.

"You will not have this Key," he said in the strongest voice he had heard from himself, strengthened in power by the anger and hurt and torment in his soul. And then he drew his hand back as if he was going to toss it to her, but then he flung it forward, launching the Key into the air straight over Elspeth's head toward the wall of the Specters.

Time seemed to slow as they watched the Key flying forward; the Specters fought one another, their hands scratching against their prison as they reached for it. The Key struck the wall, and an explosion of magic filled the cave.

Chapter 33

The Pool of Life and Death

The green, vaporous hands of the Specters burst through the wall the moment the Key touched their crystal prison, spilling out over one another. They all seemed to seize the Key at once, and the moment their hands touched it, their forms hardened and were laced with lines that crumbled back to the wall. The wall blasted out into tiny, crystalline pebbles that spilled like waves, clattering and filling the chamber with a deafening noise.

Everything had gone into disarray, and then Bran realized what had happened: when he had thrown the Key to the Specters, somehow the power to control them had been passed into their command, and this was enough to free them from their prison. Their souls poured out and fell into the water like stones. But through the noise and the flashes, Bran heard a voice scream, and out of the corner of his eye, he saw someone struggling in the water. Though the water was dragging her down as it rocked tumultuously, Bran only needed a glimpse to know who it was.

"Astara!" he shouted, so loudly that his voice echoed off the chamber ceiling, which had begun to crumble around them, stones raining down and smashing against the pillars, as if the room were falling apart. He dashed in her direction, ignoring Thomas as he called after him, and dove into the water.

Immediately he was pulled under, as if hands had reached from the depths and wrapped themselves around his ankles. The water was so cold that it burned as he flailed his arms and legs, breaking the surface once and drawing in a deep gasp of air.

"Bran!" He heard Astara call his name, and it was the most glorious sound he had heard, for she was real and only a few yards away. He called back at her, but she was pulled under the water again, so he dove down and kicked toward where he had seen her. The waters, though, were eager to fight him, bubbles swirling and blocking his view, even as the waves themselves seemed to glow. He saw a tremendous motion near the source of the light where stones were still tumbling into the water from the Specters' prison. As the stones were engulfed, they turned once again into the forms of people—opening their eyes and their mouths in a wordless scream, before their bodies sank into the darkness and turned to pale, lifeless corpses, their faces filled with final peace, disappearing into the black embrace of whatever was at the bottom of the abyss.

Lights flashed above the surface, and Bran could hear gunfire and magic. In one of the flashes he saw Astara ahead of him, her body unlike all the others: she flailed about, struggling to get back to the surface. He realized that she, unlike the Specters who had been cursed, had been taken alive, and through this she must have still had mortality, though they had been freed to die. Seeing this brought new strength and hope to Bran as he pushed toward her, his muscles burning with the effort as he moved inch by inch closer. He saw Astara begin to sink and felt his lungs scream for air.

But he could not go back to the surface. He saw her falling deeper, like she was being pulled down with the corpses by the water. Her eyes met with his, and there was a moment of recognition, but her motions became slower, her body losing strength.

Bran struggled all the more to reach her. Her eyes were beginning to close, the darkness swallowing her body. She was so close, and Bran fought terribly. But Astara was slipping away from him yet again.

No! he thought frantically, watching her fade and feeling his air running out. As it did, his feelings burst within him, everything that he had put into saving her seeming to rush forth into powers that flew to his fingers, and he threw magic toward her, only making the waters even more turbulent. His mind clouded, and he could not think over the roaring pain his lungs brought forth. He kicked his legs frantically as her head tilted up to look at him from below.

Her gaze had become serene, and she ceased to struggle. She stared at him with a blank expression on her face, but her hand moved forward, reaching to him, as if in her last bit of strength she might touch his.

Don't leave me... he thought, wishing that he could say the words aloud to her and that it might convince her to fight just a little longer, his fingers just inches from hers. The thought seemed to cross between them, magic pushing it to her mind so that she heard his voice in her head; her eyes opened a tiny bit more, and her hand reached further, and for a second, the ends of their fingers touched.

Bran curled the ends of his against hers, linking them together by one small finger. It was enough, and all thoughts of their imminent death seemed to fade away into the murky water.

Astara, though, closed her eyes, and Bran was suddenly pushed away from her by a mighty blast. He could feel that she was using her Netora powers to push him back to the surface, so that he might live though she hadn't the strength to save herself. He felt her finger leave his, but in a burst he shot forward with powers of his own, his mind screaming that he would not let her die after all he had done to save her. He thrashed about and caught her arm strongly, and they were flying toward the surface together. Bran gathered whatever strength he had left and felt a burst of power to add to hers that pushed them through the heavy waters, the lights and the sounds growing as their strength faded, until they broke through the water's surface and landed on the bridge.

Bran heard a gasp but could not tell whether it was his own or if it came from Astara, who lay beside him, coughing and choking. He could not move, for the final small piece of magic he had used had sapped his last bit of strength. He could only feel his hand still clutching Astara's, his mind not allowing him to let her go.

"Bran!" he heard her gasp, rolling over the stone bridge, the sounds of the crumbling chamber blaring in their ears once more.

"Breathe!" he commanded Astara, struggling to sit up so that he could lift her, ignoring the pain that wracked his own body. She choked the water free from her lungs, gripping him tightly as if the pool might draw her back if she let him go.

Bran held her so she could breathe more easily, and he opened his mouth to say something to her, though he didn't know what—but he was stopped by a massive boulder falling from the cave ceiling and smashing into the bridge just a few feet from his leg. The very cave had begun to tremble as if by an earthquake, and he saw Thomas fallen to the side, Elspeth finally escaping him at the other end of the bridge.

"Bran!" he heard Thomas shout frantically, just as Elspeth stumbled forward at the bridge's end, and he saw her seize something that had fallen there.

"She has the Key!" Thomas yelled, trying to stand. "Don't let her get away!"

Another boulder fell, snapping the bridge from its end. The gem in the handle of the Key was empty of its light and power, though a wild smile of victory crossed Elspeth's face, and Bran realized that she still had some use for it.

He got to his feet but was thrown down again by the impact of a rock larger than himself slamming into the ground. He was up again though, pulling Astara with him, and he saw his mother's wand rolling toward the opposite edge. He held his hand out, and it flew to his grasp.

Thomas was going for Elspeth. She saw them but seemed unconcerned and drew something from her coat, flinging it at the bridge before her. There was a dazzling flash of purple light, and smoke burst from it, swirling into an oval before her, with a black space in the middle. She leapt toward it, but Thomas had gotten to her in that same instant. She fought with him and broke free just as Bran and Astara drew near. She leapt through the smoke, and half of her disappeared through it, but Thomas grabbed hold of her arm, and seizing Bran with his other hand, the four of them tumbled through the portal, leaving the collapsing temple caves behind.

The noise of the chamber vanished and was replaced with a blast of echoes. Bran rolled and looked up and saw that he was in a manufactured tunnel, and his back rested against something metal. It was train tracks.

Elspeth's magic had not thrown them far, as proved by the sign against the tunnel wall that said they were in the Subway Imperial, which ran through Dansby and Harrison until it stopped in Wadsworth farther north. Everything was dimly lit by fluorescent lights, but far ahead, Bran could see the platform, which appeared abandoned, for there were no people or voices coming from it. Everything was very dirty, and columns separated the sets of tracks. Just ahead, Bran saw Elspeth running from them.

"Elspeth!" Thomas roared, and Bran heard a blast from a gun; Elspeth spun with her wand in a blur and sliced the bullet in half. She still clutched the Key in her hand, her eyes filled with rage and determination.

"Do you dare fire upon me, Thomas?" she said. She lifted her wand, and a burst of fire blasted from it in an arc. Thomas leapt to the side behind a column, where the flame struck in a magnificent beam and broke tiles free. Bran covered his face with his arm as they shattered and tiny pieces shot in all directions, sizzling and burning where they hit. He had his wand up instinctively, and without even thinking, he seized the shards of the tiles with magic and sent them flying in a whirlwind toward Elspeth. Caught by surprise at Bran's quick action, she barely had time to dive out of the way, the pieces slamming into others like them and cracking into dust as they collided.

"Are you all right?" Bran demanded of Astara, pulling her up and diving behind a pillar with her as another blast of magic shot from Elspeth's wand. Their reunion had been so short-lived, and it had hardly sunk in that she was there at his side.

"I'm OK," she coughed, struggling to stand but falling against the wall. "What's going on?"

"I can't explain it all now, as you can see," Bran said, ducking as Thomas let off a barrage of shots in Elspeth's direction. "But if we get out of this alive, I'll tell you everything."

There was an explosion behind him, and the ground rocked at its impact.

"Just don't die again!" Bran shouted. "That's all I'm asking. Stay here!"

Astara was about to say something, but Bran did not wait to hear it, spinning around the corner with the wand and just in time, as something black came hurtling toward him and the pillar. A blue, transparent shield erupted in front of him, deflecting Elspeth's blast into the side wall, drilling a hole and sending dust flying all over the tunnel.

"What missiv is she?" Bran shouted, because Elspeth had used so many magics that he could not tell, though she obviously held a wand that bore many enchantments of its own. Bran dashed after her, and Elspeth moved from behind her cover, throwing her wand out again. Bran was caught unprepared and was seized from the ground by the power of her rage, his back slamming into the ceiling and knocking the air out of him. He drew his hand forward, and a shield appeared again, blocking

Elspeth's power momentarily so that he plummeted toward the ground—but landed on his feet in a crouch, the same way he had done with Astara off the water tower.

There was the sound of a different gun, and Bran saw another figure had leapt off the subway platform ahead. It was Joris, and Bran realized that this escape had been in Elspeth's plans all along, for she had had Joris waiting for her. He fired at Thomas, but when he leapt into the light he spotted Bran and turned the gun in his direction.

Astara, though, had regained her senses and pushed beside Bran with her hands out, and a shield surrounded both of them, the bullet and the second that followed both ricocheting and striking the walls. Thomas seized his chance and let out a blast of shots, rattling all across the tunnel wildly. Joris fell behind a column, and as bullets tore at the concrete, Thomas shouted with rage as bits of it flew into the air.

He ran out of ammunition and fell back again, flinging his backpack onto the ground and drawing out more bullets. Joris didn't hesitate to fire, and a bullet grazed Thomas's arm, sending him back against the wall with a painful shout.

"Thomas!" Bran called, but he was alive, though bleeding from the gash that had torn through his jacket and shirt. Elspeth began to walk backward, closer to her escape, with Joris covering her with his gun and firing at Thomas, who was forced to remain behind the pillar, covering himself as debris flew in all directions. Bran managed to pull his arm around, readying the wand to blast at Joris, but before he could, there came a sound.

"Stop!" a voice shouted with such power and command that both Elspeth and Joris faltered. All eyes turned toward the figure who had leapt from the platform and onto the tracks between Elspeth and Joris's escape. .

It was the last person Bran had expected to appear from the shadows: Gary, his eyes blazing with anger. He stood strong and still, his gray coat swept over his legs. In his right hand, he clutched the key-ring map, wadded in his fist with the red mark glowing on the subway stop. And in his left hand, Gary held a golden wand at the ready, pointing straight at Elspeth's heart.

"Gary," Elspeth spat at him in recognition.

"Elspeth," he hissed in return, his voice taking on a power that made his words echo in the tunnel. He lifted his wand higher. "You shall die here tonight."

Chapter 34

The Key and the Train

Gary's command struck Elspeth as an insult, and she flinched. "You?" she shouted. "You dare to order what I shall do?"

Gary's wand did not waver; he held it resolutely, his expression unchanging. Her hands had begun to shake with sheer rage, and Bran, seeing her back turned to him, flipped his wand forward, but she was faster, turning once to deflect his magic and then flying toward Gary, her teeth bared in a wild hiss. Gary leapt to the side in a blur, springing to the wall and grabbing hold of the tiles with the ends of his fingers, using magic to cling with one hand like a spider and moving his wand to throw Elspeth to the opposite end of the tunnel.

She did not stop, rebounding from the wall with a shriek. It was as if suddenly she was ignoring everyone else in the room but Gary, flying toward him as he leapt from the wall and rolled across the tracks, bending his wand behind him. There was a deafening crack, and Elspeth hit the wall, sliding to the ground.

Joris chose this moment to open fire on Thomas once more, but Elspeth—every ounce of her attention on killing Gary—swung her arm, plucking Joris's bullets straight from the air and launching them back in a circle toward Gary. He only had to draw his hands apart in a swift motion, and the bullets turned once again in a loop back toward Elspeth, forcing her to dive to the side. As she rolled, she shot a beam of fire from her wand, the heat so powerful that Bran had to cover his face to keep from being burned. Joris dove out of the way of her magic, though Gary only drew the fire upward, where it stuck the ceiling.

All of this happened so fast that Bran's eyes could hardly register what he had seen. But then Bran heard a distant rumbling, a sound he recognized.

"There's a train coming!" Bran shouted, his voice barely audible over the noise of the fighting. He could hear it coming rapidly from the direction of Elspeth and Joris, but the fighting continued, magic and bullets tracing through the air, until Gary flew back against the wall again, and the lights of the train appeared at the corner.

Elspeth, seeing that she must escape then, began to run to the platform, with Joris ahead of her. Gary, seeing Elspeth was about to escape, lifted both of his hands over his head and began to speak words of magic that Bran could not hear from where he stood. There came a great crashing and cracking over their heads, one that caused the tunnel to tremble. And then, as if Gary was prying them loose with his very hands, the tiles on the ceiling above Elspeth peeled loose, rolling toward her. They whirled like a tornado, dust and concrete and tile all coming together at once, the wind from it throwing Bran's hair as the magic collided with Elspeth, throwing her to the ground.

The tunnel was filled with smoke and dust, but Bran saw the Key clatter from Elspeth's hand. He gasped as she fell and, without wasting another second, dashed to reach it. Thomas was going after Joris; Astara and Gary had vanished in the cloud of dust. Bran could hear the train rumbling toward them, its light flashing in his eyes, so he ran even faster.

He was almost to the Key, but Elspeth slammed into his side and drove her elbow into his jaw. He was knocked sideways, tripping across a metal rail, falling to the tracks. He saw that Elspeth nearly had the Key and that Joris had reached the platform and was escaping.

Thomas looked from Joris to Bran, his fingers white as they clutched his gun. Astara and Gary called to Bran, but the train was almost upon him, and he felt someone throw magic to lift him, but it wasn't enough, for he stumbled again, hearing the gears from the train and feeling the wheels rumbling across the tracks.

It was then that Thomas jerked into motion, throwing himself in Bran's direction, falling to the side just as the train rumbled across where Bran had been just a moment before: leaving the Key and Elspeth behind. Bran could feel the heat from the metal wheels even as Thomas rolled and held Bran tightly against himself, squeezing them both in the narrow space between the train and the walls of the subway. Elspeth's hand reached the Key, touching its edge, and she shouted in victory. But before she could lift it from the track, the train roared over it, and both Elspeth and the Key were both blocked from Bran's view.

The train did not pause, the cars rumbling by, deafening Bran, and he and his father held tightly to the concrete. Thomas lifted himself up and pulled Bran with him, rolling onto the thin side maintenance walkway as the train continued past them, and Bran bent over to catch his breath.

Thomas did not let him stay there but pushed him ahead until they had crawled to the station. The platform was above their heads, and Thomas pushed Bran up, where Gary and Astara dashed to him. Bran was so shaken from what had happened that he couldn't stand, but Gary helped him to his feet, and the train continued past in a blur of lights. Joris was nowhere to be found.

"The Key—" Bran said, but Gary pushed all of them ahead until they found a stairway and were out of view of the passengers on the train. They climbed the stair as the sounds disappeared behind them, until they reached another room—an old maintenance warehouse.

"The Key's protection was gone. It was destroyed on the track," Gary said, and it came as a giant relief to Bran—but he was even more relieved that Astara and Gary were still alive with him. He grabbed Astara then and held her tightly so that she could not leave again.

"That was nearly our deaths!" Astara said, still shaken.

"How many times have you nearly died already?" Bran said, unable to keep from laughing, because there really wasn't any other way for him to react. The danger had passed, and Astara was safe.

Gary stood, breathing the air deeply, and Bran saw that he wore an almost peaceful expression. He seemed free, and Bran realized just what had happened: Gary was out of his house.

"You came after me," Bran stammered. Gary nodded.

"I've been watching you move on the map ever since you left," he replied.

"You have?" Bran said, looking down at the charm that was still on his jacket. "Why?"

"I couldn't bear the thought of what you were going to do," Gary said, looking down. "I sent you off alone because I wasn't strong enough to go with you. And so I watched, hoping to see some sign that you succeeded and were going home."

He shook his head. "But when I saw you disappear from the desert and suddenly reappear at the Subway Imperial stop—which I recognized from my days on the Project—I had a feeling there was trouble. And," he paused to smiled, "by using Revdoor version 2.0, and the maintenance key I happened to have collected, I came to check on you."

"But you left your house," Bran said. Here Gary's eyes met with his.

"That I did," he said softly, as if realizing it himself for the first time. "But I did say when my heart had been healed, I could leave that place. I suppose it was true after all."

And that was all Gary needed to explain for Bran to understand. Bran felt his heart glow, for there he stood with his friend, alive and safe; and Gary, this man who was finally whole again; and Thomas—

"Thomas saved me from—" But Bran's voice ended there, for Thomas had vanished.

"Where did he go?" Astara said quickly. And though Bran searched the room, his father was nowhere to be found.

Chapter 35

A Welcoming Party

When Bran had first arrived in East Dinsmore, it had only been he and Oswald in the cab, with Nim hiding in Bran's things. But as Bran left East Dinsmore, though Nim was no longer there, the back seat was full, for he and Astara were returning home together.

In the cab, Bran did not speak of it, but he could not help but wonder where his father had gone without even the slightest good-bye. He didn't know which hurt more: that, or the fact he had taken Nim with him. As he thought back, he couldn't even be sure Nim had made it out of the caves with them, for he hadn't seen her in the subway tunnel. He hoped Thomas had hid her in his pocket, but he could be sure of nothing. There were so many things that Bran wanted to say and to ask Thomas: to find out what had gone through the man's head, and if he had planned all along to save Bran or had only switched sides because it would get him closer to killing Joris. When no one was watching, Bran had checked through his bags, hoping his father had left a note or something to let him know what had happened. But even though Bran checked three times, nothing surfaced, and he realized that his father had truly disappeared yet again.

Gary had decided to accompany them back to his sister, and though he said it was for their safety, Bran assumed it was more that he did not wish to tell him good-bye. Bran sat in the middle, telling Astara all that had happened between her being taken and him finding her. She could hardly speak as she listened to all that he had done, and even when he had finished, she said little. He suspected that she was tired, as was he, but the smile on her face told him that she just could not find any words that would fully express her feelings.

Oswald, who had probably never driven so many miles in a single day in all of his career, was quite sunny even as the daylight wore on and the hours of driving went deeper into the evening. Gary had telephoned him and asked that he specifically come to their whereabouts and pick them up for the drive, promising a sum the driver could not refuse. Oswald drove on for many hours, and about halfway through the trip he checked the mirror and saw that all three of his passengers had fallen asleep. He grinned, and his tentacles reached back over the seat to draw the single curtain over the window.

They arrived at the gates of Dunce, and Bran awoke to find Astara leaning against his shoulder, fast asleep, and he was leaning against Gary. Bran looked out the windows and saw the lights of the giant checkpoint gate, with the guard towers and the booths of inspectors making sure no gnomes would pass through. The cab had come to a stop, and he could see one other familiar car on the side of the road ahead. It was Adi's.

Bran and Astara were still half asleep as Oswald gently helped them out of the cab. It wasn't very late, but everything that had happened had left both of them exhausted, and Astara got into the back of Adi's car without fully coming awake.

Bran stopped, however, and left the door open, looking back toward Adi and Gary. He didn't hear what they said, but Gary had tears in his eyes and embraced his sister warmly. Gary looked at Bran and then closed his eyes as brother and sister held each other for a few moments before parting. It seemed odd that they would say so little after being apart for so long, but by their faces, Bran saw there was little for them to say to each other that could possibly describe it all anyway.

Adi walked back to Bran. She looked from him to Astara and then back to him, her own heart soaring with pride at what he had done when she had hardly believed it possible.

"I think Gary wants to tell you good-bye, Bran," she said. He turned and saw Gary waiting beside Oswald's cab. He was looking toward the setting sun, and the golden light of it seemed to be strengthening him.

Bran strode toward the man and just stood there beside him, looking into the distance. He didn't want to say good-bye, because he didn't know what was going to happen to Gary once they parted. Would Gary go back to his house and go on living his loathsome life in solitude? It pained Bran to even think of it, the constant torment and heartbreak returning to this man who had been through so much.

But as if to wipe these fears from Bran's mind, a smile crossed Gary's face. It was warm and happy, and he seemed truly at peace.

"It has been so long since I have seen the sun set on any evening away from my home," he said. He breathed in the crisp evening air. "It is truly spectacular."

"You're going to be all right, Gary," Bran said. "We've both been hurt by my mother. But we were both loved by her, too. And I think we were the ones she was thinking of, and wishing she could have been with longer, before she died."

Gary was quiet for a while.

"I still wish that fate had given me the chance to be your father," he finally said. He turned to Bran.

"But then again," Gary added, "I'd like to think of you as partly my son anyway—if not by blood or by name, then by the mere fact that I love you as my own, even in this short time we have known each other."

These words caused Bran's heart to feel lighter and happier with an emotion he could not entirely pin down. It was the feeling that he had had when he was with Rosie, how she had made him feel loved. For it was more than a name that simply went to the man who shared Bran's bloodline—it was something more, something that Gary almost seemed to hold, even in the short time they had known each other.

"It has come to my attention that I must go away for a short time," Gary said softly. "But I shall return to visit you and my sister. And if you ever need anything, you know where I am."

Gary gestured toward the gnome-hat key ring, which was still attached to Bran's jacket. "And I will always know where you are—even if you end up in some dangerous subway tunnel again."

"And what if I take this key ring off?" Bran asked, smiling warmly.

"I'll still find a way to help you," Gary said with a tone of mild amusement. Bran embraced him, and they bid farewell, departing each to their own car, and were quietly driven away.

Adi said nothing as they passed through the city and started back in the direction of Bolton Road. As they got to Deeper Dunce, the lights of the buildings began to play across the inside of her car, and Astara sat up.

"Sleep well?" Adi finally said. Astara nodded.

"Good to be back?" Adi asked. Astara smiled at that, and so did Bran.

"There's a bit of a surprise back home for you, Bran," Adi said, nodding ahead.

"What's there?" Bran asked.

"You'll see when we get there," she said.

After what seemed like ages, they finally turned onto the street, and Bran was greeted with the very last thing he had ever expected to see on Bolton Road. The street was blocked off about halfway down with wooden barriers, and cars were parked all along the sides with people bustling about. There were picnic tables spread on the lawns and streamers in the trees with strings of lights hanging all across. However, standing in the middle of the yard of the entirely repaired thirteenth house on the right side was the most shocking thing of all: a giant banner, hanging across two high poles, with words emblazoned across that read:

The Third Bank of Dunce Presents:
Welcome Home Bartley and Rosie
From the Third Bank of Dunce

"They're here?" Bran gasped, about to jump out of the car before Adi had even stopped.

"Not yet," Adi chuckled. "They'll be here this evening."

"And how did all this..." Bran started, but he couldn't finish as he took in the crowds of people, some hanging balloons and others arranging cakes onto the long tables.

"Well, after that horrible thing that went on during Fridd's Day, the Third Bank of Dunce was almost ruined publicly," Adi explained. "We had a giant meeting trying to find a way to redeem ourselves in the eyes of the public. So when I heard that Bartley and Rosie were coming back in town tonight, I suggested to the Board that we throw a giant party to make up for the wrecked one and say that through the goodness of our hearts," she snorted, "we wish to bring the community together to celebrate these newlyweds."

"And that actually worked?" Bran said with shock. "Sewey'd never agree."

"Of course he didn't," Adi said. "But he didn't have any choice after that, if he wanted to keep his job. The Board thought it was a brilliant idea, and it seems to have worked, because it's been nothing but good publicity since."

A man and a woman darted out of the Wilomases' house, carrying between them a long paper banner that they rushed to hang over the entry of the house next door. Bran noticed that the FOR RENT sign was no longer in the yard, and a moment later, he saw why. The sign being stapled over the door read:

PLEASE DO NOTICE THIS GIFT
TO THE NEWLYWEDS
FROM THE KIND THIRD BANK OF DUNCE:
THREE MONTHS FREE RENT
AND REASONABLE DUE THEREAFTER
FROM THE THIRD BANK OF DUNCE

"They certainly don't have any trouble advertising themselves," Astara noted wryly.

"They'll be living next door?" Bran said, still unable to comprehend how all this was happening.

"For a short time, subsidized by the TBD," Adi nodded proudly. "All for the sake of good publicity."

She finally parked the car and let Bran and Astara out, and all the noise of the adults ordering one another around and the children playing came out as a giant babble of sound. Adi opened the trunk and got Bran's bags out, and he was so dizzy with what he saw before him that he nearly dropped them as he got closer to the house.

He got up to the front door and was nearly pushed aside by three women who bustled their way past him, and he dropped his bags beside the door. He could hear shouting from the kitchen, and even though the voice was Sewey's, the familiarity made his heart soar.

He pushed his way to the kitchen, dragging Astara with him, but the door burst open before he even got there. Sewey came out with a giant bowl of popcorn, spilling it all over the place as he tried to carry it over the heads of the people.

"Sewey!" Bran called.

"You!" Sewey replied. "You're back. Good. Now," he pointed, "you can start by getting Mrs. Havinsworth away from sampling at the cake table, and then putting paper plates outside."

"Hello. I'm home, good evening," Bran said with annoyance. "Nice to see you again, Sewey, after all this time."

"Yes, yes," Sewey waved his hand. "I know you're home. Now get to work. And smile, or else this travesty of a party will be of no worth. Do it like this."

Sewey spread his lips apart and exposed all of his grayish teeth in what at first appeared to be an attempt to look like an angry ape but what Bran realized was his attempt at smiling.

"The public relations firm the TBD hired has helped Mabel and me practice," Sewey said, letting his face fall back into its usual position. "We've got to do it over and over and over again today. It's to reassure the customers that we do, in fact, care about them and the community and idiotic things like weddings and Bartley."

Sewey shuddered at the name. "Great rot, he's coming home. I might just eat maggots instead."

"Just keep doing that thing with your face and teeth," Bran said. "It'll make him want to leave the city again."

"Precisely," Sewey replied, and it was then that his eyes turned to Astara, and suddenly his brow furrowed.

"You?" he said, blinking. "Have I met you before?"

Bran froze, realizing suddenly that Sewey had seen a glimpse of Astara at the Fridd's Day party. However, much to his relief, there came a gigantic boom from outside that rattled the house and caused Sewey to leap into the air and forget whatever he had been thinking. Bran and Astara ducked.

"Get Balder away from that firecracker cannon!" Sewey roared. A woman jostled her way to Sewey.

"Wilomas," she said, "there's a courier at the door. He's got a package to deliver."

"Well, my hands are busy popcorning these seeds," Sewey said angrily, and he waved Bran to go sign for it. The courier was dressed in purple and was waiting at the door with a look of fear. Obviously, he was not accustomed to watching children operate firecracker cannons in the yard so close to him and was very eager to be on his way.

"Bran Hambric?" he said, when Bran reached the door.

"That's me," he replied. "I can sign for Sewey."

"Actually, it's for you," the man said, tapping the address. "Sign here."

Bran took the paper to sign and glanced for a sender's address, but there was none. The courier retreated as fast as he could, and Bran showed the package to Astara.

"I don't get packages often," he said. "Who do you think it's from?"

"No idea," Astara said. "A gift, maybe?"

"Not sure," Bran replied, shaking the box. Whatever was inside was bulky.

"Let's go open it on the roof," Astara suggested. "We can see the party from there too."

The thought of being on the rooftop was very appealing to Bran, for all the hubbub in the house was not what he felt like being in after returning home from so much of it already. They stole out the front door and around the yard. The ladder was still there, as it had been for many a month. They climbed up until they reached the top, crossed to the chimney, and sat looking over the edge.

Bran ripped the tape off and pulled the cardboard flaps apart. He set the box onto the roof between him and Astara, and she held it so it wouldn't slide off as he dug around inside and pulled out a single white envelope from the top. Inside was a piece of lined notebook paper, which when unfolded turned out to be a handwritten letter. The handwriting was more of a quick scrawl, which read:

She wasn't happy away from you, and I think we both know who she belongs with. I've got a man to hunt down. But I shall do it without her, and I have removed the devices from her eyes. But never, ever, ever, ever, think no one is watching.

THOMAS

"It's from my father," Bran said in a low voice of dismay. He looked back to the box and saw something else wrapped in paper. He drew this out and tore the wrapping to reveal the music box.

The lid was locked, but the metal lever stood from the side, as if beckoning him once again to play the song he had heard but a few times and had already memorized. His heartbeat quickened, and Astara could say nothing in her shock, even as they both stared at it.

"Did he really..." Bran whispered. But he could say no more and only began to turn the wheel. The lament started to play.

The sound was far more beautiful than any of the other times he had heard it, the notes ringing softly so that its mourning seemed to have surrendered to its origin: the lullaby that Gary had written for Emry. Bran could no longer hear the sadness or the pain that the song had come to represent but only the love with which it had first been written.

The song was over long before Bran wished for it to be, but the lock on the lid gave a click, and he slowly lifted it and peered inside. As if she had been waiting for him all the time, Nim leapt out and swirled around his head with happiness.

"Nim!" Bran said. Nim flew around and around and never

seemed to want to stop, and Bran realized that she was truly there with him and would not be forced to leave again.

"Nim," she said to him in reply, finally clinging to his shirt and rubbing her head against it. The two circles on her wings glowed in the dark, as if powered by her happiness.

"I can't believe he let her go," Astara said. "It doesn't seem at all like him."

"No," Bran said, shaking his head. "It isn't. But I've learned to never expect anything when it comes to my father."

And Bran couldn't think of anything else to say about it. So they sat there as the night grew darker and the crowd grew larger. Lights continued to be hung from the trees and the tables, and the lanterns were lit until the whole street was aglow.

"You don't remember anything from being with the Specters?" Bran asked Astara after a while. It was the third time the question had come up since he had found her, and she had already given him the same answer each time.

"I just can't," she said. "It was there a little, but it seems to be fading away. I can't really place my finger on any of it."

"It's probably for the better," Bran said with a sigh. "At least they're free now. The Key is gone. And you're back."

He grinned at her, and she punched his arm.

"Look, I thought you were dead," Bran told her with mock disgust.

"It'll take a lot more than that to get rid of me," she said slyly.

"You say that as if you were able to save yourself," Bran replied. Astara laughed.

"I just can't believe you'd go all that way when you didn't even know there was a chance of me being alive," Astara said.

"Well, I wasn't about to just let you go," Bran said. "It'll take a lot more than that to get rid of me."

Astara laughed when she heard her own words used against her, and she leaned back so that she could look at the sky and lie against the rooftop. Her hair spread around her head on the roof like a halo, and the gentle wind pushed it about.

"It was still very brave of you," she finally whispered. "I know you don't want to hear it, but I've got to thank you for saving my life, as plain as that sounds."

"Nope, don't mind hearing that at all," Bran said with a cough. "Saving the lives of girls abducted by spirits—do it all the time."

She punched him hard in the side, and it hurt so badly that he doubled over in pain. He winced as he caught his breath, but she only grinned toward the sky.

"Don't think you're getting thanks a second time, Bran," she said to him, as he slowly managed to start breathing again.

"Next time I might just leave you there," Bran croaked.

"No you won't," Astara replied, and Bran could not argue. He blew down in her face and dodged her fist another time, then saw a car turning onto Bolton Road. The crowd below started to cheer and wave flags. Astara sat up quickly and looked over the edge.

"You think we'll even get to say hello to them?" she said as the crowds of eager neighbors bustled forward, forcing the car to stop. The doors were pried open, and though he strained to look, Bran could hardly see Rosie or Bartley as the people pulled them out and blew party horns and miniature trumpets. He wanted to see Rosie so much, but he knew that his reunion with her would be tarnished if he went down now into the frenzy.

"Probably not for little bit," Bran replied, settling back reluctantly. "They'll all have their party and look respectable and then be on their way."

"Leaving Sewey and Mabel to clean up the mess," Astara finished for him.

"More likely leaving me to clean up the mess," Bran laughed. Astara grinned at that.

"Maybe we should stay up here for a little while longer then," she said, nudging him against the chimney. He pushed her back.

"That's probably a good idea," he agreed. "We both know what happened at the last party here."

"Ah, it didn't turn out quite so bad," Astara countered.

"For you," Bran replied. "Next time, it's your turn to save me."

"I've saved your life more than once," she said with a laugh. "But all right. I owe you a favor."

"It's a deal," Bran said, and he settled back against the chimney, with Astara at his side, as they watched the people. The lights from below reflected in Nim's green eyes, and the glowing circles on her wings lit up as she flew around their heads and slowly climbed up toward the night sky.

Epilogue

Mr. Rat lazily pushed his mop across the cold concrete of the subway tunnel maintenance passage, his earbud headphones playing snappy show tunes that masked the swishing noises as he cleaned. He was dressed in a dreary gray jumpsuit and had on black boots that squished across the floor, leaving tracks behind him as he mopped ahead. He was not accustomed to janitorial work. But thanks to the Ex-Prisoner Exchange Program, otherwise known as EP-EP, it was his way out of the Dunce jails.

He hummed to the tunes on his cassette player as he pushed the mop. It was late. The passages were narrow and only lit by fluorescent bulbs, many of which needed to be replaced. He wasn't the light replacer though. Davey was the light replacer, and Mr. Rat did not like Davey at all, so as he walked he made sure to punch some of the bulbs out with the wooden end of his mop, littering glass all across the floors he had just cleaned.

He tugged the mop bucket, but it had become stuck on some pipes in the corner. He struggled to pull the bucket free but slipped on the wet floor and fell flat on his back, spilling the contents of the mop bucket everywhere.

"*Greatness!*" he squeaked, flipping and flopping all over as he tried to stand. He scrambled up and then slammed against the wall, which shattered on impact, sending him and the bucket flying through.

Mr. Rat shouted, though no one heard as he fell into the darkness beyond. He rolled down a set of stairs and was hit at the bottom by the bucket, which tumbled after him.

"Aye, can't a man have a bit of mercy now?" he said to the air around him, shaking like a dog in an attempt to get some of the water off. He looked up then and saw that the stairs went up to a door that had been covered up with a fake wall.

"Now what idiot puts a door out 'ere?" he grumbled to himself, kicking the mop bucket with disgust. It was much harder plastic than he had thought, and he hopped around cradling his foot as it throbbed with pain. As he turned around, he realized that he had stumbled on an abandoned subway stop.

He fell back against the wall in surprise at all the open space before him, for he hadn't realized he was in such a large room. There were sets of tracks far ahead of him and abandoned benches and things against the walls but no people and very little sign that anyone had been there, besides some tracks across the dusty floor.

"Don't think I'm gonna be cleanin' this now, do ye?" he said aloud, punching the air. "Just walk along back up them stairs, Rat. No one'll notice it ain't been mopped."

Still, his curiosity got the better of him, and he walked forward, wanting to look down the tunnel. He knew that the subway had many abandoned stops, closed down for financial reasons. He reached the edge of the concrete and looked down and then started hollering to hear his voice echo around the corners.

"Your mother's a pig!" he shouted, and he heard it echo back, up and down the tunnels. He started to shout again, when he saw something flash down the tunnel. It was in the middle of the tracks and glimmered suddenly, as if beckoning him with a flashlight. At first he thought it might have been the eye of a rat, because it was green, but as many of his closest companions were rats themselves, it only made him wish to introduce himself and perhaps invite the rat and its family to dinner and scones. So he leapt off the edge and started toward it, listening intently for any trains that might come to squash him.

He had a flashlight on his belt, which he pulled out and waved in front of him as he walked. The faraway object flashed green every time the light passed over it, which only caused Mr. Rat's pace to quicken, until he was practically dashing to it.

He finally reached the spot and bent down and saw a solid green, shining gem, entirely unblemished and larger than any he had seen before, even in all the houses he had burglarized.

"What's this now?" he said aloud, crouching down to wipe away some shards of metal and seize the gem. He held it above his head, letting the flashlight reflect off the gem onto the walls of the tunnel in a dazzling green display.

"This is bound to be worth a thousan' sib, maybe two!" he said with a maniacal laugh. He wondered how it had gotten there on the tracks but figured perhaps some rich fiend had tossed it out the train window or one of the tunnel rats had been bored and left it behind.

"Well, isn't this grand?" he said, chuckling. Mr. Rat took another quick glance around the tunnel and then grinned to himself as he pushed the gem into his pocket, feeling that today had truly been his lucky day.

Acknowledgments

Without these people, this book would not have been possible:

Daniel Ehrenhaft: for your editing magic that made everything shine.

My agent Richard Curtis: without whom my writing would have remained a stack of papers.

Brendan Forsling: for remaining my friend even when I got the manuscript to you two years after I promised it.

Catherine, Anna, and the rest of the Biewers: for knowing all my book secrets years before anyone cared...and keeping said secrets.

Lauren Suero: for going with me on the first stops of the book tour, armed with blue pens and mints.

Rachul Gensburg: for her salty, salty lies, and talking crows.

Jaden, Kim, Becka, Gum, Nicoleface, Zane, and the rest of the FTW Crew: for late night Skype calls that kept me alive through far too many days spent indoors, acting like a serious business adult.

And the BranFans: for your general awesomeness.

About the Author

As a child, Kaleb Nation was forced to write one page a week in creative writing. But after he finished his first story, no one could make him stop. At age twelve, he telephoned the editor of a major publisher to pitch his book but got to talk with security instead. Years later, his books are being produced by publishers worldwide...including the one that first turned him down. Aside from writing, Kaleb is a blogger and a former radio host. He turned twenty-one in 2009 and currently lives in California.

Visit Kaleb online at www.kalebnation.com.

DISCARDED